happiness is too much trouble

other books in the sandra hochman collection
from turner publishing:

Walking Papers

Endangered Species

Jogging

Playing Tahoe

Streams

for children:

The Magic Convention

forthcoming:

Loving Robert Lowell

Paris 1959-1960

The Shakespeare Conspiracy

Portraits of Genius Friends

sandra hochman

happiness is too much trouble

a novel

TURNER

My thanks to Stanley Kunitz, Sophie McConnell, Patricia Irving, Anna Thornhill, Julia McFarlan, Susan and Mark Straussberg, and Don Townsend—who helped.

Turner Publishing Company
Nashville, Tennessee
New York, New York

www.turnerpublishing.com

Cover design: Maddie Cothren
Book design: Glen M. Edelstein

Library of Congress Cataloging-in-Publication Data

Names: Hochman, Sandra, author.
Title: Happiness is too much trouble : a novel / Sandra Hochman.
Description: Nashville, Tennessee : Turner, [2017]
Identifiers: LCCN 2017002567 | ISBN 9781683365198 (pbk. : alk. paper)
Subjects: LCSH: Women--Fiction.
Classification: LCC PS3558.O34 H3 2017 | DDC 813/.54--dc23
LC record available at https://lccn.loc.gov/2017002567
9781683365198

Printed in the United States of America
15 14 13 12 11 10 9 8 7 6 5 4 3 2 1

For:

My mother Mae Barrett,

My daughter Ariel,

And for my friend Shirley Bernstein

Every day
A deal is made. Every day someone drops down
And the film industry flashes its own
Message: Awake awake. The industry—
That mistress with big tits larger than a goddess
And good enough to suck: the film world
Where business and teeth and power and lips
And aromas and sights take flight with the insane: the industry.

happiness is too much trouble

the dialogues

By accident. The way things sometimes happen—
I was about to be reborn.

It was too bad. What was too bad? That—

My father wasn't alive.

He would have been very proud of me. Or perhaps he was turning over in his grave. He always thought of me as a little schlump who would not amount to much. That was because I liked to read. I trusted people. I liked to make up songs. Dance in a room by myself. Make music with a comb. Wanting to be a stand-up comedian.

"What kind of occupation is that for a girl?" he would ask. His main fear was that I would fall on my face.

Now by accident I'd been picked by a computer to be the boss of one of the world's largest film studios. I was an executive by accident. That often happens to women. Or madmen. Or unsuspecting people. It sort of fucks up the entire system. When someone comes to the party who never wanted to go to the party in the first place. Here I was, little dreamer, daddy's own little Lulu entering the world of profit and loss and big and little movie deals. I was now bankable.

3

"You'll never amount to much," my father would say.

"Why not?"

"Because you have no ambition, Lulu. Because you wear your heart on your sleeve. You're too emotional."

"I wear my heart on my sleeve because I'm free of ambition," I used to say.

We used to argue. We loved each other for being so opposite. "Why can't you be practical?" my father used to ask. Ask? Lament.

"You're a dreamer in a world where dreaming doesn't count."

"What counts?" I asked.

"It counts to know about money. It counts to toughen up. Why can't you toughen up? It counts to know how to budget. It counts to know something about real life. I didn't have your education. I didn't go to school beyond the eighth grade. But I taught myself to think. To be tough. To know what the real world's about. Can't you wise up? You're too good-natured. A scatterbrain."

I remember my father trying to teach me how to buy a car—check the tires, check the chrome, check the glass, the suspension, leaks, chassis, is the horn working? Are directional signals working? Is the steering wheel safe? Are the floor mats worn?

"But, Papa," I would say.

"Don't interrupt—"

"But, Papa, I don't want a car. Why do I have to learn all these things if I'm never going to buy a car?"

The fact was this: It pained my father that I really didn't want anything he wanted. I wanted to travel, be an actress, be a comic. *If you don't want, you don't get.* But I wasn't interested in my girlhood in frames and engine transmissions and bumpers crooked or straight. I didn't want to *get* anywhere in his world. I wanted to tell him. I was now in his world. But he was dead.

Under grass. He probably wouldn't have understood anyway. He might have told me what not to do, and worried about what would happen if I failed. But how could you fail? There was no failing. That was the answer. The records filed away in memory. All the pressures of girlhood and womanhood and lonelihood recorded there for the rest of my life. I had just bumped into success.

I wanted, despite everything, to tell my secret to someone close to me. I thought of my ex-wife. It was really my ex-wife that I wanted to contact, to share the great news with, to tell all that was happening.

I wondered where Dumbo was. The last time I had seen Dumbo he had come over to my apartment to rub my feet, to show me how he could "cure" me by all the methods of reflexology. It was odd that now, three years later, so much had changed in both our lives. I was moving into a new life in California, a new life complete with new judgments, new people, new gardens of contacts where the unprofitable had to be weeded out. Never had I felt less weary, more able to change my life and live it in all its absurd mazes and wanton complexities. But one old weariness stayed inside my gut, the fear, even the unwillingness to share the frightened part of myself. Dumbo, my last lover, my ex-wife as I called him, was the last person that I had shared that old self with. I thought I was over the "obsession" with Dumbo—that need I had experienced to see him, the need to reach him that was almost an automatic reflex. I had deadened the pain. Cut him off like a hangnail. And it seemed forever finished. Except at this moment of—triumph and yes, extreme loneliness—the only thing that would cure me of the frailty of fear was this: to talk to Dumbo. I had made him into a fairy tale jester, I had seen all his pratfalls in perspective; I had divested him of all the attractions he held for me. It was almost as if he were now dead. But I had to tell him. Telling *him* was everything. It was

5

almost as if reality which seemed more like fantasy was not happening, not happening at all, until I *told* Dumbo. It seemed at that moment that living was nothing, telling was everything, that the event did not become alive or meaningful until I spoke it. I had to reach him.

I called his number. Predictably it had been changed. The voice inside the phone referred me to another number. The phone rang. I suddenly looked at the clock next to my bed and realized that it was ten o'clock at night. I wondered if he would be out. A strange voice answered the phone. A pleasing woman's voice. It was his mother. So he was now living with his mother. Dumbo adored his mother and had carried her with him, like a bunny's foot, from city to city, as if there were no good luck without her. During the time we lived together in Manhattan she had been working in a factory in Canada, but she had come to visit Dumbo often. I remember riding with him in the Cadillac I had bought him as a gift, to pick her up at the bus terminal. She was a frail woman with a lovely speaking voice. She remembered me. "Dumbo is in Ohio," she said proudly. She advised me to call him there and gave me the name of a Holiday Inn where he was staying. I thanked her. I poured a scotch before I picked up the phone again. I wondered what the point was—calling across the country trying to reach an old lover, my ex-wife. Why would Dumbo care what had happened to me? And yet—he would care. I phoned the number and was connected to his room. I almost could not bear the excitement in my stomach as the phone rang.

"Yes?" he said.

"Dumbo," and then I couldn't say anything to him.

"Lulu." He laughed. He did not seem surprised to hear from me. "How are you doin'?" he asked. It was a particularly obnoxious form of greeting, and I remembered hating it.

"Hello," I said. And I said it again. "Hello." I was so happy to be able to say hello to Dumbo, whom I hadn't spoken to for so many years. I told him what was happening. He told me what was happening to him. He had started a chain of reflexology centers throughout the country. He had also opened up a chain of shoe stores which were "modifications" (a fancy word I'm sure for rip-offs) of the Earth Shoe—a new brand of shoe which lowered the heel and raised the toe and cushioned the sole.

"The soles are different," Dumbo said. "The soles are really the important element, and so many people overlook that very basic piece of information. I've mastered the natural shoe, the shoe that bends with the entire foot, the shoe that fits over your foot and cushions it. I'm branching out—using the principle of the natural shoe and the basic a b c's of reflexology."

"Oh," I said.

"I wish I could see you," Dumbo said.

Suddenly I felt horny—and all the horny moments that I had been pushing away and blocking out came back from the underground of my imagination. I stubbornly fought them off. "I'm going to head up the world's largest studio," I said.

"What kind of benefits are you getting?" my ex-wife answered.

I'm no longer an applicant for your affection, I was about to say, but it all seemed mindless.

"Dumbo, I somehow wish you were here."

"You'll see me soon," he said.

"When?"

"As soon as I get my headquarters set up."

Those were the realities of separation. We would probably never meet again. And I still hadn't told him anything. And so it happened that I hung up the phone not having anyone to share my news with. I didn't want to talk about heels and soles. Instead of sharing my news with my ex-wife, I was going to get into bed alone, drink a scotch and water, alone, listen to a Brahms woodwind quartet, alone, read an article on the eventual revision in the capital gains tax, read a tax-shelter report compiled by Fundscope, make notes, turn out the light, masturbate a little, and wake up in the morning and talk to my secretary. Alone, alone.

My secretary had the odd name of Itzi. It was originally Mitzi, but she had changed it when she went into show business. She was an odd-looking person, very short, with extremely large breasts. She seemed to be sculpted out of styrofoam, was always complaining that while all the world tried to have large breasts, her agony was that she was constantly trying to reduce them. The problems of a middle-class mammal. Itzi waddled like a duck, her clothes were always black to conceal her eccentric body, ah, Itzi, if you would stop trying to be what you are not, but I could never say that. Dear Itzi, I have such compassion toward you, toward Dumbo, toward everyone I have known. But now it is time to put all those feelings to rest and to park my feelings and injuries inside the sheets and sleep for the evening. Love, Lulu. I wrote a memo to myself before I signed off. "Don't call Dumbo again."

Sometimes I think I can never forgive people. But I always do. I always do . . . Sleep. Foam. Earth Shoe. Car. Move. Dome. Warranty. Perform. Down deep into what you are. It was a habit. Saying any old word until I fell asleep.

I forgave Dumbo. And forgave my father for wanting me always to be what I wasn't, and I forgave myself because I was becoming what I always was, a little Amtrak of the imagination who refused to be shoved off the lines.

This was really the most exciting time of my life. I knew it. It was being born again. And to hell with my ex-wife. Why did I need to reach anyone? I could reach deep into myself and pat myself on the soul.

The next morning the entire world heard of Lulu Cartwright. It had never been in my dream to wake up and be on the front page of every newspaper in the world. But it happened that morning.

8

My housekeeper, Emma, had brought me the papers. It was there in the papers. In black and white.

"What are you going to do with us, missus?" Emma wanted to know.

Always protecting her own neck. Emma, the cleaning Gestapo, was wondering if she was going to be ordered to the Coast. I hated her but accepted her as a necessity. A pain in the ass. Emma. Reading my mail. Listening in to my phone calls. Quietly getting all the messages wrong. Emma was a blister on my life. Sometimes I wished the blister would burst. Or go away. But she was a necessity. She bore the job of taking care of my son, David, cheerfully. She loved him. She helped him with his homework. Took him to gym classes. Practiced boxing with him. Gave him sports encyclopedias. Enjoyed him. Kept his clothes clean. Found his hockey stick when he lost it. Remembered to give him his vitamins. Didn't embarrass him by looking like a nanny. Spoke his ten-year-old language. Understood his problems. And was good for him. She cleaned well. Refused to cook. Refused to be nice to me. She was a blister all right. And now this woman was actually thinking of the power she would have in HOLLYWOOD. I had once heard a joke which reminded me of Emma. It was a joke about a movie star at a commissary. He was, the joke went, standing in line at the commissary when an unknown guy came up to him and said, "Do you know Piper Laurie?"

"No," he said. "Do you know Piper Laurie?"

"No," he said.

"Are you sure you don't know Piper Laurie?"

"Yes, I'm sure. Why do you ask?"

"Well," said the man to the movie star, "I just fucked her *maid*."

And Emma was now wondering if she was going to have a lot of power as my maid. After all, she was mentioned in the *Times* as housekeeper when the story broke. *Now* she hoped to be fucked by a movie star. Keep hoping.

9

"Emma?"

"Yes, missus."

"Do you want to move to California?"

"Oh, yes, missus. My family in Belgium always said I would be doing something in films if I came to America. I appeared on television in my Easter bonnet many times. The largest bonnet in the Easter Parade. David helped me cut out the lilies for three years now. I want to go to California. It's good for the lungs, too. The climate, missus, is better than New York." She giggled. "Will I meet Cary Grant?"

"Probably."

"Will I meet Rock Hudson? Frank Sinatra? Sammy Davis, Jr?"

"You'll meet everybody."

"I won't cook. I won't serve. We . . . oh, well . . . I would cook for Cary Grant."

"You might leave David for Cary Grant," I said.

"No."

"Why not?"

"I love David. Will we have a big house? I won't climb stairs."

"What do you mean?"

"I won't climb stairs. If your mansion in Hollywood has stairs, I won't go."

"It won't be a mansion."

"And why not?"

"Because I intend to live in a hotel."

I was amused by Emma's disappointment.

Hello. It's me, Lulu. A Lilliputian historian of myself. A fate computer watched me. A committee botched me. And I'm caught in a life machine that is more like a gag machine.

A certain weariness has set in. I mean to say that it is a difficult decision to make. I suppose that this is the pot of gold at the end of the rainbow, but don't forget, the rainbow may be made out of alloys other than sunbeams. It's a fairy tale, but I'm

10

not sure that the princess is supposed to wake and turn into an executive of a studio. She's supposed to want romance, not power. That's from a children's book I am writing, *The Emperor Godaigo*. It's about an emperor who lived in Japan and who was exiled from his court and forced to think about the simplicities of life. But it's weird. The opposite is happening to me. I may or may not be exiled from my life amid the water towers, my office where I write comedy scripts, my friends, my tennis teacher, my accountant who runs my business holdings, my filmmaker friends, even my cleaner, butcher, hairdresser, doctors, my lover, my troublemaking activities, my childhood memories on Riverside Drive, my beloved Asia House, where I lecture on Japanese art, my civic involvements in the Park (I'm in charge of Change Central Park—a committee I set up to bring poetry to the parks and make the park into a classroom), from the buddies of my son who go to the Knicks games with me, from the tomatoes and oranges and mangoes at the Venice Market, from pigeons, doctors, and book stores and banks and the empire of my own private life. I'm about to decide if I really want to exile myself from all this for the inside-out riches of the movie empire being offered to me. It's funny. It's very funny. Then why am I crying?

LULU CARTWRIGHT NAMED HEAD OF LEADING STUDIO

One morning I woke up and entered life. A new life. The phone rang. The first person to call me was Martin Loktar, my closest buddy and business manager. Martin runs an insurance firm that insures most of the stars and superstars in show business as well as many other clients, many of them with large incomes. I first met him when I got divorced and had to take my insurance into my own hands. Since then he has helped me with all my projects, and even though I have a degree in law, he knows more about investments and about what I should be doing financially than I do. He is a tall dark angel who lives in Manhasset with four kids and a wife.

"Are you kidding?" he asked. I heard his voice in the phone.

"Kidding about what?"

"Mary gave me the *Times* this morning as I was eating breakfast, and I almost choked on my eggs and chopped liver. Page one. Lulu Cartwright named first woman head of major Hollywood studio. I read the story and I said to Mary, 'My God, Mary, she's not going to have to worry about being *tapped out* now. Didn't I tell you if she produced *All in a Day's Thrills* as a porno film it would pay off?' Remember when you said to me, 'Martin, I'm a comedy artist. I'm a director of documentaries. I don't know anything about lighting insertions other than the fact that our pathological society seems pornographic,' and I said to you, 'Lulu, keep your social opinions out of this. You can do a film about life and death and lovemaking and fantasies and make it come out a winner. Don't worry about names.' Wasn't I right? Wasn't I right, kid? Come on. Give Martin his due. Think of the *fun* you're going to have on the Coast. My God, I'm jealous of you."

"What fun?" I asked. I was still hardly awake.

"Come on. You're joking. You can be another Sam Goldy—a female Selznick."

"I can see it all now—the Cartwright Boys. I can do a review in which I get a couple of cuties to star—Paul Newman, Steve McQueen, Warren Beatty. I can hold meetings in my office. I can turn Suck City upside down."

"Yeah," said Martin.

"I can make the lion that roars into a lamb. I can do away with Oscars and make porno the new art form. I can drive around town on a one-speed bicycle to show that power doesn't corrupt. I can substitute overweight women for thin women—and everyone in America will be able to eat again. Are you listening, Martin?"

"Wild!"

I continued. "I can throw out the Walt Disney crap and make movies for kids—not about bunnies or elephants that suffer anxiety losses, but about real life—and I can have kids' films scored by people who know how much kids love music. I can turn kids on to science and satellites and all the things that really interest them. I can make films that talk about what's really happening inside the minds of women, criminals, bakers, bankers, and here's the hitch. I can change the entire fantasy life of a generation. I can throw out the multimillion-dollar concept and show how movies can be made on a small budget. I can—oh, God, I'm exhausted.

"Are you joking?"

"No. I'm not."

"Then why hesitate? The papers say it's a deal."

"Because of my nerves. Because every never-to-be-gotten-rid-of agent in the world is going to be after me. I'll give an Agents' Ball at the Beverly Wilshire and all the agents can come dressed up as their favorite client—and I still won't satisfy those mothers. The packagers of the world will be after me like lice. So will every hustler-booker in America, which is about twenty-three percent of the population. My life will be ruined. And all I'll have to show for it is a couple of bucks, which I'll be too nervous to spend anyway."

"You could always go back to writing a comedy."

"No, thanks, Martin. I think I'll just gear myself for success and the big time. Did you hear, by the way, that I'm writing a special based on the children's book that I wrote ten years ago?"

"Which one?"

"The Measles Convention. It's about kids who want to catch the measles so they can stay home from school. They find a measles convention in the Hotel Commodore, started by some other kids, and it becomes their school. I don't know who it's going to star, but they're thinking of—hold onto your hats—Carol Burnett. As the oldest kid's mom."

"I insure her. And believe me, she'd be perfect. But why are they talking about specials to you? You'll be creating your own specials. Yea, God—you can make or write anything you want, you lucky son of a bitch, while I'll just be selling insurance."

"Martin, I love you. Let me call you back."

"Better yet, come down to the office."

Bart was in California when the news came out in the papers. He thought Hollywood in general, with its hustlers, money-makers, frauds, great money-makers, and front office, was ridiculous. Bartel was an odd person in my life. Someone I liked rather than loved for so long that I couldn't tell where the like left off and the love began. Bartel baked bread. He was in the pumpernickel business and had invented the first fast-foods bread operation, which began in San Diego and now had branched out into Barts Enterprises with offices in New York and fast-food bread restaurants all over the country. He served twenty-five kinds of sandwiches on a variety of black bread and pumpernickel. For a dollar, you could get a sandwich, dessert, coffee, beer and sit as long as you wished at his restaurants, which were aesthetic and comfortable. He owned his own bakeries in Australia and California and Japan and operated his food chains in France, England, Japan, Indonesia and all over South America. Bartel, Bart, B.J. (the J was for Jansen—Bart's family was originally Danish and Norwegian) was born on a large ranch in North Dakota. He was not a millionaire, had been a widower for six years, and planned to stay single the rest of his life. He had adored his wife and now loved his children and grandchildren and good friends, but Bart was a loner and had few friends. At sixty-two he looked better than most men looked at fifty. His body was in perfect shape, outside of a slight stomach, a body he created years ago when he was a boxer. His white hair set off a rugged, lined face, his eyes slanted slightly, and the outstanding quality about Bart was his energy, the energy of a cowboy, the energy of a loner, that quality of life which has a pull of its own.

I never went to Bart for advice. And Bart never asked me for any. The reason I liked Bart was that he was the first man ever to treat me like an equal. He was a tough and sturdy person, and so was I. No one had ever broken his spirit, and no one had ever broken mine, although many hustlers and suckers had tried, but those days were over. My Dumbo days—that's what I called them—were over, and Bart knew it. I spent a lot of time trying to shield Bart from the knowledge that I needed him; he knew I did but never took advantage of that need. That odd need to be loved, to be happy with a friend. My own character tended to be overly emotional, sometimes impractical, creative, zany, and spontaneous. Bart was just the opposite. He was practically calm all the day and night. His voice, a North Dakota drawl, never went up or down. He was even, smooth, and I liked that. We had made a pact never to live together, never to marry, and I liked that best of all. I was trying to make life worth living for myself and my son, and Bart never got in the way of the way I lived. And I tried to stay out of his heart, which was easy. Bart had no heart as far as women were concerned. Either you were a friend or not a friend, and that was it. So easy. So relaxing. Friends. Lover friends. Buddies. You buddy me, I buddy you. My God, after all those years of "relationships" and "marriage" and "looking for happiness"—Bart always said "happiness is too much trouble" and we both laughed. When he came back from California that morning, he called me. As usual, I was delirious to hear his low and calm voice.

"Lulu? It's Bart."

"I know your voice."

"I was reading about you on the plane this morning."

"It's a little overwhelming."

"Lulu, I can see you screwing up the industry. Giving them business advice on how to run the studio. Well, you always liked being a director. Here's a whole universe for you to direct. I'll buy you lunch, and we can talk about it."

He was chuckling. When people are used to being in charge, it amuses them when other people are in charge. Bart was extraordinary. He wished me well. And he had confidence that I could do anything. And he was right, of course.

I loved Bart. And I still love Bart. And I'll always love Bart. Because he's the most controlled person I've ever known and ever will know. He let me finally turn from a victim into a person. You may not believe it, but for years I suffered one humiliation after another as I went from one creep to another saying love me, love me, I'm good, I'm a great fuck, I'm talented, I'm funny, love me, love me—and finally I found this oddball, this wizened cowboy, this level lover; Bart. We sat at a back table in a small restaurant on the West Side. On several occasions I have given parties there, and they often turn down the music when I arrive. I hate background music.

Bart didn't ask me if I was going to take the job.

"I'm not the Lulu Cartwright that the studio thinks they're getting," I said to Bart. "They may be thinking they're getting some token woman with a law degree who has produced one film that brought a combination of porn and karate and artistic values—a combination of women's fantasy and sexual identity—to make twenty-three million dollars. I'm not the madwoman turned comedy writer turned executive that you think I am. I'm someone at the end of youth. I'm trying to decide if power is insanity. If power is a joke. Or if power is something that really interests me."

"*It's not for you,* Lulu," Bart says.

"I'm not so sure," I counter back.

"Look, this has nothing to do with me. You make your own decisions. But you're too creative for this job. You're not really

16

an executive. You'll get in there with all that wheeling and dealing and you'll be lost."

He lit a cigarette.

"I'll be a new kind of executive. One that shakes things up. I think of all the things I could do. I could put some of the most creative people in the world on the payroll. I could bring poetry into films. I could make films about imagination, about thoughts, about the world that is filled with fantasy."

"That sounds to me like a lot of crap. What makes you think that they are hiring you to get artistic films? Do you think they care about messages? They care about money. You're just a monkey that they have bought to bring them some publicity. You're like the Charlie McCarthy on Edgar Bergen's knee. So what? Do you really want to be a bought monkey? Stick to what you know best. You've made personally a million dollars on your film. You make money from your comedy writing. You like that. You're better off working with people like Lily Tomlin and Joan Rivers and Milton Berle than trying to be an executive at a goddamn studio. So you'll be the first woman president of a studio. So what? It'll be just another token job. You'll be dealing with a group of dudes who are all much smarter and tougher than you."

"I could always use another million," I said.

No point in approaching Bart in other ways. He was tough, and he understood money. No point in telling him that I wanted to make Colette's novels into films, that I wanted to produce Alain Fournier's *The Wanderer*, that I wanted to make a different kind of children's film, that I saw porn films as the great new art form, that I wanted to take satellites and sell films on satellites all over the globe. No point in telling him that I was going to bust up the unions and use camerawomen, sound women, women directors, that the films I was going to make were going to reflect the lives of the people who saw them. I found myself saying to Bart, "I like making the money.

17

I'm so tired of this noble nigger role that we are supposed to play. If you could make an extra couple of bucks as simply as this, you would take it."

"Me?" He laughed and took another sip of his scotch. He saw me laughing, too. "I only know about two things—women and pumpernickel. I've been a cowboy all my life. And I've sold blue sky. But I want to stick to what I know. And I think you should, too."

"What do you mean?"

"Look, sweetheart. I never tell you what to do. But I think you're doing too much now. You've got another comedy film that you've just written about——what is it——Mafia women who get hold of satellites and smuggle people to death, the perfect crime. You're writing another porn film for the bicentennial. What are you calling it? Seventeen seventy-suck. You've been asked by Bantam to write a comic sex manual called *I'd Like to Spend the Morning with You* or something like that. Then you're running your portfolio, playing around with real estate, you're running a seminar at Post Business School on film production, you're ass-deep in your project about teaching kids in the park, you're fighting the Parks Commission on that one, you're bringing up your son, you're constantly working. Do you really want to add to your headaches the fact that you're now heading up a studio? Do you realize how you'll have to drop everything else? I'm not talking about me. You know I don't need anyone, and I don't need you. But I just can't see you wasting your time doing something that is not that important to you. You're a comedy writer. Write."

The lunch ended abruptly. B.J. got an emergency call and had to go back to his office. I walked back to my apartment. Not once that I can remember had he ever said, "Don't do that because I want you for myself." He never said that. Which is why I saw him.

I called Elizabeth Ludman, my lawyer, and I called Emma to find out what David was doing, and I called a couple of other people, and then I took the phone off the hook. I decided to go to see Dr. Lutzman.

Dr. Lutzman, otherwise known as Lutz, dropped his other patients when he heard I was in the office. "That's fame," I thought to myself. Lutz liked famous patients. He liked to brag how he had cured Philip Roth's asthma and Liz Renay's hives. He talked a lot about the women's revolution and how it was affecting the health of a lot of his patients. "For the better," he said. "I'm going to write an article about that."

He lived on top of the store, so to speak, in a brownstone on East Seventy-third Street. His wife worked on political campaigns, and he was proud of her. He was the only doctor I knew who could make me feel better by just talking. He was smart. And I guess I trusted him as much as I could trust any doctor. I sat in his office and noticed how he looked younger when he smiled.

"Are you looking for an ulcer?" he said, talking obviously about the *Times* article.

I know it sounded strange, but I was now beginning to call it THE TIMES ARTICLE. It had suddenly, in twenty-four hours, changed my life. My son's governess wanted to go to Hollywood to fuck Warren Beatty and become famous in Europe. My best friend, Helen, saw this as some terrible Faustian compromise to my soul. My mother was proud. My father was dead, so he couldn't have an opinion, but as a self-made businessman from the Lower East Side, he would have loved it. This was better than marrying a millionaire. This meant being a millionare. This meant power. This was Cartwright's daughter, Lulu, unfucking her life. My dog was also dead—beloved Flops—so he didn't have to be subjected to the move. But he would have hated it. He had hated new cities. My son had not yet been consulted. My analyst was somewhere gloating. The analysis had turned one of the world's greatest masochists into a famous film executive. I had once said, "I'll know I'm cured, Dr. Bears, when I make a million dollars."

This wasn't a joke anymore. This was serious. My schoolmates would hate me. My elevator man asked for my autograph. My Aunt Julia was flying down from Boston on the shuttle to make sure I had the right wardrobe. She was bringing with her nine pairs of pantyhose with the hope that I would now stop wearing pants and begin wearing dresses. My ex-decorator was in seventh heaven. He imagined bookcases and plaid and paisley bedrooms in the ghettos of Beverly Hills. My ex-boyfriends who were in show business were all probably cutting their wrists— or their cocks—for not staying with me. My ex-husbands were probably figuring out my salary. My old orthodontist was probably saying it all happened because I had straight teeth. My bladder doctor, Dr. Grimes, was probably wondering if I was now peeing in my pants, a nervous habit which I kept from childhood. My druggist was probably adding up in his mind how much Librium I would be buying before leaving for California. He had read *Valley of the Dolls*. Ah, fame. Ah, brave new world. That has just so many idiots in it. I was fighting—for time. It was hard to decide—hard to decide whether the political act of taking this job and using this power to get women in on the action was worth it. Obviously no one in their right mind wanted to go to the Coast and work with those morons. The ice-cream-parlor intimacy of Stars and Stripes, starring Lulu Cartwright, didn't make me do anything but laugh. Dr. Lutzman seemed to be reading my mind.

"You look big, Lulu. You've put on a lot of weight. I guess this whole thing has made you nervous. Other than that, I'd say you're in good health. Take some diet pills and knock off twenty pounds before you get yourself into this. Also, I'd get a lot of sleep before you get into this thing. How's your love life?"

"Better than yours," I said.

That was the only strategy to use with Lutz.

"Are you still using a diaphragm or have you gone back to the pill?"

"I'm just giving blow jobs."

"Seriously. . . ."

"I've got a diaphragm in every famous city in the world. Along with my satin sheets. That way—when I travel. . . ."

"I don't need any more of your lousy jokes," Lutz said, laughing.

All this was happening around the time I let my body go to seed. It was as if all the unhappiness of my life had been checked by mental discipline. The fear doctors had gotten me to believe that I could succeed—if I wanted to. I was convinced that I could do anything I wanted to with my life. And after all, my life wasn't that bad. All the old dreams and crazy people and bad memories and guilt-ridden family—ride a cock horse—all behind me. The only telltale sign of misery was the fat flesh hanging out of my clothes—the desperado pounds. That was always a problem. The weight problem. The wait problem. I was always waiting. Like many people. For what? What was I waiting for, for Christ's sake? I was weighted down with the waiting for what? For touch? For feeling? I could give a good case against flab vs. feeling. What I was waiting for, I guess, was just this. This Hollywood weirdo event. This crowning of the unsuspecting head. What the hell—my God—it was an accident. The crown was falling on the wrong head. So be it.

(Based on the minutes of the board meeting)

The meeting was held in the offices of the studio. The twelve men on the board of directors arrived on time to discuss the serious situation. Hall, Croft & Guinzberg, the executive consultant firm, had given its seventy-five-thousand-dollar advice. It was now time for the studio to push ahead and hire a broad to run the studio. The case of ITT which recently made the front pages of the *Times*—the silly thing about minorities, sexism and racism—had now become not so silly. They had to pay reparations to the women in the company—and most of all, the negative publicity was not good for any corporation. The fact that the studio had been a lily-white organization had affected them badly five years ago. The scare that went through every stockholder's spine was now beginning to take its course in the destiny of the studio's future. Harry Sedwick, the bright young man whose fate it was to care for the studio as deeply as a lover, made his final report. A woman had to be found. A token woman to head the otherwise all-male organization.

Sedwick had pointed out that an organization of a thousand women called Coalition Against Media Arrogance, located in New York, had already been picketing companies catering mainly to women but refusing to support production costs of the CAMA's programs. A certain Miriam Bogert, the Celebrate Women's Event Director, had presented proposals to seventy-five outstanding companies. These companies, she had said to the New York *Times* and the Washington *Post,* refused to deal with women's concerns. She had presented a program called *Celebrate Women* on WPIX-TV following the format of WBZ's production in Boston in January, 1974, and WJZ's production in Baltimore in 1975 created by a Ray Bonwo and co-produced by Stephanie Meagher. Sedwick warned the studio that it was the major Hollywood target on the coalition list. This group of women had written letters of protest stating that women resent being last on the list of programs sponsored by the companies they had chosen. The memo which had gone to the studio heads came directly from Sedwick. It was a memo of companies, corporations, unions, and foundations that had rejected the Women's Coalition Funding requisite. These firms were now being boycotted regularly, such firms as Morgan Guaranty, Avon, Woolworth's, Getty Oil, Bristol-Myers, etc. Some of the slogans used by the coalition were dramatic enough to have attracted the media's attention and were appearing on the news on CBS and NBC.

The studio was on the list. The slogans against the studio said simply LET'S KICK THEM WHERE IT HURTS MOST—AT THE BOX OFFICE. They weren't all that smart-ass, but still, the whole women's thing was turning into a bad joke. It was not good for studio distribution. It was not good for studio image. It was not good for studio product, especially for the shopping market theaters where the studio product was formerly doing good business. Sedwick had been asked to fulfill a specific assignment. It was this—how to counteract the bad publicity. His answer had been swift. A management opening had to be found at the studio. A top management opening. And it had to be filled by a woman. Sedwick, after research, and flipcharts, decided one couldn't take the time to test the market in management. His market target was women—the largest and fastest-growing new market. The president, yes, the male president, of the world's largest film studio had to go. He was, of course, directly responsible for the distribution and image as well as the product. He had to be replaced by a SHE. A she who could target the women's market. A she who could target women's distribution. A she, not a he, would pacify the radical fringe who were no longer the fringe. A she in other words who would guarantee the product for women smelled squeaky clean not only in the race department but in the sex department. Women, after all, were the largest buyers of the studio's product. They not only wanted to be entertained, but wanted to stop being insulted. The day had arrived. A she had to be found. Image was everything. Product was all.

The king was dead. New management was essential.

The meeting took place at nine o'clock. The twelve men were brought to order by the chairman. Sedwick explained the situation. He had obtained a list of women, selected by computer at the management consultant headquarters.

It was a sad day. The meeting was more like a funeral. Sedwick read the names of the women. They were all "possible" candidates for the position but had to be discussed.

Lita Schwartz, a studio lawyer, was the first woman whose name was mentioned. The suggestion was put down.

"She's a ballbreaker. Forget it."

The next name was Lady Bird Johnson. Somebody laughed. Nobody spoke. Then Schwitzer, who had been with the studio for years, said, "Wrong image."

Streisand?

"Are you joking?"

Mengers?

"Pass."

Betty Friedan.

"Too old."

Shirley Chisholm.

"Too much soul."

Mary Wells?

"Too pushy."

Twelve studio men were uncomfortable. Twelve management men were miserable. Boycotts. Women's inter-arts centers. Target dates. All this new patter about broads. It was—unbelievable.

More names. Bella Abzug. Eleanor Perry. Gloria Steinem. Mrs. Danny Kaye. Dr. Joyce Brothers. Other outstanding women were candidates. All shot down. At the end of the list was one no one had ever heard of, Lulu Cartwright. Lawyer. Comedy writer. Single but divorced. Film producer. Still young. The new executive. The new Eastern Hollywood. Written a book on film production. Producer of *Kill, Kill,* which was the sleeper of the year, grossing twenty-three million. Former writer for Steve Allen. Friend of the Kennedys (nobody knew what kind of friend. The computer hadn't answered that one). Good-looking. Bonded to no corporation. Not a company person. But a female person. The credentials were read off in a funeral list of accomplishments. Age thirty-nine, graduate of La Bellson Progressive School, graduate of Bennington, graduate of the Sorbonne École de Droit. Master's at NYU in film production. Comedy writer for ten years. Film producer recently of first female kung fu sleeper. Intellectual. Father wealthy businessman in New York, now deceased. Divorced. One child aged ten. No drinking. No smoking. No loud voice. No ballbreaker. Nothing bad. NOTHING BAD, the computer said.

"We can manipulate her," a voice said.

"We can use her."

"We can bear her," said another voice.

The meeting closed mournfully. A broad had been chosen.

"Helen?"

"The door is open."

I opened the door to Helen's house. West Side, large studio. Helen, poet of weird poems, prophecies, old-time buddy from college. Skinny. Casual. Sloppy. Smart. Going into her late thirties comfortably, still wildly strange and neurotic, Helen looked at me over her glasses.

"I read the paper."

"Do you believe it?"

We walked into her kitchen. Pots. Pans. Books. Newspapers.

"I believe it."

"The studio's in trouble. Who are they going to call in? Allen and Company? This is *cinéma vérité*. And I'm the *vérité*. Thus, instead of a lot of knowing hands, one knowing hand."

"What is the sound of one hand clapping?" Helen asked. We sat down in her kitchen. She walked over to the sink, and made us both a drink. We had strega on the rocks.

"How did it happen?"

"Helen, it's the biggest mystery of all time. Right now I can't put all the pieces together. I gather that there was an

25

executive-search committee that got my name from one of the large head-hunting firms. They must have followed the film I produced and gotten a copy of *Producing, Financing and Distributing Film on a Low Budget,* my funny producing book."

"The book you wrote while you were studying law? How did you ever write that?"

"It was during the time I lived in New York City with husband number one. I was thinking all the time that no one really had a practical book on film, so that anyone who had an idea for a film could put one together. I started keeping track of all the things I would want to know about films if I knew nothing. I wrote about optioning film rights, copyright search, clearance procedure re titles, relationship of option price to purchase price, varieties of distribution media. Oh, God, I researched agents, production financing. I began writing notes to myself in my sleep about studio facilities, agreements. It was all like a game. Finally, when the book was printed, I added some jokes, and it sold quite well. I guess my book, the fact that I've been married twice, have a kid, write for television, and that nobody's ever really gotten to hate me helped. And of course, they wanted some sort of twist. Something radical but not too radical. Not a Black Panther. Not a Muslim. A woman. The first woman president. Ha-ha. That's me."

I took another strega and then changed to a scotch.

Helen looked at me. "Are you really going to do this, Lulu?"

"Yes."

"Can you imagine how your life is going to change?"

"Yes. I'm going to go bananas. A million dollars' worth. I'm going to be one of the highest paid packagers in the world. I'm going to deal with agents, other packagers, creative pishers, production pishers, salesmen, producers, film executives. I'll never have another serene day for the rest of my life."

"Yes, you will. The day you're canned. And that will be what everyone wants. Greek tragedy wasn't exactly made up out of nothing, darling. Everyone will be waiting for your downfall. Every two-bit actor and actress in the world will have your number and will lay in wait for you. Every gossip columnist, accountant, hustler, Stanislavsky actress, everyone in the women's movement, in the women's inter-arts centers, every relative and ex-lay you have ever had, everyone who went to school with you will be after you. There will be no more time for chess. For friends. For Lulu. You will be doing strictly bullshit managerial work. You'll have lunch with someone in your office and they'll say, 'Lulu, are you still writing comedy?' and you'll tell them no, you're *management* now. You'll be up to your ass in contracts, properties, warranties, indemnities, liabilities, production schedules, overhead, attorneys' fees, a whole list of horrors. You'll need an analyst for your analyst."

I looked at Helen. "That's old-style thinking," I said. "New-style thinking is to take anything on. I've been complaining for years about not being able to have something which challenges me. This will not only challenge me, it will humor me. It'll be fun to make trouble in Suck City."

"It will be?" Helen looked at me. "You want some advice from a friend? I'm going to give it to you anyway. Don't take it, Lulu."

"Why?"

"Faust didn't particularly dig life after he sold his soul to the devil."

"This isn't the devil, Helen. Look at it this way—Hollywood is responsible for the sick dreams that we grew up on. Who taught us what we think life is? The movies. Where did we go to duck from our parents and find out about our own absurdities? About horniness? Didn't Hollywood teach us to shave under our arms, to let happiness go just so far, to keep on trying to win the man even if he turned out to be Frankenstein,

27

Junior? Didn't we get our adventures, our poetry, our sense of failure, of always being out of things, of the void, of the human body, of fleshy pictures, of fame, of reaching out and touching the world from those little sick poems pawned off on our brains as movies? Didn't they instruct us on how to be pretty? Weren't we controlled through our girlhood by movies? I'm going to make good movies."

"Stop," said Helen. "It just hasn't been done. For every *Citizen Kane*, there's a million and one *Guiding Lights* and *Razor's Edge* and *I Love Lucy*. For every divine Fred Astaire tap sequence, there's a million sad films showing crap."

"But they're all lies. There isn't one honest film about kids' imagination. Films are just commercials for the system. There's no imagination."

"That's because there isn't any. Occasionally in Italy you see it. A Fellini makes *Eight and a Half*. A Lina Wertmuller makes *The Seduction of Mimi*. Sometimes you see a film that comes out of Asia, like *The Glass Harp*. . . ."

"But films are just this—a continuation of pushing products. And they're all so ugly. There's a formula. Rich is beautiful. Poor is ugly. And then for Christ sakes, there are the trends, the trends about films on monkeys and aborigines, a whole group of films on the romance of innocence or what it's like to back up into the Tassadays, or there are the coming-of-age films, all the films that show women waking up and deciding they too want orgasms and stop doing the dishes. Then there are the Mafia films, the disaster films, the war films, the black films . . .

"You get into markets, and everything's a market. . . ."

"Porn. Give me porn or give me death."

"And all the truly rococo artificial freak show people in the world are trying to go down on you or up on you and make it seem glamorous. Hollywood is the forest where manslaughter is always appropriate. All those floating kidney swimming pools. All those wise-guys looking like gurus. Okay, go live with the impotent showoffs and think you're making some progress."

Helen sat back. She had concluded her lecture. But it didn't convince me. I wanted the fun of being out there with those people MARKETING, dreaming up their sick fantasies so they could get rich and have big cars and diamonds as big as your pancreas, that almighty place that manufactured fantasies. I was curious.

And I told Helen. She listened to me.

"Can I come visit you?" she asked, laughing.

"Yeah," I said. "Let's go get some pizza."

"Fuck *pizza*. I'm going to make some dinner for you. Now that you're a celebrity, don't you like a nice home-cooked meal?"

"What do you have?"

"I cooked some stuffed cabbage."

We sat up drinking. We sat up all night talking. Until morning. Sun through windows. Helen laughing. Smoking. Old times.

"What are you thinking?" Helen asked before I left.

"I am thinking how I will miss you. I am thinking of how much we meant to each other when we were in college. I am thinking of how you sang 'Deep Blue Sea Baby' and married a sad and beautiful college professor and had four children and came fresh and idealistic into the oh-it-hurts world. I am thinking of how I once used a Ouija board in college and pretended to be a seer. I was Madame Blavatsky! Right out of Yeats. I am thinking how we used to talk." Sunlight. New York early morning. Pain. Friendship.

"Good-bye, Lulu," Helen said. She kissed me good-bye. Hugged me. And sent me out into the morning. Empty streets. No cabs. Walking home.

DARE. DARE. DARE.

It was a dream that was happening to me. The next morning, I woke up and knew. In some dark back part of my

29

mind, I knew that I had become a *producer* of films only to make it possible to have my own words known.

I walked into my lawyer's office. She had her office in the World Trade Center. I said to the receptionist, "Please tell Mrs. Ludman that Lulu Cartwright is here."

Elizabeth Ludman is my age. We both went to law school at the same time. She went to Columbia University, and I attended the École de Droit in Paris, taking classes in law while I was married to my first husband, Abraham. Later I finished my law degree at Columbia when I moved back to America. It was at Columbia I met Elizabeth. I became a writer of comedies. She became a writer of briefs, torts, letters of opinion, another sort of comedy. I hadn't seen her in years but asked her to represent me on my second divorce. We have since been friends. When I came in her office, she was eating an egg salad sandwich.

"Want one?" she asked. "I'll ask my secretary to order one for you."

"No. I'm back on a diet. At the Kennedy Clinic."

"What is that?"

"They give you shots. It comes from nuns' pee. It's called by some fancy Italian name, named after the doctor who invented it. Then you get a little baggie with four hundred and fifty calories a day, all nicely packed for you. It's really the food that causes weight loss. It's a pain in the ass. If you cheat one bit, I mean, have one stick of chewing gum, you're finished."

"I don't have time for that," Elizabeth said.

She picked up the phone. Spoke into the receiver to her secretary.

"No calls."

She relaxed in her chair.

"I read the papers," Elizabeth said. "It's impressive."

"Impressive?" I said. "It's incredible."

"How did it really happen?"

30

"First of all, let me say that the whole thing has a dreamlike quality about it."

"In what way?"

"First, I get a phone call. I'm being considered for the head of the studio. Then I am flown in the company jet to the Coast. Then I meet with men who resemble jailers. They are the guards of the studio fortune. I sit in a tiny boardroom that resembles a jail. Only it's an office. Water is in front of me. They face me, smiling. They ask me questions."

"What kind of questions?"

"Elizabeth, they want to know everything about my life. My political life. My personal history. My financial life. My professional life as a comedy writer. My experience producing independent films. What I would do if I took over the studio."

"What did you tell them?" She continued eating the egg sandwich.

"I told them nothing, of course, about the women's movement. I spared them. I figured that their egos were too fragile. They're all on a power trip. After all, they think they are hiring me as the token woman. They want me to stay in my place. They want my brains, but not my pains. I tell them that I was involved in the arts and letters campaign for Robert Kennedy and that I wrote position papers for Congressman Ottinger when he was running for the Senate. That doesn't impress them. I tell them I've been married twice. *That* impresses them. They're basically suspicious of anyone too happy or unhappy. I give them my law credentials. And then I talk about marketing. Flip charts. Creativity."

"What did they think?"

"They thought I was a nice gal they could handle."

"And what else?" She laughed.

"They are all interested in energy. Cosmic energy. Body energy. They are all dead inside, so they need other people's energies. That's why everyone out there plays tennis. They

31

have to move. They always have to *move*. Even if they're miserable and dead, they have to move. They all have to be famous producers. Famous executives. And nobody who's famous sits still. They thought they could put up with me. And they liked the fact that I play tennis. Besides, I look feminine. That's what they want."

"What would you do with the studio portfolio?"

"You manage it with me."

Elizabeth looked at me. She was expecting me to say that. And she couldn't pretend otherwise.

"I'll have to get a copy of all the holdings. Then we can sit down and decide what to keep and what to sell. Money is a very strange subject out there. It's not money, really. It's 'communication.' They put fifteen million into a development of a new system of tape films to be shown on home TV sets because they think that is the communication of the future. I'm supposed to be an expert on 'home entertainment,' and they tell me the more money they put into it, the more they are going to communicate. They figure fifteen million is one kind of communication. Twenty is another. The more money, the more communication. Four million in a film is four million worth of communication. It's all ridiculous."

"Hello, little Flip-chart world," I said.

Elizabeth continued. "What are you going to do about tax shelters? You know that sheltering has become a very risky business, and with the new rulings, it borders on being illegal."

"I'm getting rid of sheltering. It's a tax dodge, and sooner or later the studios will be in a lot of trouble. It also gets rid of the lawyers. You know I hate lawyers. That's why I write comedy."

Elizabeth pushed her chair back. Smoked.

"Then you're going to take it. Okay. I'll draw up the contract. What are the terms? You haven't even told me."

"They are offering me a salary of two hundred thousand dollars a year for five years, with stock options. I told them to make it three hundred and forget about stock options. And I get a piece of any film I produce. And all expenses, of course."

So much money. I left my lawyer's office and went home.

It was beyond what I dreamed of. Those businessmen who worked on the production side had chosen me to be their number one packager. I thought of the few years I had spent in the Rawlins agency working with production ideas, writing scripts. My dog days as a comedy writer, the years in law school, the years of being a prisoner in two marriages, the years of fucking up and being an emotional loser, all the years of being poor and *terrified* of myself and others didn't mean a fucking thing to these people. Little Lulu's Loss-years. They just never saw *me* as Lulu Cartwright. To them I was someone who could be a good image of the new Hollywood. Cut costs of production. Bring "new ideas" to their record division. Change family entertainment. Create "home entertainment" films that would sell to the new public now hungry for more sophisticated skin. THE HEAD OF THE STUDIO. It said that in the papers. As soon as I walked into my house, the phone rang. It was my father's oldest friend, Hughie Farber. Oh, Papa, I wish you were here.

"Lulu?"

"Hughie? You must have the papers in your hand."

"Listen, Lulu, it's too bad your old man isn't alive to see this. Can you imagine? He never thought you were any good at business, Lulu. He always thought you were some kind of a nut. He loved you. Don't get me wrong. But for God's sakes, the head of Hollywood. Lulu Cartwright. It's just a shame your old man can't be here."

"Thanks, Hughie. I'll be in touch with you."

The phone rang. Another phone.

"Hughie, it's my other phone."

"Dat's all right. I'll hold on."

I picked up the other phone. It was my mother. She was crying.

"My baby" was all she was saying into the receiver.

"Mom," I said into the white phone. "Hold on. I'll be with you in a second. Daddy's old friend—do you remember him?—Hughie is on the other phone."

"Hughie. Listen. I can't talk to you now. But I appreciate your congratulations."

Hughie refused to hang up.

"Listen, Lulu. I gotta ask you somethin'. When you get to California, if you got a moment, could you see my cousin-in-law, Ronald Berkson? He's been out there for years working with the television commercial people at Universal. He looks like Clark Gable. The fact is they give him a draw. Only one hundred and thirty-five dollars a week take-home pay. Is that enough to support a family with? With three kids, could you live on that? For your father's sake, for old times, Lulu, I want you to interview Ronald. He could be very big in your organization."

"Okay," I said. "Can you call me back this evening?"

"Yeah. Remember when you and your dad and I used to go to the races? Remember Belmont? I'd put you on my lap, and you'd look out of the binoculars. Did you ever think you were going to be so famous?" Hughie asked.

I had no answer. I threw him a kiss. "I'll help Ronald," I said.

I hung up. The phone rang again. It was Mrs. Linel, my son's teacher at school.

"One moment, I can't talk now," I said to Mrs. Linel. "I'll call you back."

"That's all right, dear. I just wanted to congratulate you." She hung up.

"Mom?"

"I'm still holding," my mother said proudly.

"I didn't tell you about any of this because as long as they were considering me, I thought I wouldn't get your hopes up, Mother. Yes. I am very happy. I think I am."

My mother had a few words of encouragement. It was almost as if I were getting married again.

"You will make a wonderful head of the studio," she said, substituting studio for wife.

"All these years I've believed in you. I knew you would find yourself. So many nights I prayed for you. I said just make Lulu find herself. What's it going to be like out there? Can I visit you?"

"Mom, I'm not going to Siberia. Of course. As soon as I get settled."

"Will you meet a nice crowd?" my mother asked.

"Are you kidding, Mother? Those people are all con men."

"Don't say that," my mother said. "Your grandfather was in show business. And you know there must be very interesting people out there. I want you to dress nicely. You're going to be in the public eye. Will you have a car and chauffeur? What will your accommodations be like?"

My mother always used big words for little words. Accommodations.

"Mother?"

"Yes?"

"Why don't you take the plane down from Boston? We could spend the whole day together."

"I'm still working," she said doubtfully.

"But, Mom, I'd like to see you. I love you. I miss you. Come down and help me get everything arranged. Okay. I know you don't like the shuttle, so take the bus. I'll see you later. All right, sweetheart?"

"If you really want me."

"I do. Good-bye."

The phone rang another time. It was my French teacher and oldest friend, Marianne. She was a surrealist.

"My dear. This is mystical. This is a miracle. It's positively hilarious. You. As a successful businesswoman. I never heard of anything so absurd. Think of all the men you can make love to. My God, with that kind of position, you can do it with almost anyone."

She always thought in terms of genitalia.

"This whole thing is a nightmare," I said into the phone. "Can you believe it that this phone hasn't stopped ringing? And it's not even ten o'clock in the morning."

"Are you going to make changes?"

"In what?" I asked.

"In the studio."

"Of course I am. I'm going to make kiddie movies for adults and skin flicks for kiddies."

"*Merde*," she said. "I mean that as good luck."

We were laughing. But I was aware that I had a lot to do that morning.

"Come by and have breakfast with me," I said.

"I will be there. What time? I have to teach."

"I don't know, sweetheart. Any time."

I could hear the other phone ringing. It was incredible. As if I had awakened all the fantasies of everyone I knew.

"Bye."

"Au revoir."

I picked up the phone. It was another lawyer, Donald Fine, who worked with me on my last film.

"Lulu?"

"Fine?"

"There are a couple of nuts-and-bolts facts and procedures in the industry that I want to talk to you about. It's often confusing."

"Go ahead," I said.

He usually spoke to me as if I were a bewildered dwarf, but I felt like one this morning, so I just let him keep talking, grateful for the fact that he wasn't hysterical.

36

"It's about financing and distribution. You have an opportunity now, Lulu, to change the way that's done out there. It's not that you don't know about acquisitions and financing and distribution agreements. And you're so goddamn bright I don't have to talk dollars and cents and percentages with you. I just want to sit down and have lunch with you and talk about the details. But you're going to have to make a lot of changes out there. I know that's not what they're expecting. But I'm telling you, Lulu, that we should sit down and talk about a whole new way of handling cash advances and guarantees. Also, Lulu, there's a lot of stuff I have on my mind that can be helpful when it comes to dealing with the P-D rights. And also the shorter distribution purposes."

"I appreciate it," I said. "I'm not even thinking of all this at the moment."

Through the long cord of the telephone which led from his secrets to mine, which led from my bedroom to his office in the Brickman Building, to his desk with the pictures of his family, to my bed and my books and my flowers and my memos about exhibition agreements, to his desk—from my bed—to his desk—he began laughing.

"You haven't signed the contract?"

"No. I'm still thinking about it. . . ."

"It said in the papers. . . ."

"I know. And I'm pretty sure I'm going to take it. They think I have taken it. And I'm supposed to fly out to the Coast. They've made their company plane available and I'm supposed to go to LA tomorrow. But I'll call you before I go. Thanks."

I hung up the phone. I then took both the phones off the hook. And walked into my son's room.

He was up. And putting on his clothes for day camp. His room looked like a Kung Fu Palace. Pictures of Bruce Lee everywhere. My son. I loved him more than myself. It was hard for anyone to believe that unless they had a child of their own. But there was this *person*, this little *person* in front of me who loved me and whom I loved. He had just finished changing the water for his goldfish.

"Mama?"

"Yes, sweetheart?"

"Are you going away?"

"What do you mean?"

"I heard you talking on the phone. And, Mama, you look frightened. Are you going away?"

There was sunlight in the room. Room of plants and hockey sticks and tiny books and large books. Room of my sitting on the edge of the bed during earaches and colds. Room of being friends. Room of spanks. Room of my son. I wanted to say, "I love you."

When David looked at me, sometimes I felt as if I were at the bottom of the sea. The waves knocking against me. I swallowed water, surfacing and floating and talking to him. David was my only child. After his father and I divorced, we had clung to each other, and we were still roped together in that kind of love that comes when something has gone wrong with the family and only survivors remain.

"I'm not going anyplace without you."

"Where are you going?" David asked.

"I am going to take a job in California. I'm going to take a job with a film studio. So that instead of making films independently here or trying to keep writing comedy programs, I'm going to be putting together films in California," I said to my son.

"Am I coming?"

"Of course. You and Emma and I are going to move to Los Angeles."

"Do you know anyone there?" he asked.

"A few people. And I'll know more people."

He went back to the fish tank and began putting some crumbs into the fishbowl. I saw him counting out five crumbs carefully.

"I don't know anyone there, Mother," he said. "And I will have to start at a new school, where nobody will know me and probably nobody will like me."

I started to say something to him nutty and odd, like "Everybody has nobody," but I said nothing.

"And besides, Mom, when we get to California, how do you know that you'll like it? Won't you miss your friends?"

"I'll miss them, but I can always see them when we come back to New York. It's only a few hours away by plane."

The floor of the sea. I remembered all the men in my life since my husband, staying at my house and David saying, "Who is that, Mommy? Who is that?" and wanting to be part of my life, closeness with everyone. David, who won me over every day with his homework and crayons and pictures that had comic-strip words coming out of them. David, who fled with me during holidays when I went to Florida because I couldn't bear to be alone in Dead New York and hated Christmas trees and carols and Christmas sales and false activity and no family. David, who shadowed me, who tugged me in the dark, who talked to me as a friend. With David I was in an ocean deeper than the dark mystery part of the sea, the two of us swimming. I loved him.

"Mommy, I won't go there."

"Why not?" I asked.

"Because I'll be lonely," David said.

"Who says so?"

"I say so. I won't know anybody. You will be at your job. And I'll be left after school with Emma. I'm too big to have a nurse, Mommy. You told me when I was ten years old, I wouldn't need a nurse anymore, and we still have her."

"She's not a nurse," I said.

"She is a nurse."

"She's not. She's a housekeeper, David."

"What's the difference? She's still a nurse."

David began packing some books into a backpack.

"I hate California," David said.

"Do you? So do I. But we have to go there. Because I'm making a living. And my living takes me there. And it's an opportunity to change things."

"What things?" David wanted to know.

"A lot of things. No more Mickey Mouse."

"What other things?"

"No more Mickey Mouse. And really good movies you can see. So you can go sit in the dark movie houses like I did when I was a child and eat ice cream and popcorn and really have a good time. Mommy will make movies about lousy hospitals and bad insane asylums."

I figured nobody in the world would understand all this but David.

"Why do you want to do that, Mommy?"

"I don't know, David, I just want to. Sometimes you want to do things very much, don't you?"

"Yes." He looked at me in a strange little-boy way.

"Come hug me."

"I don't want to."

"We are going to live in a wonderful place."

"What kind of place?"

"I don't know. Maybe a hotel."

"Do you like living in a hotel?" David asked.

"Wouldn't you like a hotel?"

"No. I hate hotels. Sometimes I stay with Daddy in a hotel."

"Well, that's different. That's the Galapagos Islands. I mean a Hollywood hotel."

"Which one?" David asked.

Now he was at least accepting the move.

"The Beverly Wilshire?" I said meekly.

He didn't know the difference. We were all swimming. The bottom of the sea. The bottom of the sea.

"Okay, Mama. I'll go. When do you go?"

"I leave tomorrow. Then you all move out to be with me. You and Emma and me. Grandma will come down and stay with you while I'm gone."

"Everybody is gone away in the summer," David said, changing the subject. Then suddenly he looked at me.

"How come Daddy didn't want to see me this summer?"

"I told you that he did want to see you. But that he's moving his office from the Galapagos Islands to Manila and a move sometimes takes a long time. He's going to come and visit with you in the fall."

"Will I like Manila?"

I hugged him suddenly. I held him so close.

"Of course you'll like Manila. You'll visit Daddy next summer. And we'll be together in our own place in California. And we will go swimming. And we will have a good time. You'll see, David. We will really have a good time. We will go into the sea, just like two fish, and have a good time. Into the fishy sea."

"Bye, Mama. I have to go. The bus will be waiting for me."

I took David to the elevator. I hugged him. He hugged back. I hugged again.

When he left, I was again at the tip of the ocean's edge. I had a hard time to keep from crying.

"Sasha, I may be going to California," I said, under a mirror and a stuffed fish.

Sasha was working at a film production studio. She was a close friend, beloved friend, tall as a temple goddess, with deep green eyes that you could swim inside. She always made me feel happy, like a little girl. I loved to see Sasha. We giggled. We looked at things as if through a spyglass. She reminded me of once a long time ago in boarding school when one had best friends, friends that always made you feel good when you saw them. Friends you could tell secrets to. Friends into whose beds you could even come at night and look through a flashlight at books and letters from home. Friends you could hold hands with. Sasha was married for the second time to an imperative verb, a man so dynamic and charming that it was sometimes difficult to see her. He was one of the great futurists who had worked with Kennedy on the space program and was now a consultant and lecturer.

"Sasha, if I tell you all this, you won't tell anyone?"

"Of course not."

"This whole thing is a nightmare. It's more than a dream coming true. It's a dream I never had coming true."

"Don't be silly," Sasha said.

We ordered our fish.

"You've always been ambitious. It's not unusual that you should be successful."

"You call this successful?" I said.

"Well, sooner or later they were going to let a woman head a studio. And they weren't going to pick Sue Mengers or any of the straight agency people because they had too many enemies. You're a maverick. Someone who has always been successful, always had talent, but who nobody knows. What are you going to do when you get there?"

"Seriously, Sasha, the first thing I'm going to do is make the studio resign from the Academy of Motion Pictures. Not only is the Academy Awards pure fakery, but they *award* little golden statues for films that simply reflect racism and sexism and exploitation. They call that entertainment. The whole concept of entertainment has to be changed. It's not entertaining to see a film where a woman becomes a drunk because she can't get a job. Or entertaining to see two closet queens running from their own hometown because they can't come out of the closet. Anyway, the films they have been turning out stink."

"But they make money," interrupted Sasha.

"They may be making money, but they couldn't be making that much money because, Sasha, the company is bankrupt. I'd like to cut out the Oscar crap and all the awards crap to begin with. Secondly, I'm interested in documentaries. There is so much about this country that can be combined in filmic fictional form. I'm not talking about films like *Z* but films like *Nashville*, for example, where you really get a piece of *knowledge* about this country. There are so many goddamn renaissance happenings going on that no one has ever really documented successfully. I'd like to show corruption. Through comedy if necessary. I'd like to crack open the unions."

"What about the agencies?" asked Sasha, neglecting her fish.

"I'd like to take most of the agents and send them a letter and tell them nobody at the studio needs their services," I continued.

"Anyway, Sasha, I'm not going to be the unpaid servant girl of the studio. Faithful. Honest. Carrying the burden uncomplaining. If they think they have hired a noble nigger, they have another guess coming. I'm not going to be just another fatty playing cards with the guys in LA. I've convinced myself that I need to do a little investigating. I might even hire a few people to form a quiet little investigative unit. And after that, when I've looked into the corrupt way everything is done, I'll recommend to the studios a few solutions. After all, don't we still believe in fairy tales?"

"Meaning . . ." asked Sasha, leaning over her coleslaw, looking at me like a goddess of apples and warm weather.

"What I mean is this. There is no Cinderella. The golden Warner Brothers' pumpkin was chewed to a pulp by MGM a long time ago. The gown was covered with blood by Universal. The clock struck out at Paramount. Columbia took the golden slipper and broke it until all that remained was shards of glass in everyone's eye. Then Universal maced the coach. Fox ate the stepsister and the stepmother. Cinderella is dead. So, you ask me what I'm going to do?"

I stopped eating my lunch.

"I'm writing a memo to David O. Selznick. Even though he's dead, I'm writing a memo to him. 'Dear David. Go fuck yourself. For years we sat being spitted upon and farted at and shit on. We are going to make a few little changes. And then we're going to start all over again.' "

Sasha had to go. She shook her head.

"I don't know. You're going to be very unpopular," she said.

I kissed her good-bye. We split the check and left the restaurant. She went back to her office. One of my favorite friends. Sasha, the golden one.

It was funny. I was standing in front of Lincoln Center where they showed a film festival every year but rarely showed American films. That's another thing I'm going to get rid of. The bullshit cloak and suiters who pick the films for festivals. It's going to be a whole new ball game.

I was going to do my best to make different kinds of films. To get them shown in different kinds of festivals. Oh, yeah!

I felt powerful. And good. Yippee. I was the unbroken token.

And I felt for the first time as if I had a voice in the pathology called movies. I, Lulu Cartwright, was going to do something about the death of the soul.

memory on the plane

On the company airplane I began thinking of the past. I was jogging to my new life. My new job. I would have appointments every moment. On the trip, I had brought an attaché case filled with memos for projects. Filled with financial plans and stratagems, fantasies and dreams for fulfillment. I had run up a two-thousand-dollar long-distance phone bill conferring with financial experts, novelists, specialists, poets, playwrights; I had written memos to myself. Memos that would unsettle a lot of people. I decided not to read them. Instead, I just tilted my head back and looked out the window. It was night. I watched New York City become smaller. I allowed myself to bob into the giant stars and dwarf stars. It was all like a dream. "In dreams begin responsibilities," the poet Delmore Schwartz had written. I began thinking of nothing. Then of the past. Then of the men in my past. The past which I tried to keep away kept coming back. The old life. The old lies. The affairs. The childhood. All jumbled and mixed together. It was the me I used to be. I couldn't stop it. I just let it run all over me. The pain. The pain and the weird sense of the past amputated Lulu. The person I used to be. I had to laugh. It was painful.

I was once Little Lulu. You may have read about me in the comics years ago. In case you didn't read the comics, I'll tell you about my old self. I always wore a smile. I was good-natured all the time. I was always in the same dress, and I had ringlets. Most of all, I was a schmuck. I was always being generous to other people, especially to the boys I knew, and they paid me back by not wanting me around. Nothing good ever happened to me, but I kept coming back for more every Sunday. There wasn't anything to really remember about me except that I was always getting myself into trouble. I was a fool. I was slightly wacky. I remained little. One day, I had a nervous collapse. They asked me what my name was. All I could say was Ul Ul (that's Lulu backwards). As Ul Ul, I went through the tortures of hell.

I wanted to be a functioning person, not just like the little girl in the comics who was Everygirl. I also wanted to be loved. For myself. But I had no self, and that was the trouble. It's taken me a light-year to find out who Lulu is.

My name is Lulu Cartwright. I am about to be president of a large studio. Now I am moving away from an East Seventy-eighth Street town house next to Doris Duke's sad mansion, which is now a library. I am a renovated woman, with high blood pressure and a temper that I am trying to subdue. My life has been a fight for self-control. About ten years ago I began writing hunks for comediennes and comedy programs for a living. Then I wrote and produced a film called *Kill, Kill*, which is about women's violence.

Before I forget, I want to admit that I have made stupid mistakes in my life. If anything can be said at all, I guess you could say I have been living out a pilgrim's progress, and in my own way, I am a pilgrim. I do not avoid myself. I am not afraid of growing old. In fact, I no longer even know what age means—except at this point in my life, I feel I have suffered enough. Not that you ever stop suffering, but you stop letting other people know you are—except through jokes, of course. You know the old Pennsylvania Dutch saying (also found in fortune cookies at upper-class Chinese restaurants in New

York City) WE GROW TOO SOON OLD AND TOO LATE SHMART? Well, I want to say that it's not too late. My life isn't over. I, Lulu Cartwright, through a series of desperate acts with desperate people (none more desperate than myself) made life, which is a beautiful thing, into a terrible thing. That's over. But some people never learn at all. It takes a long time to learn how to be your own self, depending on no one and shmart before you're too old. Especially if you're a girl.

I've made mistakes, mistakes. I have a genius for mistakes. I've been a Comedienne, Writer, Mother, Daddy's Little Girl, Fast Fuck, Troublemaker, Analysand, Huggee, Touchy Person, Housemaid, Pillar of Strength, Mistress, Bookkeeper, Lawyer, Professional Wife, Masseuse, Massagee, Teacher, Executive, Demonstrator, Ex-Lady, Ex-Cupcake, Ex-Wife, Dignified Woman. Oh! The fantasy world of feeling . . . of creating jokes and not knowing where the life left off and the joke began.

Sometimes I, as good old Lulu, otherwise known as Ul, used to get up in the morning and be fucking tired of being funny. To write jokes was no joke. I remember that the man who gave me the biggest pain in the ass was the leftover liberal at United Artists who had a name for every kind of humor.

"This script doesn't make it," he had said without wasting time on what my father used to call the niceties. "There's the humor of fear. There's the humor of attrition. There are many kinds of organic humor. But none of it's here."

I sat there. This guy had to be joking with all his philosophies about organic humor. Didn't he realize that women were tired of seeing themselves always up there on the non-organic screen as Lassie and always coming home? What did he mean by the humor of *attrition*? I had written a funny script—but they wouldn't buy it. They wanted a script that was *engaging*. What's so *engaging* about female rage? It wasn't funny.

"We don't get it," said the Important Mammals at United Artists.

49

"See how funny you can be?" my agent Morty said.

He was reading *The Last Laugh*, a TV female comedy hour I had written with my friend and sometimes collaborator Jacquie, on the Coast. It began with a new look at Washington (Washington revisited). It had a hunk called "The Man in Your Life," another section called "What Are the Women Doing This Week?" and a slapstick section called "Masterpiece Theater," showing how women had been left out of literature and the Bible. It had Ophelia and Rapunzel and the Moses legend retold, and it ended with a wacky takeoff on how women never asked for recognition, going back to the Old Testament.

Morty read aloud from his favorite part of the script.

SCENE: An office of a Hollywood agent. Enter his secretary, Miriam.

MIRIAM: Hello, Mr. Moses, how are you this morning?

MOSES: I have a hangover.

MIRIAM (*gently*): Thou shalt not drink.

MOSES: I don't know what I'm going to do. I have an appointment with God this afternoon to close a deal. With God's help, I'd like to get out of talent management and into producing. I'm tired of handling the careers of people like Pharaoh. I want to get into the Big Time. And so I've optioned this great property from God. Oh, I have such a headache.

MIRIAM: Listen, if you don't feel well, why don't you lie down in the bulrushes and I'll go and close the deal with God?

MOSES: What a good idea. The industry is such a bulrush business. You know, Miriam, I think you're the smartest secretary in show business. I'm so glad I found you. Now I want you to go to God. He should have eleven commandments that he wants me to produce. No one has ever seen the property—it's hot. First we'll make it into a book. Then a movie. Then I have plans for a lot of spin-offs.

MIRIAM: What's it about?

50

Moses: I don't know anything about it. All I know is it's not dirty, it has no sex, no violence, it's R rated. The kind of thing you can take your kids to. I'd like to show it to my neighbor, Marty. He's with one of the big agencies.

Miriam: Oh, Mr. Moses, don't show it to Marty; he might covet it.

Moses: If he coveted it, I'd kill him.

Miriam: Thou shalt not kill. Where is God staying these days?

Moses: He's at the penthouse in the Sinai Hilton. But the elevator is broken. You'll have to climb the steps.

Miriam: Climb the steps? Do you know what a climb that is?

Moses: Believe me, when you see the property, you'll know it's worth it. The only problem is, there's only one copy. He hasn't taken it to studio duplicating yet. That's your job, Miriam. Now he's going to hand it to you in slabs.

Miriam: Excuse me. If I'm climbing all those stairs, if I'm taking it down in slabs, and if I'm translating it from the original Hebrew and bringing it up to date, you know His archaic style, if I'm doing all that work, couldn't I at least be the line producer?

Moses (*getting tough*): Look, I told you when you took the job that you'd have to do all the dirty work and that the salary wasn't so great. But it's got prestige. It's a glamor job. Don't forget when you answer the phone, you represent *me*. How many gals would love to be in your position?

Miriam: I'd like to be in your position, Mr. Moses.

Moses: Well, maybe if you're here long enough—if you stick around, for, say, two thousand years—who knows?

(CUT to pantomime of Miriam climbing the stairs, then chiseling commandments quickly in shorthand. CUT to office. Miriam wheels in shopping cart with ten tablets.)

Miriam: Mr. Moses, I've got them, the Ten Commandments. And they're terrific.

Moses: Ten? I told you there were eleven. You forgot one.

Miriam: Well, God only chose to give me ten. He also thought it was very unfair that I shouldn't be given any historical credit.

MOSES: You know, Miriam, it's because of pushy dames like you that every morning when I get up I thank God I'm not a woman.

"But it's not *funny*, Lulu. In the television sense. It's funny in the funny sense, but in the television sense it's not *funny*. If you see what I mean."

"How about the *Alphabet World of Sidney Cooper?*" I asked. "How do you like that fable?"

"I don't," he said. "I just don't like it at all. It *stinks*. It's *sophomoric*. It's not your best *stuff*."

"Humor is supposed to be *sophomoric*. Humor isn't *geriatric* or *mature*," I protested.

The agent had his own *ideas*. "Stop writing dreck that won't sell. Stop writing about comic-strip characters. Be witty. Be sophisticated!"

I had begun writing "jokes" in boarding school. I was the funny one in the class, the butterball (always overweight) joker. When I was fifteen, my father, old Seymour the Ribbon King (Seymour had invented a new kind of typewriter ribbon), used to say, "With your jokes and your ass, you can get any guy in the world. But you will never hold on to him unless you learn how to cater. A guy can take just so much. Ha-ha-ha. Then he wants someone who delivers. You don't want to bring home the bacon to a comedienne."

"Who wants the bacon?" I would say. And who wants those serious dark-haired men anyway that most rich men's daughters married in the game of blindwomen's bluff? The men who make good livings? You call that living? I call that a dying, not a living.

"Remember this, Lulu, this is a dog-eat-dog world, and you are not a dog."

Woof.

But I found, finally, a man who catered to me.

One thing was apparent: Dumbo loved himself. He adored his own ass, for example. That was why he always posed with his ass raised while lying on the fur rug I gave him. Dumbo posing on his white sheepskin looked like something out of a baby picture. His hair was curled in a cute babylike way. He smiled. He sang his goo, goo songs, "I love youuuuuuu for sentimentalllllll reeeeasons," looking at me and using his eyes in a babylike way. He played baby. I played baby nurse. Madame Lulu Cartwright. Sent from the Save the Artist Baby Nurse Agency. References? But he was good to me.

My name is Lulu. Forgive me if I keep repeating my name over again, but it is only to remind myself that I exist.

And don't give me that bullshit about I am, therefore I think, or vice versa, because I do a lot of thinking and here's the rub. I still question my existence every day of my life. It was because of this that I got involved four years ago with Dumbo Lavitch. He made me feel good, at first.

Dumbo is now in the foot business. Reflexology. He rubs *feet* in New York City for a living. Straight out of a fairy tale—Aladdin rubbing his lamp, the prince looking for a glass slipper, Puss in Boots, Jesus in drag. Dumbo rubs toes, corns, souls, and believes all this will make him a *healer*. He takes off your slipper (if you're a client) and then he rubs your feet (how depends on your bank account). Dumbo the Heel is now a Healer. But he was once my wife.

Back then it was necessary to understand Dumbo's pathology. And my own. Once I even had considered murder. That's right: assassination. Better than contraception. Look the other way. Put a diaphragm over his eye and call him Moshe Dayan. Do something to him. Wound. Slap. Get even. But of course, you can't get *even*. You go to jail. You can't do much in jail. They don't even let you make license plates in the women's jail.

They don't even let you protest in jail, and we all know that women in jail just wait to die. But why die? Why not get back at the motherfucker? But how? Put glass in my feet so that when he rubbed them he'd cut himself? So many memories of dear Dumbo lying in my arms, saying in his monotone voice "You turn me on," as if he were a faucet. And the little drip kept fucking and sucking——for jackets and suits.

Dumbo, my beloved, with your curly hair and your magnificent hands and your small white onyx ass and your eyes that slanted into brown travertine almonds and your Roman nose and your lips which were always cold and your torso all bony and rich as alabaster. My golden alabaster gardener and godhead and Goliath.Why on earth did I think I needed you?

I remember getting life and fantasy all mixed up with Dumbo. I needed a wife——someone to take care of me——or so I thought at the time. Dumbo, was it only four years ago that you were my wife?

Dumbo Lavitch. I see Dumbo as I saw him the first time. Thin, in shiny maroon pants. The crotch shines in the dark. He is waiting. Suddenly, three cameras switch on in my mind. The cameras start rolling. They start recording the tragedy. I can't stop them.The cameras, the cameras, they are turning so quickly.The sound equipment turns on. Dumbo walks toward me. Footsteps. Then switch to another time, the time that he left me. It begins with his showing up at my house a little late, then very late, then not at all. *Where* is he? He had been living by my side, practicing the guitar, playing the chords of "On Top of Old Smoky" over and over again. "On Top of Old Smoky," then suddenly the breakup. Dumbo is gone. Old Smoky is gone. Everything over.Why was it so difficult to say good-bye? Why did it frighten me? Was I so afraid of myself? I hung on to this *moron*. Was it like a child at boarding school on a cold Sunday hanging on to her mommy's hand?

Dumbo walks into my house one day and says, "I'm leaving you forever, Lulu. You no longer turn me on."

He is still wearing his blue poplin raincoat. The cameras record now quickly. He steps toward me, puts his hands around my neck. He is choking me. "You don't turn me on," he is saying. My breath goes out of my throat. Suddenly, he is the enemy. We are two opponents off-balancing each other. I try to fight back, to bite, to hit. Suddenly, I think of Jerome Mackey and the karate I might have studied but didn't. Little black belts dance back and forth in my mind. Why wasn't I a black belt? A blue belt? Any kind of belt? I kid myself. I could whack Dumbo around, chop him up. I could be a strong person, not a helpless, yelling, divorced, frightened woman with a kid whose lover, younger and stronger, a male whore, wears tight maroon pants and is choking her.

Lulu Cartwright has fallen prey to Dumbo Lavitch, a model and singer, a professional extra who takes vitamin E and rubs his hair with coconut oil and eats health food and uses a juicer and believes in reflexology and the occult and reads how-to-do-it books and you-can-if-you-want-to books and books on other lifetimes. Lulu Cartwright, comedy writer. Her own life is more grotesque than the comedy she could write. Her life funnier (more tragic?) than anything she could write. Lulu Cartwright, who works for Odyssey House, Cancer Care, the Collegiate School, the Help Save the Refugees Committee. Lulu, mother, good friend, lonely woman, scared-to-death animal. Lulu Cartwright will not continue her reversed-role relationship with Mr. Dumbo Lavitch.

Follow the footprints. . . .

Isn't life a bitch?

I'm a woman laughing at myself. Dumbo, you were just one of my mistakes, although at the time it seemed to make perfect sense in the Female Comedy. At first you were a wonderful wife. You were a whore in bed. A cock in the kitchen. Tired of my old Step-and-Kvetch-it female role, I let love go to the dogs, where it always belonged, and reversed genders. You played wife. I played husband. I let love go to the mad dogs and made myself live out the fantasy of what you called *helping* each other. I needed a wife. You needed a husband. I thought I was using you. You thought you were using me. What a perfect relationship.

Dumbo. Even though your love making did resemble touch typing (all automatic), I was an equal opportunity employer and you were the best typist possible. But your mind was always elsewhere. As it always is in the mechanical arts. Anyway, old whore, old gigolo, oddball gangbangbuster of the desperate show biz world, with your perfumed armpits and your K-Y Jelly and Bain de Soleil and your imitation Gucci loafers and your open sports shirts and your Hollywood pretensions and your name-dropping and your singing lessons and your baboon subnormal intelligence, your turned-off soul and your available asshole along with your astrological prophecies and fantasies, your cockamamie beliefs, your occult politics, your upward mobility, your well-massaged but balding head, your hair blower, and you, the human blower of contacts, alas, old chap, as I was saying, you are nowhere and never will be anywhere because you are a loser, a cheap, boring whore, and a phony liar.

I didn't know that because fantasy plays tricks on us all. I believe I *needed* your love for my happiness. What *love*? What *happiness*?

Dumbo darling, you controlled your narcissism when you were living at my house but couldn't wait to run home to your own mirror. There you could parade in front of the mirror and make phone calls to secretaries of casting agents. While you washed me off your body in the shower, you sang all your favorite tunes, especially "Fly Me to the Moon."

You had trouble speaking English correctly and used to drop your *ing* endings, so you would say speakin or bein or comin or goin, and you generally used a toothpick, and the look on your face was one of studied cheerfulness and perversion. Your patois consisted of one banality after another. At first, when you started talking in banalities, I thought, you're joking; no one talks like that. I thought, who knows? Maybe this guy is clever. He really is a homespun philosopher. You used to say to me, "I really fell in the fat when I met you." Or "the proof of the puddin is in the eatin." Or "my heart's been to school." Or "water seeks its own level."

"Dumbo," I said, "please stop talking banality."

"It helps me over the rough spots," you replied.

Dear Dumbo Lavitch, my ladies' home companion, who used my energy and who left behind a few glossy photographs, some shaving cream, and the K-Y Jelly, not to mention a copy of the latest show business newspaper, *Casting*.

Dumbo Lavitch was born in Montreal thirty-six years ago. Life history: He left school in the tenth grade and went to work in a vacuum cleaner factory. From vacuums he went into baseball and joined the minor leagues. According to his clippings, which he always carried with him in a tan Samsonite briefcase, he had played third base for the Kansas City Athletics. He would have stayed in the minor leagues but decided to become a U.S. citizen and joined the Air Force. In the Air Force he played "ball" in Japan and was sent all over Asia. While he was in Japan a movie was being made, and he got a job as Cary Grant's stand-in. Mr. Grant asked him for a glass of water.

"Thank you, Mr. Grant," Dumbo had said, star-struck.

He decided to become a movie star. But when nothing "clicked" for him in Hollywood, he drove east to try to "make it" in New York. He lived at the Y. Slowly, through Jerry, a leading casting director, producer, and neurotic faggot whose preference was for "straight"-looking homosexuals, Dumbo learned the ins and outs of New York City and show biz. He left the Y and lived with Jerry.

I met Dumbo New Year's Eve. (Should auld acquaintance be *forgot*.)

An old flame called Heartbreak Henry took me to a New Year's Eve party in New York City in a town house. It belonged to a man called Jeremiah Morris. It was there that I met Dumbo Lavitch. Only he called himself at the time Dumbo Drak. He began talking to me as I stood at the edge of the party. I felt deaf and dumb. His shirt was open so that you could see his chest hairs, if you were interested. And he said in an attuned voice, "I'm a singer. What do you do?"

Dumbo began humming in my ear. His voice sounded like Drano down the pipes, and I thought, If you are a singer, I'm Maria Callas, but I didn't say anything.

"Where do you sing?" I asked, slipping a cigarette into my shaking fingers. I was very nervous at that time.

"On cruise ships. I also work in this gallery selling paintings."

At twelve o'clock, Dumbo Lavitch kissed me. Henry was too busy talking to someone at the end of the room. The next few days I thought about Dumbo.

Dumbo received a telephone call from me a few weeks later. I asked if I could come over for a cup of coffee. He thought I was saying, "Can I come over and make love?" But I really wanted just to talk to rub out the bad memories of Heartbreak Henry. I entered Dumbo's block, which was Ninety-second Street between Amsterdam and Columbus avenues, and began to feel frightened. It's a block crowded with those West Side dogs that look like wolves. I rang the buzzer that said "Drak." Dumbo awaited me behind a door with a steel bolt attached to it. He was dressed for the occasion. His hair had been obviously just fluffed into ringlets by one of those blowers, and he was wearing the same perfume which made underarm odor smell delicious in comparison. He wore cowboy boots and those eternal maroon pants, and when I entered his apartment, my intuition told me immediately that Henry was a prince compared to Dumbo Lavitch. But it was too late. He had been burning incense in anticipation of my visit.

In his hallway were huge Keene-like oil portraits of two women, both naked except for suggestive veils around their bosoms. They were on the order of naked "playmates" or like the Varga girls my father used to collect when I was young. Dumbo's hallway was pink. The living room looked like a twelve-year-old boy's room in Scarsdale. It had in it all the things that little boys like. It had maps. It had a big desk. It had a hi-fi set with records. All the record jackets were displayed against the wall, side by side. He liked Nat King Cole, Tony Bennett, Billy Eckstine. There was a huge mirror in the middle of the wall. Later I found out that Dumbo would sing to himself in the mirror ("If I Ruled the World") while he listened to his own voice played back on the tape recorder.

Worst of all were the colors.

"I like earth colors," he said.

His carpet, which had big swirls, was maroon. His walls were brown. The huge plastic couches he had picked up in a thrift shop were brown. And there were bars on the window since he needed a lot of "protection" on the West Side. His pretensions were unbearable.

"This apartment is my castle," he said. "I like it to be cozy. I could sell it for a fortune."

Cozy? It was as cozy as a cell in Leavenworth. Pictures of Dumbo all over the place with his name on the glossies and his big smile coming at you like a huge spray of dentures.

Dumbo took my hand and led me to a fireplace. He began singing a song about popcorn and fires. I sat down on his plastic couch, petrified. What was I frightened of? I don't know. But I sensed that something wrong was going to happen to me with Dumbo.

"Relax," he said. "Would you like a drink?"

My hands were ice cold, and I drank some of the liquor he gave me. I think it was apricot brandy. I noticed that on the wall he had a high school diploma which came in the mail. I had always seen them advertised on matchbook covers, but I never knew anyone who actually sent for one. The books in the bookcase were all weirdo works.

"I go in for the occult," Dumbo said.

I noticed a huge yellow book on the prostate gland. He saw me looking at it.

"The prostate gland is the key to all sex," he said.

Dumbo's voice was like a preacher's. He made pronouncements on everything. He had an opinion about everything. He had a phrase for everything, such as "Understanding is love" or "We are all eternal," and he said each statement in the way that the Prophet might have spoken, had the Prophet spoken. He talked Khalil-Gibranese.

It was late. Dumbo stared meaningfully at me. He lay down in front of the fire and started posing. I suppose I was supposed to be the frustrated divorcée who would jump on him. I sat on the couch petrified. Dumbo began singing, "Your lips tell me no, no, but there's yes, yes in your eyes."

My new body. Dumbo, in the beginning, awakened a newness of life, erotic sensations I'd forgotten I had.

"The body is the vessel of the gods," he would say in that monotone voice of his that always made pronouncements, little

60

program notes that came from nowhere. And somewhere in his freaky numerology world of secrets that told about finding the center of the earth, *the power of the pyramids, the footprints left by astronauts from Venus seventy billion years ago,* I heard him speak, but I wasn't listening. I didn't *care* what he was saying. Just put your tongue on me, dear Dumbo delicious. Touch me. And Dumbo was sort of dumbstruck that he had found this touch-starved divorcée, this successful comedy writer with a kid and a dog who might really care for him, might be a good contact for him, might do things for him.

"Her connections are unbelievable," he told a friend. "I want to get into her life."

Dumbo, never the intellectual. Dumbo. Suddenly he was with me always, his skin linked in mine, his hand touching me in the place that made me wonder why it had taken me all those years to be so womanly, sexual, and, most of all, motherly. I mothered him, my baby, my Cary Grant, my darling, my aphrodisiac. My wife. Dumbo.

I loved Dumbo so much I wanted everyone in the world that I knew to meet him. I wanted to show that after Heartbreak Henry, who was so charmless and so difficult, I had found the perfect companion. I wanted Dumbo to meet my Aunt Julia, my closest friend and former girlfriend of my father's who had given me so much wisdom and kindness while I was growing up. She lived in a small apartment outside Boston, married to a furniture executive, who was rarely home. We drove to Boston.

"Dumbo meet Julia," I said as we entered the apartment.

Aunt Julia, a huge, jolly woman, embraced Dumbo with a kiss. She was on crutches, because of a hip operation, threw down the crutches and gave him a hug.

"I'm so happy you are taking care of Lulu. We love her so much." She looked at Dumbo, then at me. "At last you're keeping company with someone who isn't out for all he can get," she said.

Taking care of? It was the other way around. I paid for Dumbo's tap lessons and French lessons. He carried around a small blue book called *French Verbs* which I had bought for him. But he never learned to speak French. Julia had it all wrong. But it didn't matter. Julia drove both of us around Boston, first to the historic Oyster House and then to Harvard Square. Dumbo wasn't interested in history or Harvard. He had a complete disinterest in things academic. I tried to interest him in the Lamont Library and showed him a house on Irving Street where I lived when I went to Harvard summer school those summers when I was getting my master's in performing arts. But Dumbo was more interested in driving past the suede boutiques and department stores. I could hear my father shouting at me from his grave in Valhalla Cemetery, "Lulu, you have a master's degree. What are you doing with this Vaselined moron?" But to each academic, a chorus boy must fall. Dumbo was holding my hand, pinching my cheek, saying, "Hello, gorgeous," in a way he alone could say it. And, thanks to him, I felt *gorgeous* at that time.

But I had noticed a couple of odd things. For example, when we arrived at Aunt Julia's apartment, Dumbo seemed disappointed. He only liked great wealth. It gave him an opportunity to impose his tastes on those already there. And he considered himself another Louis XIV when it came to furnishing. Aunt Julia's apartment was simple and modestly furnished. Dumbo sat down and began looking through his book on French verbs.

"Want a little cognac?" Julia urged.

She was hopping around the house like a large, excited bird. Maybe Lulu had finally found a "friend." Dumbo smiled his Mona Lisa smile. He was an astrological guru personality——Dumbo the healer. The things I had to listen to just to get loved——physically and transcendentally.

Dumbo: "According to Far Eastern medicine as I understand it, there need be no therapeutics or remedies because the mother of all life is the universe. We seek creative spiritual cure——a life without fear or anxiety——a life of freedom, happiness and justice——the realization of self. This is the medicine of the mind." I wished he would stop *reading*. We had planned to spend the weekend on the Cape and I couldn't wait to leave.

Anxiously, I kissed Julia good-bye and promised to call the next day. Off we went in Dumbo's new green Cadillac, driving to Gloucester, beyond Gloucester. Late that night we stopped at a motel and watched the sun going down. Alone in the motel room, we hugged each other. I watched Dumbo prepare a radish drink. We made love; then we slept. The next morning we made love again. I paid the bill. We got in the car and stopped by the Gloucester fishing boats. Made love. Drove. We kept driving. Stopped and made love. Ate oysters. Drove. Stopped and kissed. Drove. Made love. Stopped. Drove. Sex on wheels. All the time, I was nervously thinking about the time Dumbo might grow tired of me——or I might not be able to afford him. What would I do without him? Restless in my Cadillac, down the highway to New York, I began wondering when he would tire of me. The only thing to do was to be so "indispensable" to Dumbo's singing career that he had to stay with me. Or keep giving him presents and cash and taking care of him so he would get so used to the security of my money he couldn't afford to leave. I indulged my wife with trinkets to keep him happy. I promised him trips, interesting contacts that would help his career (but he had no career). I was a demanding person but a *good provider*.

When he stayed with me, Dumbo's day went like this. Up every morning at seven thirty. The Mickey Mouse clock went off by our bed with music and news. Then he brought me breakfast. After he made breakfast, he took David to school, and then he vacuumed the apartment. Answered my phone. Kept track of my business appointments. Typed my manuscripts. Drove me to my office. Took my slacks to the cleaners. Planned our menu. At the breakfast table he felt the need to make intelligent conversation. For example, over coffee he once told me he had read that there was really a *hole* in the earth, the center of the earth, and that was the place that Martians came from. He produced a mimeographed text, complete with drawings, which proved that Admiral Perry on his long trip through the Arctic had discovered, as if by accident, a center of the earth, a hole through which people could descend into a place of sunlight and justice. There, Dumbo explained, children were taken care of by a group of adults in the community so that child rearing was a joy and not a problem. Given my domestic situation with my son (my tomboy kid, eight years old, whom I loved more than anyone else in the world but who played on my nerves with Indian screams that went up and down the scale and not forgetting that an army of housekeepers had come and gone in my household, clicking their power heels with Hitleresque regularity, stabbing all working mothers in the back with their jigsaw nursese language that was composed of voodoo, Swiss, spankings, F.A.O. toyboy, and paranoia), the idea of the center of the earth appealed to me as a possible alternative. There, in the center of the earth, Dumbo explained, seriously giving me maps to study, charts, all people were allowed to follow their destinies, doing what they wished to do, eating fruit. The vegetation was unique. Trees never stopped growing, and the air was pure. He prattled on. I didn't pay attention and tried to humor him. Because he was such a good wife, what did I care? I needed him. But after a breakfast like that I was glad to get out of the house. His chatter drove me mad. I needed an intelligent woman to talk to after a breakfast with Dumbo.

Memory. It attacks me with its spear until the blood comes. Dumbo, I began having fantasies about you. Fantasy fulfills the desire to be loved. But it is not love. It is fantasy. The preparation for love is long and intense. I thought I had found you, in you the other half of the orange. It is terrible to come home—nadir of loneliness—and find the bed empty. There are the pictures we took in Florida. There's me, the fish on the line, my mouth bleeding. Pictures we took at nightclubs where the lights continued popping. Florida. . . .

One day my wife, Dumbo, turned over in bed and said to me, "Lulu, I need a vacation. I'm tired of housework. Let's go fishing in Florida."

We went to the Automobile Club of America (Dumbo, in his commander period, loved maps, charts, planning), and the two of us, complete with a tape recorder and tapes of the worst singers in history, began our vacation that he needed.

As we left New York early one morning in his green Cadillac convertible, it occurred to me, quite suddenly, that once away from the frenetic rhythm of my scriptwriting and household we had nothing to say to each other. We were to be locked together in the prison of the car. Driving out of the city, past the smog towers, out, out into the winding tape deck of the highway, I had nothing to say to Dumbo. In my mind were all the romantic things to do on the way to Florida and I hoped he would talk to me about something else besides speed limits.

Keeping the car perfectly in the middle of the road, Dumbo wore his suede jacket and drove like a good chauffeur, a professional chauffeur. One of his favorite accomplishments which he used to brag about was that he had driven back and forth across the country six times. *What on earth for?* I had asked. It was all in his career as a traveling professional extra. Car driving, as well as being a good housekeeper and cook and wife and lover—all this was his specialty. And so on that trip, we drove to the Wittenaur Gardens in Delaware. But when we got there, the gates were shut—no tulips, no daffodils, nothing to be seen. It was spring. The green everywhere was intoxicating. I was in love with Dumbo, my wife, who steered the car expertly past the small houses and gardens of Delaware. But the gardens were closed.

It rained. The trip was becoming nightmarish. In Virginia I wanted to stay at an old "historic inn," but Dumbo preferred a Holiday Inn. We argued about it. He wanted a Holiday Inn or Ramada Inn or nothing. I yearned for a creaky old romantic hotel where Washington had slept. Finally Dumbo drove to the Cherry Hill House, an inn that was remodeled along the lines of the early colonial houses in Scarsdale. But he hated me for staying at that hotel. We fought. Shown to our Lysoled room with a bed, Dumbo said, "Everything here is so *old*."

"Including me," I shot back.

He wanted new sheets, new towels, and a color TV. I wanted antebellum charm. We didn't make love, didn't embrace. Dumbo slept on one side of the bed, I slept on the other. During one wild moment in the lobby I wanted to go to the public phone and telephone Aunt Julia and say, "Help me out of this." I wanted to say, "I'm down in the fucking South with this freaked-out *zombie* wife who's talking constantly about palm reading and foot reading and what is your sign and astrology, and it's driving me stark raving mad." It was as if I had lost touch with my real life—whatever that was.

But Dumbo's kindness, his genuine sweetness, made me change my mind. Just when I was most angry, he would pinch my cheeks and call me Salty Dog and kiss me and behave like a sweet and attentive lover. And so the trip progressed.

Dumbo: "A fortune-teller once told me that my life would take this turn for the better—it's my destiny—to be with you in this inn—life *is* love—and no one can take away your self-respect." The lonely lost jargon of banality. Would we *ever* reach Florida?

While I paid all the bills, he droned on and on about self-respect. It occurred to me that Dumbo was a gigolo and that he was only my "hired companion." But so what? I thought. As long as he does what I need him to do. And after all, I adore him.

Once, during the trip, he turned to me and said, "I'll marry you, Lulu, if you put three thousand dollars in the bank."

Three thousand dollars. I had been surprised that he would sell himself so cheaply.

"Yeah," he said, continuing the driving, "I have to have a little security. Suppose we get divorced. I'll need a thousand dollars to put as a down payment on my own apartment. Then I'll have to buy wall-to-wall carpeting. That's at least five hundred dollars. Standing lamps, about fifty dollars each. To furnish the bedroom, I'll need at least five hundred for the bed, the dressing table, and the bedside table. Then I'll need to buy at least a few comfortable chairs—that's another eight hundred dollars. And a grate and screen for the fireplace, another five hundred dollars."

And so Dumbo had his hearth and home all planned. He was all mine for three thousand.

"Why the fuck do you have to marry me to get your grate and screen? Why don't I just lend you another three thousand dollars and you can fix up your own place immediately without the emotional detours? If you are such a little homemaker, just forget about me and get to it." Dumbo continued driving. I lowered my voice. I had to be careful not to insult him. One high-pitched tone, and it was all over. Dumbo wouldn't stand for screaming or a shrill voice. His idea of being reasonable was listening, obeying, going quietly from one dream scheme to another. I wanted to continue this Magoo tour through the South with Dumbo. I wanted desperately to stop at the side of the road, get out of the car, and start making love. I had never known what it was like to "want" to caress anyone as much as Dumbo and one yell could spoil everything. One yell could fuck up your setup.

My dear Dumbo—beloved chorus boy, occult nut—I must humor you. Dumbo stopped the car in some deserted place in the South off the road. He took off his pants and took off my pants. We made love in a rest area. We rested. Then we drove and ate lobsters, drank beer, and took a walk in a deserted Southern town. Did I care that I was paying for all this? That it had cost me (I had figured it out) about a hundred dollars a come and that only Mrs. Jock Whitney would have the money to sustain Dumbo's love of cars, suede, lobsters, French lessons, singing lessons, radios, tape recorders, bank accounts, canes, shoes, books on the pyramids of Egypt, jersey shirts, jewelry, tape decks, nightclubs, fishing poles, denim hats, white linen slacks, sweat shirts, subscriptions to *Moon* magazine and *The Foot*, hair blowers, vitamin E capsules for very long, although he always said to me, "With you, Lulu, I'm happy with just bread and beans." Some beans. Some bread. I must have been off my beany, but I didn't care. I thought I needed him. It was still cheaper than a housekeeper, chauffeur, and nanny. Driving ninety miles an hour to Charlotte, North Carolina, or Orlando, Florida, it didn't matter. He was *with* me. That was the main thing.

Finally, arriving at the Keys, we stayed at the motel Dumbo chose, the Sportsman's Lodge. How weird, I thought, lying back on one of the green cotton goyish bedspreads, to be here at the Sportsman's Lodge when I know nothing about sports. Dumbo was reading *Sports World* magazine, engrossed in an article on fishing. He was very excited about the bait and the fishing and going out on a boat. Slowly, he took a bath and got into his terry-cloth monogrammed robe (a present) and took off his gold wristwatch (a present) to comb his hair with his new Kent hairbrush (a present). I slipped into my pink cotton nightgown. With all the presents for Dumbo I could hardly splurge on myself. I lay on the bed like a poached salmon. A poached someone. A poached woman?

Desperately I tried to talk fish talk. To sound as if I came from the backwoods of Canada the way he did, to sound like just home folks. To talk about hooks and bait and things. *Nomen est omen,* I thought. The name says everything. Dumbo. I'll have to be dumb, too. Just to suck his dumbo-dinghy, I'll say anything—until it is time to entwine myself in his arms. The unicorn in Dumbo's captivity. I felt safe there. After lovemaking, Dumbo would lie back in bed and talk about his pre-Lulu-ian life. As the big orange Florida sun slipped down over the frisky palm trees, I lay back in my Dumbo's arms and listened to his secrets. Dumbo. Florida.

"On top of Old Smoky, on top of Old Smoky." In Florida Dumbo bought a guitar with my money and started playing the guru-guitarist. It must have been right after Florida that Dumbo sat locked in my bathroom picking away at the guitar and studying his guitar manual ("The Old Gray Mare, She Ain't What She Used to Be" and other horse songs), when the idea struck him of becoming a healer. What is beyond the ego principle of the *entertainer* but the *healer?* If he couldn't make it as another Cary Grant or Babe Ruth, he would make it as a rip-off of Foot Guru. A psychologist-healer.

Why was he hanging out in my bathroom? His motives for being in my life in the first place were simply to have a good "touch," to find a husband to support him until he found "his thing." Suddenly, his thing could be not making a touch but touching. He didn't like the hours involved in being a house-wife. But he liked the hours involved in being a masseur. It was rub-a-dub-dub for an hour—twenty dollars—and on to the next client. (Rubeee.) And so it was in my bathroom that a light went on in Dumbo's illiterate head, which was that he could conquer the universe by using his own two hands.

"The idea is to go into the reality of the body away from mere appearances," Dumbo was later to explain.

Dumbo had been reading at night, in my bed, his favorite book, *The Man Who Tapped the Secrets of the Universe*. The book begins with the following testimony: "All my life I have been looking for a man who has discovered the universal law which lies in back of the Sermon on the Mount, who consciously uses that law with full awareness of its meaning." It was the combination of reading that book, his disgust with having to take my dog, Flops, to the veterinarian, and a small volume on feet that he found in the Good Fatima Bookstore that threw Dumbo into a career change, from wife to reflexologist. His revelation took place in June in my bathroom.

Dumbo's illumination: On June 3, while studying his foot book, Dumbo discovers that the Chinese charts show 657 strategic points along 26 energy or meridian lines. On June 4 Dumbo becomes a healer. On June 6 Dumbo sets forth from my apartment—and connections—aiming to make a place for the new him in the world of aches and pains and feet. On June 13 Dumbo receives his foot massage license. On June 15 Dumbo prints personal cards of Shiatsu treatments. June 17: Dumbo discards Lulu Cartwright.

One day, after he left me and told me I no longer *turned him on*, Dumbo dropped off his card. It was in the shape of a foot. The foot card was orange. It was grotesque. It said, in black letters: "If you're feeling out of kilter, don't know why or what about, let your feet reveal the answer. Find the sore spot. Work it out. Call Dumbo Lavitch." And then his phone number: 555-4700.

I looked at the card. So now he was passing out foot cards. He had metamorphosed from a singer and my wife into a foot rubber. No longer a live-in wife, his hustle now was rich women with a need to be cured and/or amused for an hour. His answer to their aches and pains was in the reflex to adrenal glands, the reflex to the bladder, the hip and the shoulder and the pituitary. That's it, Dumbo, get right down to the sinuses, spine, spleen, and stomach. Go into the zone markings. Find Shiatsu-prone women and men, and rub them the right way. Rub your way up the ladder. From live-in wife to day work. From *extra* to foot *rubber*.

Before long he called me up and said in his Dumboesque voice, "Can I give you a treatment?" I was still a sucker for Dumbo.

He arrived with his briefcase, formerly filled with his clippings and sheet music (all stamped "Property of Dumbo Lavitch") but now filled with mineral oil and towels. Without even mentioning our past life together, he began by breaking down the "crystals" in my feet, all the time talking about "zones" and "bladders." Dumbo, the whore without a soul, was now rubbing feet and was trying to hustle me, a year later, as a client. He told me how he had taken away another client's headaches. The metamorphosis of my singer/extra/wife into a masseur was almost too much to contemplate. I gave him my foot.

At the end of the foot massage I said, "Can I pay you, Dumbo?" and he smirked.

"I couldn't take any more money from you, Lulu."

(Of course not, you still owe me for rent, lights, guitar, French and singing lessons.)

"I just would appreciate it if you would *spread the word* and let me come back and give you another treatment. *Spread the word*," he said in his Dumbo zombie voice. He stood in my bedroom holding his Samsonite briefcase. My ex-wife.

He was still wearing the same shiny maroon pants he had worn all the time, six months, as my wife, during which he had pretended to be in love with me, living with me. The same maroon shiny pants, the same vest made out of imitation leather, the same gold ring with the pyramid on it. He had bought me a ring just like his and had his friend at the jewelry center (an old character actor—could I get him a part in a TV show or a film?) design it. The old man thought it was a wedding band and blessed us, the happy couple. Dumbo had been Mr. Bridegroom himself in those days, putting his gold ring with the pyramid (his own design) on my finger and looking into my eyes, saying, "Lulu, we were married in ancient Egypt many centuries ago. In another incarnation, I was a chariot driver and you were the queen of Egypt. It was to you that I devoted my life." Now he was merely a reflexologist paying a house call.

Memory: I really didn't believe in all that reincarnation crap. But Dumbo, Mr. Adonis, was so gorgeous and so convincing that I began to think maybe there is something in all this. Maybe—just perhaps—who knows?—we did meet in another lifetime. *Nomen est omen*. The *name* gives you the game. Dumbo Lavitch—the dumb itch of my life—and what damage done by Dumbitch. *You grow too soon old and too late shmart*. Well, I was old, but at that time, not smart enough. The night of the last rub I lay in bed smoking a cigarette and staring at a white wall covered with a child's—my child's— drawings. His life was lines on a wall. He had gotten all the child-world on paper—in holy crayons—red and blue and green gulls, sparrows, dogs, faces, facts, stars, father, cloudy world, blue water, pine trees, wind, more clouds, more faces, markings of his own dilemma in the life farce. Sometimes I thought that only a child's drawing could encompass my experience with Dumbo. That, or a temple rubbing. Rubbing, that was it. Dumo was rubbing feet now, and I was ribbing while he was rubbing. Rub-a-dub-dub. My ex-wife in the reflexology business. After all that, he had come by only to break down my crystals. Life was bizarre. That was the rub. Little world of souls and heels and zones. Who was I anyway? I had no toe hold on reality. Or did I have one foot in the grave? I always wanted to believe in someone. He would rub me out. It was so easy to have one's life rubbed off the blackboard so that one became, quite by accident, invisible. First the head disappeared. Then the shoulders. Then the arms. Dumbo might really be able to rub me away. That was the trouble. I mustn't let that happen. To me. To me. But it was happening. Memory.

My childhood: I was born a normal human being. Born a girl and wanted a good life. The doctor spanked. Mama wailed. Into my childhood I was jailed. I went to my house. Papa wept. Mother hated him. The nursie slept. And I grew up. To keep from crying, I laughed myself to sleep. God bless Papa. Let my life keep. Nazis kill Jews. Jews die in camps. Mama, when will I have menstrual cramps? In boarding school the rule: Don't pet. Don't be a fool. I remember all the litany of the boarding school. I remember. I remember. I was writing an essay on freedom versus authority. I didn't know what freedom was: to be free of my fears. I fear union and I fear solitude: the human comedy. And because I got tired of the crap I had to put up with with being a girl vis-à-vis my father and his expectations of how I, as a girl, had to live, because of my two husbands and what they expected of me, I had taken a man as my helper instead of the other way around. But that didn't work either. My wife left me.

I used to be the youngest. I'm not anymore. I can no longer be liked for my *youngness*.

I can no longer be *little*, Lulu.

Actually, my first demonstration, "Why Are We Afraid of Growing Old?" had been held in front of Henri Bendel. Hundreds of people had gathered on the street and watched me and five other women in the arts, in masks, pantomime the idiocy of old-age fears. We had brought some folding chairs and radios and mimed women in nursing homes while I passed out brochures, saying:

73

"Women—don't fall for the myth of age—you are not old cars to be junked in the junkyard when you are no longer shiny—defeat the idea of the sick male paternal system which sends old women out to buy ya-ya clothes from Henri Bendel and old men out to advertise cigarettes. Let's have more dirty old women as well as dirty old men."

We had gained nothing except a mention in the *New York Times* saying, "Comedy writer leads women in the arts in demonstration against the myth of age." But it was true, of course. Getting older was not an ugly thing. It was a good thing. My God, I wouldn't want that childhood back again, that miserable child-world that I walked around in like a dwarf, that childhood where I was always trying to reinvent love and invent who I was. TO THINE OWN SELF BE TRUE, wrote Mr. Lubowitz, my tenth-grade history teacher, in *The Berry Pit*, my boarding school yearbook—but who the fuck was *MINE OWN Self*? And who was Mr. Lubowitz anyway to tell me to be true to it? Childhood sucked. Adolescence sucked. With all those sick parents and teachers meeting to discuss my problems when they were all so sick themselves. They all talked about my needing help when *they* were the ones who were insane, bored, and basically unimaginative. Was it my fault I was born with a comic sense of life and a desire to make trouble? While they were born complaining, yelling, tormeting, crying and hadn't the faintest idea how to be spies on life.

It was always my deepest middle-class tragedy that I did not get into Sarah Lawrence. But Bernice Barry was screwing the English teacher, and he gave her a good recommendation and he gave me a bad one. Anyway, I misspelled Sarah Lawrence fourteen times on the application and when they asked me one of their banal celebrity-game questions like "Who has been the most important man in your life?" I wrote my father. And when they asked me, "Who is the man you most admire?" instead of writing Mahatma Gandhi or one of the sociological schlock answers that they required, I wrote Edward R. Murrow—because he was my favorite man. I was fascinated by the media even then, and as a senior at high school I loved watching his craggy face, his marvelous hands, his huge, zero-white eyes, black eyebrows, and the elegance he had when he went into some dumbbell's home and made that putz look good. He was such a gracious and elegant man, as no man in my life ever had been. After all, neither of the sides of my family had any elegance whatsoever. In the Proustian sense, my Guermantes Way and Swann's Way were hardly anything to boast about. On the other side, the Cartwrights (I always kept my maiden name), and on the other side the Bloomingtons. The Cartwrights were all earthy, crass, self-destructive Lower East Side vulgarians from Galicia. No one in my family was like Edward R. Murrow.

Memory: My mother was an outstanding tennis player with a secure career in musical therapy. She is someone who gave birth to me not so much out of will but out of career problems. I came howling and screaming into St. Vincent's Hospital (deluxe suite) partly because she couldn't find work as a concert cellist and partly because of my father's insistence that she have a child. The old saying "Stick with your own class" must have been invented after people took a gander at my mother and father. Two people verily out of different shoes, different classes, different backgrounds, and so different that it's a wonder that they ever made me.

My old man was Seymour Cartwright, better known as the "tyrant" to his friends and to his final girlfriend, Julia, who always referred to him lovingly as "the tyrant" even in the most absurd circumstances such as "Shall I get the tyrant his pants?" in the morning. My father, a biggie in the typewriter ribbon business and in the hotel business as a para-banker and para-politician, was not a weakling. You knew when he was around. He was the bull, and my mother was the china shop. My mother had terrific manners and came from a very "comfortable" family on Park Avenue where my grandfather kept his "nest." Her father was a chippy chaser on Broadway, known in the best bars from Broadway to the Bowery for his spiffy dressing. He always wore dark suits and polka-dot shirts and he loved women. Remember *Tomorrow the World* and *Arsenic and Old Lace* and *Carousel*? My mama's papa put his dough into those shows. He was Larry the magnificent, a leading Broadway producer.

Anyway, my mother was, first and foremost, a Bloomington, which had a great deal of distinction connected to it in the show business world, if nowhere else. Her mother, my Grandma Anna, was a gentle dark saint. She was constantly making "sacrifices" for her children and staying home and cooking, embroidering and tap-tapping on a sewing machine. She always did good works for the poor. She taught herself how to read English. She was always available for people to cry with and on. She ran her household so perfectly that there were always the good smells of food cooking, of fresh linen, of fresh ironing. She was a martyr to show biz and Grandpa. Another madonna for mankind. My mother made up her mind, I am sure quite early, that she wanted to be where the action was and not stay home and be a saint. In fact, all her five sisters and brothers were people who couldn't wait to "get out of the house"—such was the example of my grandmother's sainthood. She was the only "good" person in the entire family, perhaps in my whole history. Nobody else was good. It was a family of baa, baa black sheep on my mother's and father's sides.

My mother was rich. Smart. An intellectual. Musician. Good-looking. Well educated. She finally wound up with a master's degree from Juilliard—*and* my father. Strong, witty, she had a great sense of humor about everything *but* my father. My father was a mistake. A big one. Although an eccentric successful man, he was still an illiterate from the Lower East Side who couldn't do anything but look handsome and make money. He came from the traditional "poorer than poor" background, and he played being a self-made man. He was a guy who did it alone, starting with selling newspapers at the age of three, carrying suitcases as a babe for people coming out of the subway, worked his way up the financial circuit selling lemonade, then candy bars, then hot dogs, and then, with a sudden career change at the age of eleven, he went to work for a certain gent who was in the typewriter ribbon business, a Mr. Landerson, where my father learned that the typewriter ribbon business was open to anyone with brains, that it required a lot of political smarts, a lot of hustle, and a lot of charm.

My father had more charm than Valentino—he was a Jewish Valentino, standing around with no expression on his face he could make women swoon and people laugh by the magnetic field of his personality. He found out that politics had to do with knowing the right people and that led to business contacts—especially the Irish—and he appealed to the New York Athletic Club Irishmen as a genuine primitive. He had the grace to hustle but not to make them feel "stupid." My father was a divine joker. You could tell he was a ladies' man, but he was also a man's man. He knew just how to play up and down to people, to be smart and give orders and still gain everything he wanted. His magnetic brain picked up the typewriter ribbon business in two years, and soon he had left Landerson and started his own ribbon company called Arrow Ribbon because he figured out it would come first in the phone book. Arrow put Landerson out of the big time, and it was the first time a Jewish hustler made it in the bachelor button, Irish whiskey, Irish mafiosi typewriter ribbon world. None of those guys was a match for Seymour. They were outraged by his ability to get everything done quicker than everyone else. He was a go-getter and got all the business.

My Papa cornered the typewriter ribbon market by the time he was sixteen. Then came his own Park Avenue apartment. A snappy Packard car. Girls. Finally, the prize: my mother with her huge green eyes and her gracious personality. And finally fights, disagreements, scenes, the agony of two people who are divinely mismatched. My father stood for thrift. My mother loved to spend a buck. Several. She would spend money on things my father thought ridiculous— like all-white furniture, white everything. She was never very good at "budgeting," and my mother's lack of respect for Papa's pennies, nickels, and dimes was one of the causes of his heartache. The other was, of course, that my father was a self-made man and my mother was always trying to educate him.

During World War II my father tried to join the Army. They wouldn't take him. Since he was 4-F, he used to pose in uniforms borrowed from friends. Sucking in his stomach, he would fit into the uniform. All over the house were pictures of my father in dress military, even in general's stripes, in uniform in his imaginary progress through World War II. It was from him that I got my fantasy life. My mother worked for the Red Cross on the weekends. She took me along with her to the blood bank, where the blood was frozen in the jars that looked like canning jars for stewed prunes or stewed tomatoes.

After the separation Mama and I went to live with her family, and my mother gave up teaching and studying in order to sell housecoats. She was broke. My father gave her no money, to punish her, since it was she who wanted the separation. My grandfather's show business investments weren't paying off and the best he could do was to let us live with him.

At my grandparents' house I loved to try on Mother's hats and housecoats and pretend I was a Cossack or a queen. During the day I was sick as much as possible so I didn't have to go to school. Just try on housecoats and listen to my grandparents' radio. Like many children in the American tradition, it was through the radio that I developed my idea of human relationships. All men were Lorenzo Jones. All women were his dizzy wife, Belle. Serious women had nothing to do but concern themselves with the immediate problem of soap powder. Rinso Bright. Rinso White. Soap filled my nightmares. What was so important about foam? Why did the world care so much about armpits and asses when there were so many other things to care about? Were soap and suppositories all there was to life? At age seven I read *Hamlet* in bed, the *Classic Comics* version. At one point in the *Classic Comics,* Hamlet said to himself (since he was always alone), "To be or not to be. That is the question." No. To float or not to float. That is the question asked by every woman on the radio. If it could float, it was good. If it just sank, it was not good.

Spying on my elders, I became an investigator of my grandparents' apartment. Inside the house, besides my grandparents, were an aunt and uncle. My Uncle John was a surrealist. He took blue and red paint and painted circles on the piano. All over the piano, so if someone put down a glass without a coaster, you wouldn't be able to tell the ring from the other circles. My Uncle John hated me and referred to me not as Little Lulu but as Little Poison. And sooner or later, my peeing in my Aunt Poll's bed got on her nerves. She was tired of changing the sheets. A girl of seven shouldn't wet her bed even if she was sleeping with her aunt.

At my grandparents' I used to wait for my father's telephone call. The phone in the hallway was a black seduction machine that beckoned me to visit my father, who made it perfectly clear—clear as the sun—that he loved me. My father would make an arrangement for me to come and spend a few days at his hotel. At that time he owned the Greenside which faced Gramercy Park.

"I will pick you up at your grandparents' at seven," he would promise over the telephone in his husky, breathy voice.

But he always came at nine. I sat waiting in the living room, looking out the window, while my grandmother cursed him for being late.

"He doesn't want you now, while you're a child," she would say bitterly. "He'll want you when you are sixteen and the difficult part is over."

What difficult part?

At age eight, after one year of living with my grandparents, I was sent to a concentration camp called La Bellson School. I remember waving good-bye to my mother as I got on the train. I didn't know where I was going or when I would come back. There were other children on the train. All miserable, weeping. We all had name tags. Mine said "Lulu." My school was the Final Solution. At eight, my family was rid of me.

When I arrived at La Bellson, I was shoved into a wooden station wagon with the other children and driven to a strange place where there were a lot of trees and horses. We all slept on a screened-in porch where it was cold. We were told it was good for us. We were made to stand up in the dark if we cried at night. I stayed there for eight years. In the lower school, my porch changed to a room. I had a roommate, and every year there was another one. But I sucked my thumb and continued wetting my bed. The nurse at the infirmary told me if I kept wetting my bed, she would take out my bladder. So I cried instead. The nurse said if I kept crying, they would take out my eyes. So I got earaches. They said they could not keep me at La Bellson with bad ears. I went in and out to New York City on the trains to ear doctors. I also went in and out on the trains to see an orthodontist, Dr. Limmerman. At his office, I saw hundreds of plaster-cast teeth behind glass. I was so proud that my teeth were behind glass with the name "Lulu Cartwright" on them. My life was spent at boarding school or on trains going to doctors.

At La Bellson I learned basketball. I learned social dancing, and I learned how to read books. My favorite book was the Bible. I wanted badly to be Mrs. Moses with my husband a nice Jewish boy bringing me home a gift, the Ten Commandments. Sometimes I wanted to be simply Joan of Arc.

In boarding school, I modestly rewrote the Bible:

When Adam found out he came out of Eve's rib, he felt hurt, upset, henpecked, ribbed off, ejected, and neglected. So he got so mad he turned against her, and bullied her, and convinced her she really came from his rib.

As they left the Garden of Eden to go shopping at the supermarket, Adam ran away and Eve ran after him.

Eve said, "What are you doing?"

"I can't help it," he said. "I came out of your rib. I'm just another rib."

"So what?" said Eve. "What difference does it make where you come from? Suppose you came from my lip?"

"I'll never live it down," he said.

And so Adam invented "having his own way."

And Adam became a doctor. Eve became a nurse. Adam had all the instruments, and Eve had only a typewriter and a phone. Eve had a little office and a reception desk, and Adam and Eve played doctor and nurse.

One day Eve said, "I've had enough, so long. I'm going back to college to get my monster's degree."

And Eve studied to be a monster. Grwwwl, grwwwl.

81

Lulu Cartwright, aged ten. I got an A+ for daring something more original than a long comp on collies or cats. It was my preoccupation with Eve. That surprised my teacher, being left out of the action. I was no fool.

Sometimes on weekends I would go to my father's hotel and feel like a little orphan. I had no friends in the hotel. Only elevator boys to whom my father would say, "Isn't Little Lulu beautiful? Some hips on that kid!"

And I would feel unlovely. My father often made embarrassing remarks about my breasts to his friends. He felt uncomfortable with me because I had breasts and I was a girl. I know he would look at me and wonder how he had "created" me, and in his eyes was always that perplexed look, amazement that out of his cock and sperm came this living, breathing little girl with a life of her own. But what could he do with her? He moved in a set of bachelors and chorus girls. He was seen mostly with nightclub beauties, blond demi-call girls he had by flashing money at nightclubs like the Copacabana. Raising a daughter had no place in his life. But there was no place for me in my mother's life either.

At night, during boarding school vacations, while the other kids were at Radio City Music Hall or home with their families carving turkeys or doing something *American*, I sat alone in a whore's room in the damp, rotting hotel on Gramercy Park. I looked out the window. Nothing but the park. Its gloomy trees and sassy little paths all reminded me of the diagram I had seen in a book about hell. This was hell, I thought. I was Daddy's little whore. I used to think of that whenever they sang "Daddy's Little Girl." I had no one to love.

But why was Mother always making me feel guilty? If she wanted to marry a guy from Palm Beach who didn't want me in the house, that was her prerogative. But why did she always "invite" me there to make me feel even more unwanted? Why did she always make it so painfully clear that she couldn't "help" herself? Bill wouldn't have married her, she claimed, if he had to put up with me. So she got rid of me. But why was she always saying how much she loved me? Why didn't she just admit that I was a pain in the ass? But I was behaving like a brat only to attract a little love and attention. Fat chance with my mother. Her love was devoted to Bill, a good-looking young Gentile doctor, blond, from Palm Beach. *He's just my Bill, an ordinary guy. Too ordinary.* Her love was mostly pinned to survival. Survival as a professional musician. Survival as a woman. Most of all, her new husband, Blondie, was a professional man. They were all so goddamn professional. They only mixed with professional people. Other doctors and musicians.

My father, of course, wasn't a professional person. What was he? A Lower East Side cowboy. A grubby, self-made, gruff Panda man. A white Panda businessman who couldn't read or write but energized and bossed his way to the top. He was the first Jew in the typewriter ribbon world. People said he had a couple of million bucks. If he did, I never saw it. Daddy Warbucks. He hid his riches magnificently. He lived on bread alone, but what bread. Corned beef on rye sandwiches. Hot dogs from pushcarts. The cheapest clothes from Barney's. Only he always went out with flashy dames. I wasn't going to grow up to be a flashy dame, and that was the trouble as far as he was concerned. I was good-natured Little Lulu who wanted to be loved. A person. A real *poison*. A person who had no one to love.

That was why I read books. At night, I read about the Rite of the Goddess, Kali, the black one, Kali, the bloody one, Kali of the hecatombs. Was she unique? By no means. Far from India, in pre-Aztec Mexico, the name of the Terrible Mother was Chicomecoatl, with the seven snakes, goddess of voluptuousness and sin, but also of renewal of vegetation, the sexual act. As moon and earth goddess she was the goddess of the

West, of death and the underworld. She bore the death's head, and the female sacrifice offered up to her was beheaded. That's me, I thought. Little Lulu reading in Daddy's hotel room. That's me. Goddess of voluptuousness and sin. I looked in the mirror of the Greenside Hotel. I looked myself over. One head of brown hair worn in ringlets. Large eyes. Upturned nose. Funny lips. Nice lips. Smiling large lips. Braces. Two breasts which are shaped like hubcaps. Pink little hubcaps with motorcycle heart whirring around inside my body. The heart too big. The engine of the heart too powerful. Always whirring the heart. I never wanted to be a flashy dame. I was always Little Lulu. Chubby, good-natured. Walk all over me. All that I wanted was to be loved.

In my yearbook at La Bellson School I had a "quote." They wrote next to my picture, "Though she is little, she is fierce." And fiercely, through a machination of events, I always wanted to be a professional writer. It was my "way out" of my life, the secret door that would lead me into the wonderful world of words. Make no mistake. My intention as a child was to lead a good life. To levitate. To transcend. To be. To get out of the concentration camp of boarding school.

How had I lived through La Bellson? Lived through the mornings and the mornings and the mornings. Read poems. Felt something inside me growing like a bulb too large for its pot. The desire not to be me, to try to be, oh, someone else, someone floating in the universe not tied by earth and roots, someone floating in the being of things, powerful and lovely and talented and strange, not ordinary, beyond the curlers, the cold cream, the doom, beyond the habits and saying what must be said, beyond my country, in a world of turrets and soft pillows. I slept. And wished my mother was with me. I cried in the childbed of La Bellson School where there was no privacy. I dreamed. Possible plays and movies I would be in. I danced in futures of theaters and red velvet. Wonder Woman bracelets let me through the universe. I performed miracles. I was a magician. And mistress. And madwoman. And President of the United States of Umbilical. I was doing everything that the men I admired did. I tamed animals, ran countries, discovered new vitamins, vegetables, countries. I gave orders. I led armies. I broke barriers. I flew planes and spoke with kings. I slid into the Olympic world of politics and plays and put myself into the front, marching down the galaxies with dwarfs and giants and FDR. I would march with Gandhi, give to the rich, take from the poor. I was Mozart and Marx. I was miracle woman, Superlu, and nobody kept me locked in the pantry. In dreams began possibilities. My English teacher showed me that anyone can be like the Hopi Indians if he or she only tries hard enough. One little, two little, three little Indians.

On the war path I discovered that Mother was definitely finished with me. No warmth there. Too bad. Father kept saying I was "all he had," but it was just to sound good. He couldn't put me in his business, and he didn't know what to do with me, so he wished me luck and let me grow up in La Bellson Institution.

Song on graduation day, in time to "Pomp and Circumstance":

> La Bellson Institution
> Cause of Our Misery
> How can I go to college?
> Look what you've done to me —
> La Bellson Institution
> Look what I have been through
> How can I go to college?
> I belong in Bellevue. . . .

But I knew I didn't have to go to Bellevue. The *world* itself was an institution and all us people merely inmates. If Buddha doesn't go to Bellevue, Bellevue will come to Buddha. I was always unsure of myself.

How I hate being Little Lulu. Something is wrong. I'll tell you what's wrong, you little brat. You're a girl, and you want to be a writer. You might as well give up now. No matter how much crap they hand you at La Bellson Progressive Bullshit Boarding School about how privileged you are to be a girl, it's a crock. It's not a girl's world. Why do you always talk in the masculine? Because the world is masculine, my dear Lulu, or hasn't the shit hit the fan yet? You see all these books? Well, my darling, they are addressed specifically to the He. They are written for men and of men. If female eyes happen to cast upon them, that's okay, but they are written as if only men read. And you know what? You will heretofore be referred to as a man for the rest of your living life. Mankind. And you know what? You will live in a country run by men. That's right. And all the powerful corporations will be run by men. And even all revolutions will be run by men. And women (you will be a woman someday, Lulu) will always be minors. They will always be little girls. Little Lulus. And without a dingdong you can just forget it. Your comedy writing won't be taken seriously. Everything important will be written for men. Like, King Lear *won't be written about a woman, my darling. Who cares about an aging woman? Who cares about Queen Lear? You can play her to your heart's content in Bellevue, but not on Broadway. And when it comes to directing plays or directing anything, forget being a leader. Just be a follower. You remember what your daddy told you? Men like dumb women.*

In boarding school America during the 1940s, when I was still a studious virginal bratfall of a girl, tumbling, like an acrobat, from one daydream of power to another, I spent my time dressing myself up in different costumes backstage in the gym and wanting to play my part in the outside life theater. The demon of contradiction was always inside me. Should I be a wife? A professional pilot? A professional bare-back rider? With absolutely no talent for athletics, I imagined a short-lived career as a professional tennis champion. Also on my list of things to be: a revolutionary, a scientist, a comedian, a psychiatrist, a historian, a private detective. Also an architect. Anything at all but who I was.

But who was I? Who was Lulu anyway? And was I going to grow up to be happy?

I rejected the life of doing nothing but dreaming. I prepared myself. The school psychologist, Dr. Kadit, took a mild interest in me. Dr. Kadit, a fat woman with a Captain Marvel voice and great soul in her windpipe, said in her Russian accent, "You should make your dreams come true."

I mulled that one over as I took walks in the boarding school fields of Connecticut, going off by myself to look at the sun setting over the boarding school trees. My heroines were Madame Sun Yat-sen and Betty Grable.

CHILDHOOD IS FULL OF CRAP, I thought to myself and knew I would get out. I would find a way to escape childhood.

At graduation, my entire family arrived to watch me graduate. My mother (tears in her eyes) sat on one side of the graduation lawn, and my father (tears in his eyes) on the other side. I was happy to be getting out alive. My Aunt Poll wore a large red hat.

After my graduation, Papa, the typewriter ribbon king, was out of breath as he carried my suitcase down the Manor House stairs and into the car. He began driving out of the school grounds, and once we got on the highway, I asked him to tell me about business deals, property.

"Don't bother your pretty head. Girls aren't supposed to know about that. Someday a man will take care of you. Don't bother your head about deficits, credits, bonds, deals. That's a man's world. Lulu, you have no part in it. You're a scatterbrain like your mother."

I was isolated from his world.

I took Papa's advice. I looked for men to take care of me. I gambled on love. And with lovers, like gamblers, I could never win. Because nobody could take care of me.

His fingers were insured. You can't imagine what it's like to sleep with a guy with insured fingers. Like it or not, you can't exactly ask that he touch you there, just there, no, there, with his insured index finger. It's like being touched by Lloyds of London. You can't finger-fuck with Lloyds; if a finger went wrong, the whole hand was useless.

My first husband was a semifamous concert cellist. After we were married, my job on earth was to carry around the world his imitation alligator cello case. Seventy thousand dollars went into my boarding school and, later, college so I could grow up and schlep a cello around the world for someone else. That was my orientation to art. I was twenty. He wanted to be worshiped. I used to say to him, "Abraham, do you mind if I go in a corner of the room and write?"

He used to keep me sitting on the bed, listening to him slowly practice, bo boo boo Booo Boo Boo. I used to say, "Please? Can I write a little bit?"

And he would scream at me, "Write? You can write when you're older. How long do you think cello fingers last? My fingers will grow stiff one day, and then you can write. While you're able to, listen to me, listen to me. You can always write later." He was a genius. And an egomaniac.

No, he didn't say "you"; he said "we." He always spoke of himself with the royal "we."

I had met Abraham at a party given for the debut of the conductor Igor Markevitch in New York City. I was the girl with the split lip, and Dr. Rapky had said, "Don't eat or talk," so when Abraham came over and started talking to me, he fell in love with the girl, the silent girl who didn't say anything. He talked and I listened. When he walked into the room, the minute I looked at him I thought, what a gorgeous man. He was wearing a camel-hair coat, and he waddled like a duck and he had long blond hair that came down almost to his shoulders. He looked in every direction, and the woman he was with looked attractively comfortable with that hunk of man next to her.

"If I could find a guy like that, I would marry him," I said to myself, looking longingly at the food I couldn't eat because of

88

my split lip. The romantic stranger was older, worldly, charming, protective but artistic. He belonged to the grown-up world. In the ladies' room, all perfume and feathers, I wanted to say to the woman who came in with the blond man, "Your husband is gorgeous," but I didn't dare. I heard that his name was Abraham. Later he asked me for my phone number. I whispered it to him.

"But what about your wife?"

"That's not my wife," he said. "That's Vera Braun, Yahoodi Braun's wife. Are you married?"

"No, are you?"

Abraham threw back his head and started to laugh.

"I'll call you as soon as I can."

At six thirty in the morning the phone rang. It was Abraham. My old man was in the hospital, and I was living alone in New York City during the college vacation.

Abraham said, "I stayed up all night because I was afraid I would forget your phone number. Are you busy tonight?"

"Where do you live?"

"On East Thirty-ninth Street. Come over," he said.

I took a cab.

During the time we were courting, Abraham lived at the Sherman Square Studios. He had sublet Gian-Carlo Menotti's studio and was always walking around in baggy pants and sandals. He was messy, and I used to go over to his apartment and clean up after him. I was always making salads. We always ate together, and there were a lot of books in that house and I read them all. I remember the West Side, the heat of summer, no air conditioning, and the parties he gave at night where I was his "hostess" and we burned candles so no one could see the spots on the furniture. He never practiced the cello.

Abraham met my father, and my father didn't like him. Even after we were married, he kept saying, "This is my son,

Abraham Fill," instead of *Shill*. He didn't like him because Abraham was (1) poor, (2) a cellist, (3) too charming, (4) a hustler, (5) always whining, and (6) a foreigner. He asked my father for a new cello, and my father said, "I'll buy a cello for you if you marry my daughter, but there will be strings attached. No cello if no daughter. You run off with someone else and the cello comes back to me."

Do re mi fa sol la ti do.

But Abraham insisted, "No strings attached."

My FATHER: Strings. I ain't giving no cello without string attached.

ABRAHAM: No strings.

My FATHER: I ain't buying no cello unless you stay with my daughter. What do you think? I'm going to put twenty thousand dollars into a cello and you're going to walk off with it? What can *I* do with a cello? Hang it around my neck? You get the cello, but it's yours only as long as you're with my Lulu. No tickee, no washee. Do re mi fatso la ti dough.

At that time Abraham was mad. I was mad. But I also was mad about Abraham. Our engagement was off and on, off and on. When he wanted to, I didn't. And when I wanted to, he didn't. For two years we were together and apart. He fiddled, you understand—but he also faddled. He fiddled with friends—mostly women friends so he could mooch free places to love in or live in. Abraham was a collector's item. Women collected musicians, and he was a prize. One day Abraham went off to Greece. His patron was a woman called Stella Livanos. Abraham wrote to me that he was living in a wonderful house on Simunido Street with Stella (an "exciting woman," he wrote, "understanding," "sympathetic"). So there I am, arriving in Greece with nylon wash-and-wear blouses. Lulu the innocent.

Abraham had been given a huge studio with a piano in it at Stella's villa, and original Matisse paintings. But that's for

Abraham. The artist. Stella's popsie. When I arrive, I'm shown to my tiny room on the top floor of the house. The *top* floor in the middle of August. Even a roach would have lain back and died in that room. An abandoned maid's room under the roof they gave me. In Athens. In the middle of summer. No shower. No air. No window. It was a little Auschwitz. Stella said she hoped I'd be "comfortable." Comfortable. I had trekked to Greece to "be with Abraham." At night, it was a five-minute hike down the Livanos steps to the dining room. After I climbed up and down the steps a few hundred times, I said to Abraham, "I've had it."

He said, "Where are you going to go? Like, who do you know in Athens?"

He had a point. I was a prisoner. But one day I went over to the girlfriend of one of Abraham's pupils, a cultured guy named Takis who played in the orchestra. I mimed to his girlfriend, "Can you give me a place to stay? I want to get out of here." The girl, her name was Christa, gave me a postcard picture of herself in toe shoes, said okay and took me home with her. She lived in a tenement building at the other end of Athens. People took baths on the rooftop, and she had seven sisters all sleeping in one large room. The only place for me to sleep was on the dining-room table. They made up the table for me with a pillow and sheet, but it was still only a table. I felt instead of going to sleep, I was being served for dinner. A moussaka of delights. I dreamed of sleeping with Abraham. Finally, it was a choice between Stella's hot room on the fifth floor under the roof or the dining-room table with everyone speaking Greek and my not understanding one word. I went back to Abraham. And the maid's room.

I was caught in the wounds of his life, the bandages of new faces. And let's take time out to understand one thing: Abraham was very ambivalent about me because not only was he a ladies' man, he was a man's man, too. If he were just a Don Juan, it wouldn't matter, but he was a Don Juana and a Don Juan and a Juan Juan and a Don Don. He was interested with his whole heart and soul in very nearly every piece of ass that passed his way. I wasn't just competing with girls. I was competing with boys, too. What is it like to compete with everyone? It really keeps you on your toes. It was awful.

The air was murderous. Stella was a portrait painter and was always doing little charcoal portraits of me and Abraham. She hated me. Abraham always came out in the portrait looking like a million bucks. Good-looking. Suave. I came out looking like a tramp whose head had been caught in a blender. Stella really wished me dead. It didn't matter. Stella treated Abraham as if he were her private property. I suspected poison in my grape leaves.

I was exiled with Abraham and Stella. On a humid, buggy Greek day of days, when the sun was hot as an iron, we finally left Stella's house for good. We were going to visit Israel. Abraham had a concert in Israel, where his family lived. He was a sabra, and when we arrived in Israel, I had no intention of getting married. But his father lived there, and he said, "Is there a better place to get married than Israel? If you're going to marry, why not Israel?"

Then the trouble started. We wanted to get married in the woods, but his Tante Sonia couldn't walk in the woods because she had arthritis. Then we wanted to get married in a tiny hotel on top of the mountain of Haifa called Shoshanatha Carmel. But it was run by Arabs and wasn't kosher, and if the rabbi wouldn't eat there, neither would Tante Sonia. Shulamite suggested her house. His cousin Meira went shopping with me for a Yemenite dress which was a present. I forgot the veil. I was so nervous. Only three hours before the ceremony did we decide on a place to get married that would practically please everybody. A rooftop in Haifa. On a roof no one would be upset. So we got a Chupah and a rabbi, and we all walked to the rooftop.

Nervous? Was I nervous? I knew I was trying to do the right thing. I was so nervous that the morning of my nuptials, I tried to join the Martha Graham Dance Company, which was leaving Haifa for Uganda. I figured if I could just slip into a leotard and join the company, no one would miss me. But I was too fat. My friend the dancer Bette Shaler said Martha wouldn't want anyone even a little overweight in the company, so there was no way out. Stuck in Haifa. I kept stalling for time. The rabbi wouldn't marry us unless I could prove I was Jewish. Whew. Wonderful. But Abraham called my father long distance, collect, and my father had called the chief rabbi, and a telegram arrived saying, "Yes, she is Jewish," and signed by the Rabbi of Rabbis. So there I was, about to become the wife of the cellist Abraham Shill, one part of me not wanting to get married, but the other part of me, Little Lulu, feeling helpless that I couldn't do anything else with my life.

The day of my wedding I got a letter from my father. On tissue paper, five pages. "My beloved daughter, you know I can't stand the man you are marrying. He's not as talented as you think he is. He's not my first choice. He's not even my tenth choice. But if you love him, that's all I want." And to Abraham, he had written, "My son, my son, live with her and cherish her, and the two of you get to know each other and give a little and take a little and bleed a little and feel the embrace of the cosmic sound and the eternal light." My wedding present from my father was this letter. But there was no toilet on the rooftop where we were married. Only an outhouse in the yard. Abraham took my father's letter and, because there was no toilet paper, wiped his behind with it.

Abraham had been a wunderkind. He played his own cello at six. At the age of eight he had given cello concerts in Israel, and Jacques Tibaud, the violinist, heard him play and sent him to Europe. He went with his mother. His first patron at the age of ten was a nice old man who adored the cello and also, apparently, tried to seduce Abraham by taking him away to a château and sleeping with him. His mother, instead of having the old man arrested, tried to get money out of him to keep the whole thing quiet. Thus, playing the cello was connected with being a little male whore. Abraham practiced but at the same time began to hate the cello. As years went by and his mama died, Abraham became famous in France and started to give concerts. He won the Prix de Musique competition by a scandal, and all the reviews in the papers were sensational: *"Il est un génie!"*

Is it a genius? No, it's Abraham, Abraham, narcissistic, bisexual, charming as a magician, egotistical, sick Abraham. I wonder why I *married* you. I think I know: Once, a long time ago at boarding school, I had a vision on the lawn and thought, I will marry someone who needs me. You were that man. I saw you in your nervous state wearing a long cape, looking like a great blond god. Abraham, the wunderkind, the artist, twenty years older than me. I was attracted to you because I was a girl, and your "fame" meant this: a new world opening. But I played to Abraham. I thought you were "great," and the romantic myth of the artist entered my head as a delight. I didn't know that two years later I would have a nervous breakdown. I was your maid.

After Abraham and I were married in Haifa, we returned to New York City. My father was still living in the Greenside Hotel, which he owned. Abraham was preparing for his cello recital at Carnegie Hall, paid for by my father. He began practicing. Finally, the day of the concert arrived. The entire Carnegie Hall was papered with friends of my father's, friends of my mother's. We gave tickets away to all the people we knew so it would look "jammed." Abraham started the evening in a fit of nerves. He said that I "held him up" getting to the concert. When we arrived at Carnegie Hall, he was cracking jokes but was terribly nervous. But the concert began on time. My husband stepped out on the empty stage, sat down, and for one moment, I thought he was going to start to throw up. He hated being a virtuoso musician and would have preferred, I am sure, being a comedian. Then he began to play Bach.

For a moment, I thought he had forgotten the music, and I became manic. There was always some reason or other why I was having an anxiety fit. Either Abraham wasn't practicing. Or Abraham wasn't playing well or Abraham wasn't the wunderkind he used to be. Was he another Piatigorsky? Flash forward: The concert was a bomb. Abraham got the worst reviews in musical history. We had a big party waiting for the reviews to come out. The *Times* called him "a failure." The *Post* called him "a bore." The other papers slaughtered him. We were in despair. Mrs. Yahoodi Braun was secretly delighted that Abraham had gotten such crappy reviews. She took us to lunch the next day at the Plaza, and suggested we move to Portugal and Abraham could practice his cello for a few years. Abraham was sure that the critics were against Israelis. We were roped together you understand, like melons. So that when Abraham was despondent, I was also despondent. Abraham had some concerts lined up in France, so we decided to leave the United States and move there. The flight of the genius. With me trailing behind, carrying his cello.

I had a maid's-eye view of Europe. One by one I met all the great musical celebrities of our time, Shostakovitch, Rubinstein, Stravinsky, Oistrakh, Horowitz, Schoenberg's disciples, all as the valet of Abraham Schill.

La vie est étrange. We continued to live in Paris. He was the genius. I was only the little goat with a cello who trailed behind him, the unicorn he had met in America, Little Lulu, the schmuck. We lived in one room after another and never had enough money to feed us. We found a restaurant in Paris where children ate for about thirty-five cents. We could get a hot meal there. And we used to go out in the afternoons and eat with the children. I went along with him everywhere, looking always a mess. This was my routine: Get up. Buy bread at small bread store. Bring it home. Serve breakfast in bed to my husband (genius) who was still sleeping. Then do house-work. Light fire. Wax floors. Wash windows. Type Abraham's letters. Cook. Scrub. Snivel. Wash. Screw.

Boulevard Raspail market. Seeing by feeling. The touch led me like a blond blind woman to the market, where I felt the oranges, pressed my hands against the eggplants, lifted the tomatoes. Oh, no, can't forget: the bread store, where the palaces of odors and fragrances made me dizzy. The bread world. The world of round breads and long breads. Vegetables and loaves and the salami stores. Then on to the fish mart, the great fish in rows like dead chorus girls with scales. The Busby Berkeley Paris fish world where thousands of bright orange fish lay side by side. Then to the cracked mirrors of the meat market where I saw myself split into two people in the mirror before a backdrop of red meat hanging from a hook. I, too, was hanging from a hook. Bleeding. That was the loneliness no one knew when I came home loaded with bright-green lettuce leaves and breads and cooked lunches and dinners for the friends of my husband-stranger. He too liked strangers. I cooked for actors, whores, violinists, bums, fake pianists and pederasts, and managers, and all the profiteers following the cellist and his wife like parasites. I was a cook. A nobody. Abraham told me to shut up and let him do the talking.

The apartment we spent the most time in was like a madhouse. It was on the Rue de Lille and belonged to a red-haired madwoman called Madame de Carville. The apart-ment, which was on the third floor, had walls on which there were murals of the gods fucking each other in every position. Here was this very old-fashioned Paris apartment with these weird murals, all in blue and white, naked women and men having a go at it, pieces of ass all over the walls. In the living room was old furniture, broken chairs, a huge piano, A large kitchen without an icebox or stove was in the back. A hot plate was there. It was hard to make the apartment livable. It was cold. Madame de Carville had rented it to us for little money since she had gone off to a wedding in Lebanon. Madame de Carville had an old man who came in once a week to clean the house, but we couldn't afford him, so the old man had shown me how to tie rags onto my feet and wax the floor by scuffing against them in the way that had been practiced for centuries. I woke up in the morning, tied the rags to my feet, and scuffed across the floor like a skater, skating on wax. The genius was still sleeping. When the genius woke up, he was usually in a foul mood and told me to go buy some lunch because he had invited five or six people to come have a "bite" with us. I took the rags off my feet. Took out my string basket and went to the different stores in the neighborhood. I came home and made lunch. Who came? Miss Israel and some of Abraham's other "friends."

Now Abraham was in love with Miss Israel, a tall busty dark-haired beauty, unhappily married to a Polish furrier and living in the middle of the Avenue Foch. And Miss Israel, whose name was Dora, always wore couturier clothes and looked very pouty. She put on a brother-sister act with Abraham. To tell the truth, I didn't believe that act for a minute.

"Why the hell is that bitch coming here every day for lunch?" I wanted to know.

I was cooking for Romeo and Juliet. What was I? A cook for Miss Israel? Why couldn't she eat at home with the furrier instead of bothering us?

"She's had a terrible life," Abraham said to me. "Her parents were in a concentration camp."

Abraham's friends all had terrible lives behind them which made them guests and made me the cook. Just because my mother was born in America and grew up to get a master's degree and married my father and divorced him and my father was a guy who made a lot of money in the typewriter ribbon business, even though he was illiterate, that didn't qualify me for Abraham's attention. Dora's life was her come-on.

Abraham blew hot and cold with Miss Israel to the point where I couldn't stand it. One night he took us both to the theater to see *The Hostage* and Miss Israel didn't understand the play and I did, so she said to Abraham in her haughty French-Israeli accent, "Of course, I'm not as much of an intellectual as your darling wife."

I hit her over the head during the intermission with my pocketbook. I had to reach up because I'm a shrimp and she was well over six feet, but I hated her so much for making me make her lunch and wash the dishes and I did all the dirty work while she arrived at our apartment in minks and sables, looking like an ad for Miss Universe while I looked like an ad for Ajax Cleanser, and I hit her wham right over the head with my Paris pocketbook. She hit back, and a fight broke out between us in the Théâtre des Nations lobby. Everyone was shocked. They had never seen two women fighting in the lobby.

"You bitch from the furry world of Foch Avenue, get out of my life, you're sleeping with my husband, with your fur coats and fancy clothes, and I'm your cook," I screamed at her, and smashed her again over the head. As I hit her, I remembered the lunches I had made for them both.

I thought her false eyelashes would fall off. She tried to hit me back by scratching my face with her long false red fingernails. I didn't get scratched at all because I ducked and then gave her a good sock in the knockers. Abraham came over and took her side. He tried to protect her from me, his wife, as if she were right simply because she was Miss Israel. He heard her sarcastic remarks but didn't care at all if she insulted me.

"Okay, stay with her," I shouted to him, and ran backstage. There I met up with a bunch of rakish Irish actors and went out drinking with them. I didn't dare have an affair with any of the actors because in those days I thought it was sinful to commit adultery. But I just stayed away from my home for a day, drinking and having fun, and then came back. Abraham apologized and said he would never see Miss Israel again if I just came home. And calmed down. And I did. By the way, it was in that apartment with Abraham I had a nervous breakdown. It happened like this:

One day Abraham came home and found me crying. I couldn't talk, only cry. Every time I tried to get a word out of my mouth it came out in screams. Abraham, in his typically wrong way, took me to see Yahoodi Braun's diet doctor. I didn't need a diet, I needed a husband. Over my shaking body, they both spoke in French. I did not understand one word. I heard the male voices saying "spasmophiliac" and to me it sounded like "cancerous tuberculosis of the liver" or something equally horrible. The fact was this: The doctor was full of shit. Like most full-of-shit doctors in Paris or anywhere else, he found it convenient to diagnose me for something I didn't have. "Spasmophilia" meant that I had calcium missing in my bones. He said I should have two weeks' rest in a dark room without visitors and I should take calcium shots regularly. Like Little Lulu, I nodded my head in agreement. Why the fuck didn't I protest? Why didn't I say, "You are full of shit. I'm having a nervous breakdown because my husband is a failure as a husband and a failure as a cellist. He doesn't do anything except play genius all day, and I'm his maid and his whipping girl, and when he does practice, it's for ten minutes. He makes me sit on the bed and listen and he blames me for everything that's wrong in his life and makes me feel guilty and leaves me alone in the apartment and I don't speak French and I can't get a job and he won't let me have girlfriends or see anyone and I grew up in a progressive school and all the people I keep meeting in Paris are these middle-class French yentas and if I hear the word *mignon* one more time I'll grow a tumor on my tummy because, Doc, I'm lonely for everything good. I want to feel good. I want to feel like a person, not a servant. I want to have friends I can talk to, and I want to stop worrying about Abraham's fucking career and money, and I want to stop gaining weight and feel a little affection from my husband, who never treats me as if I was precious to him but as if I were the biggest pain in the ass he ever met. Doctor, I'm a person! A nervous person. But a person."

Abraham took me home and put me into bed in a windowed back room. It happened that the bed slanted. I lay in the room on a slant. No one came to visit me. No one spent time with me. Every once in a while I would hear the toilet flush in the next apartment. But I was kept in bed for my calcium shots. Finally, Abraham was going to the south of France.

"Take her with you," the doctor said.

I badly needed to get out of the room.

"Abraham, help me out of bed."

Still a servant, I went with him on the train. Sick as I was, I carried the cello. To the south. To the sun. To the tropics. To the new place of the world where I could see palm leaves. He had several guest appearances with the Cannes Symphony Orchestra. It was my job always to dress up and sit in the audience and clap until my hands were bright red. I was instructed always to be the first to yell *Bravo*.

I was in love with leaves. With palm leaves. I trailed behind Abraham, carrying his cello, so happy to be in the south. Looking at leaves. I felt new in the sun.

We all need, at one time or another, someone to love us. I was not loved by Abraham. Although he always accused me of

100

having a lover. Early in our marriage, Abraham talked about my lovers all the time. What lovers? I wanted to know. Who had a lover? I didn't. But he kept accusing me. He would go away for a concert overnight, and when he came back, he would say, "I suppose you've spent your time with your lover."

"*I don't have a lover.* Abraham, you're my lover."

He didn't believe me.

Abraham, you idiot. You were an Israeli con man. And you were a fakir. A con man. But what a good one. You lived at the Plaza Hotel in Victor Borge's suite. Yahoodi Braun liked you because he's a big closet queen and Dora Braun liked you because you were handsome and her ass hurt, and so there you were, liked, for being an Israeli wunderkind. You were charming. Funny. Sexy. Everyone adored your jokes. (Except my father: "Who's that schleppy guy you're fiddling around with? Why doesn't he get his pants pressed?") Abraham, I met you when I was at Bennington, where I majored in social science with the hope of changing society via a socialist revolution and I also wrote poetry which was printed in *Voices and Verses*, a third-world magazine, me, the little schizo Sappho of the bohemian world of careless socialist girls and would-be analysts all talking about neurotic interaction in marriage. And there I was with long brown hair and big eyes and good skin and what possibily was the biggest ass in the whole college, pretending to everyone that I was older. Me, a virgin, meeting up with you, the great cellist. It was my lucky day. Some lucky day. So long. Good-bye to life. Join with a man. Make his life your life. Because you don't have a life, sweetheart. Oh yes. And when he asked you to marry him, what did you say? I'd like to think about it? Maybe I don't need a psychotic cellist in my life? A genius? Like I have my own problems? Oh, no, you say, of course I'll marry you. And that's the end of your life. *Brava! Bravissima!*

I married Abraham for many reasons: to escape myself, and to escape my family, to escape the middle-class milieu of America, to have someone to live for, to live through, to protect me from the world, which frightened me. And *voilà*, yippee, I don't have to live my own life. I don't have to be alone. I don't have to do a fucking thing because if I tie myself down to Abraham, then the relationship with him will take up all my time tra-la tra-la. So what if I had to carry a cello through all the train stations of Europe? At least it was *Europe*. I met Stravinsky. I heard great music. It was better than slugging it out on my own in New York City, eating my heart out at Horn & Hardart's. Instead of being an artist, I married one.

My father came to Paris. I had written him that Abraham and I were not very well suited to each other. He arrived with Maria and they stayed at the cheapest hotel, Le Lutèce. He came to visit Abraham and me in our studio, and he spoke to Abraham as if he were some kind of stranger.

"Sit down," he said to Abraham. "I want you to do me a favor."

"What is it I can do for you, Seymour?"

"My daughter isn't happy with you. She doesn't like being left in Paris by herself while you go off on your trips to give concerts. I'd like you to take her with you."

"It's too expensive, Seymour. I don't have a car."

"Abraham," says my papa, "I'll buy you a car."

And off they went to buy a car. A car to take me with him. Abraham couldn't drive, which made driving with him a monstrosity. But now I became his chauffeur as well as his maid.

Meanwhile, a large, tall, thin greyhound of a woman called Baroness de Durkhem had "adopted" Abraham and me. We were invited for picnics at her summer home. I would try to cuddle up to Abraham. I was always looking for affection. But he was no longer my lover. He was gone.

"Hello, dear husband," I would say in the morning.

"Stop that," he would yell at me.

I would get up and make breakfast. The phone would ring. Immediately Abraham would put on his good-natured, friendly voice. He reserved his sour, angry, hostile personality exclusively for me. To anyone on the phone, he was cheerful.

"Bonjour, mon ami, ça va?"

The good-natured jolly musician. THE LOVER INSIDE HIM GONE, THE HUSBAND A PHONY CON MAN.

When I think of Paris, I think of the days I spent sneaking out of my apartment to see an ancient roué, Jock. (I had finally chosen a lover.) I would tell Abraham I was going to the cleaner's or to look for some material to make curtains for the new house we were living in. My sadness was this: I went out on the streets just to feel like myself. I felt too closed in, that Abraham was eating my life away with his cello and his constant self-pitying and his mistresses. I wanted someone to love me. Jock was *the* disciple of Schoenberg.

Sneaking out to see Jock, I wore old clothes. I wore old velvet pants, and I began to look like a bum. I wore a tired gray hat. I was frightened in my stomach. In my guts. I was afraid to be me. I was Abraham's wife, not Lulu. I didn't want to find out who I was.

The windows of Paris held things that I couldn't buy. But I lived inside the windows with my eyes. I saw shiny lizard pocketbooks with tortoiseshell clasps and perfectly made shoes and antiques and clothes that were cut by magical scissors. I desired these well-made things but couldn't buy them. Coats and shirts for ladies. I looked through my Rio travel material every day.

One day Jock said that he loved me. We were making love in a four-foot-wide brownstone hotel off the Rue du Bac.

"I want you to know how much I love you," he said.

Would my life change? Would I go run off for and with him?

I often thought that Jock represented death. He had died inside, and only this strange liar-person remained. This odd old man with his "love" for me. I knew he had others. Would he run out on me? Would he leave me? I imagined myself in Rio, sitting alone on a farm while Jock drove around in a large car. Jock. Death was my boyfriend. He was sixty years old. He dyed his hair. He once knew Schoenberg. I loved him.

Depressed, I sulked around Paris. I would take long bus rides that would lead me to the outskirts of the city where the poor lived. This was a different Paris from the Avenue Foch and the ya-ya boutiques of St.-Tropez doodads. On the outskirts of Paris, this part of the city was filled with men waiting in queues for work, vegetables sold outside the house with flies as big as cockroaches, coal-tar soap. Places change you. In this section of the poor, my nose became a different nose; my nose smelled sweat and the smell of leftover war and urine. Death came oozing out with its smell, too. Death came out of the streets and the horsemeat stores with the golden horse heads on top of them, the death of horsemeat. Death came with the clattering of a tram; out of the *métro* came dirty feet, indigestion, women with pockmarked faces, faded dresses, cotton stockings, collars made out of paper that haven't been changed, the couching mass of workers who won't get paid for their time, wouldn't get paid enough to eat, the lost sick children with pus streaming out of their eyes, playing with sticks in the street, the women and men who get squeezed in and out of the *métro*. And why did I go walking into this world with them? Got to admit it: to be squeezed. To feel close enough to smell someone. To feel close to people. The men pressing their dicks against me, the women on the *métro* with their arms lifted so that the hair shone under their arms like bushels of old hay. These affectionate men, these women, these were my lovers. I was pushed up against them. I looked like one of them. I felt ill and unwanted and aimless. My life—a zero. My parents were selfish souls whose heritage to me had been material things and no family. Had I ever been in my mother's arms? Had my father ever kissed me or told me that he loved me? My heritage had been divorces, judges, boarding schools, trains that led to vacations, orthodontia, and from vacations, camps, and my father saying, "Someday you'll understand what it means to be miserable." My father's legacy to me—his misery. I imagined a little circle of black crows, all of them in a row, the way the nursery rhyme went, and all the crows were my family. Now, here I was, in the Paris environs, lost, where nothing was familiar, lost among strange lavatories and strangers' faces, lost among faces that did not know me and didn't care: twenty-one years old, unknown girl, not speaking French, fucking a sixty-one-year-old man for love, lost girl of the no-touch, no-taste world, shrimp, strong, wandering in the streets, surrounded by firm, obstinate women who refuse to die, by old men who look at the sun. The underwater world of dirt and violence and no food. Looking up to strangers in the *métro*. In my loneliness. Little Lulu looking for love.

It was true. I had not conquered my greatest fear: being alone forever. But what was the worst disaster that could happen? I would be one of the old women lying in front of the bathroom in Grand Central with paper bags wrapped around my feet and a rag around my neck, peeling an apple with my hand out to all the fashionable women going inside for a ten-cent pee. Was that so terrible? Wasn't it better to be an old woman bum on the outs with material things and people, an old gypsy tramp down and out, than INSIDE A MIDDLE-CLASS FUCKING MARRIAGE? An emotional bum looking for emotional handouts?

I really believed that if I wasn't married to one man, I had to be married to another. This went back to a time when my father hysterically looked for a protector for me. Let me go back to my freshman year when my hysterical father took me on a cruise. He was so panicked that I wouldn't find a husband that he actually sprang for cruise tickets. Where was the boat going? Where? Who cared? He was looking for a husband for his daughter. Not that I was so ugly or anything. I was just little. I didn't look grown-up. And a little girl doesn't find a husband that easily. On the boat I wore my new green felt dress, the one that made me look like a walking pool table with curves. I sat with my father at a table with a man and a woman who had been married for seventeen years. They did not talk to each other but talked to us. They liked my father. They liked my "breeding."

"Where did she get that lovely breeding?" the man asked.

"At women's reform prison," I replied.

I was a regular little female Lenny Bruce—even then. But they didn't take me seriously. The man at our table knew that my husband-hunting father was not particular about who he found for me. He just had to have one thing: money.

One night, after a cruiselike dinner of poached salmon, squab, steak, pineapple turnovers, ice cream and cookies (I always ate everything), we took a stroll, all four of us, on the deck. Behold a vision too beautiful for words, an angel shining in a camel's hair coat, a final solution dropped from the news of heaven, a man of magnificence, Abou Ben Adam, may his tribe increase: In short, a bachelor appeared before us. An angel with a suntan. Who could ask for anything more? The man had been eyeing me in the dining room as I went from fish to squab. His eyes had fallen on my little breasts. My father threw himself at the man, when he tried to unclothe me. The *man*, whose name was Stan Conway, proceeded to walk me around the deck. The deck led to other things: his cabin. In the cabin, he told me, "very honestly," he wanted to put his hand politely inside my pool table dress. I thanked him for his honesty and said that I was a virgin and nothing doing. Stan

Conway was, he confessed, married to a woman in Bronx-ville who did not understand him. They had three boys. But no understanding. That was why he was on the cruise. Once I realized that he was *married*, thus not eligible for my father's final solution, I relaxed and got to know him. Platonically. I even gave him my college address.

He used to write me wonderful letters at college. And he also pursued me with a series of witty collect phone calls (he never wanted my number on his bill). As he had promised in one of his calls, he drove up Thanksgiving holiday to take me home for college, to drive me to my father in New York. He entered Stokes House and was greeted by one of the Benning-ton girls in the house.

"Hey, Lulu," the girl called up the stairs. "Hey, Lulu, your father's down here."

Stan Conway was mortified. After all the money he spent on masseurs and clothes and dyeing his hair to look young. At that moment I came to the top of the stairs. I had the Asian flu. All my friends had the Asian flu. I asked Stan Conway if he minded driving three of my friends, Ellen, Arlene, and Jerry, home, too. It wasn't the romantic trip he had in mind, but he agreed. We all piled our junk into his huge limousine, complete with chauffeur, and off we went.

As we neared New York, he took us on a little diversion. He drove to a huge park somewhere in Westchester; taking me out of the car, away from my friends, he showed me some land fenced in by wire.

"Someday all this will be yours," he said.

My girlfriends were throwing up near the car. The flu was pretty bad.

"How come?" I asked.

He smiled at me. "I own this."

"Who are you anyway, Nelson Rockefeller?" I asked, trying to be witty.

"No. *I am the King of Westchester,*" he replied. "I own thousands and thousands of landmarks and acres in Westchester. I began buying up Westchester when I was a young boy. By the time I was thirty I owned more Westchester land than anyone else. Marry me, and all Westchester can be yours."

"But I don't want Westchester," I said to Stan Conway. "I just want to get home and throw up. I have the flu. The flu. Don't you understand that when you are a diseased person, you don't want anything? Not even Westchester?"

"You poor child," he said, and walked me to the car.

Stan Conway drove me to my father's apartment in New York, where I recovered. As soon as I was well enough to go out, he picked me up in the limousine and took me out to my first expensive restaurant. It was called Cerutti's. As I walked down the aisle in my pool table green (I was addicted to this one felt dress which I made myself with felt from the dime store and pinking shears), I was aware that I could hardly walk correctly in my patent leather high heel sandals. As he was seating me at the table, the headwaiter dropped the table on the small toe of my right foot. I was in agony. I wanted to scream in the restaurant, but I didn't dare. Stan Conway kept prompting me to eat lunch. He was pushing wine and food at me, but I shut my lips tight and just sat there with my toe in agony. I was too shy to scream, so I sat there with the scream inside me, all tight and unable to come out. That was the day the table fell on my foot.

Years later, when I was going with Henry, I had to see a foot doctor. His name was Dr. Farcus. I looked at Dr. Farcus.

"And all these years your toe has been broken, just a small break, but bulging every time you have an irritating shoe over the delicate tissue. You realize that every time you put this toe into a shoe you are aggravating it and causing it to swell. You realize that you will have to go all through your life with a shoe or a boot with a hole in it?"

It was true. I had been wearing boots with a hole cut out of the side for years. It wasn't very attractive. Especially the boot I had chosen, which was an old snow boot.

"Wouldn't you like to throw away your boots? And really walk?" Dr. Farcus asked. "You're much too pretty a gal to go through life in boots with holes."

"Okay," I said, hanging my head. He was unnerving me. "Give me the name of a good foot surgeon."

And that was how I got to the offices of Dr. Lillianthal. His offices were being remodeled, and sawdust was coming down from the heavens of his podiatric ceiling. There were casts of feet everywhere. He took one look at my toe, a couple of X rays, and gave me the news: elective surgery. It wouldn't be an easy operation.

I went to the hospital. Scared footless. Under the ether, all the ghastly men in my life came back to me. They say before you die, all the events in your life pass before your eyes. Actual Homo non-sapiens who had entwined their lives with mine. Toe to toe, heel to heel, we were dancing together. John Seissman, the anthropologist, who was an anti-Semite. Sherwood "Bermuda" Stanley, with bugs in his bed. My first husband, who had his fingers insured. Jock, the old madman who took me to the back hotels of Paris. My mind drifted . . . drifted under ether to the different kinds of men I had known between marriages and before marriages—the greatest trauma in my life, outside my two husbands, had been Mahindra, the first who believed in my writing but believed in my ass even more.

Enter Mahindra, otherwise known as the Prince of Peace. He was billed as the greatest poet in the world, and he came to read at my college. I remember walking through the pine forest which led to the Carriage Barn. All the girls were seated, waiting for him to give his poems their airing in the fresh air of a girls' college, air his poems the way you air sheets in the sun, dirty laundry fresh in the sun. And he began reading to all the faces. He began singsong readings; his poems were incantations. He was originally from India, and I was overwhelmed by his Indian voice, which went up and down. Overwhelmed, but it was easy to overwhelm me in those days, those lost days, those wild days of girlhood when a dark man in a white tunic and a white turban, airing his poems, seemed like the Prince of Peace. I picked some pine tree branches and placed them on my bed, on the dresser in my bedroom, placed his picture next to it and went to sleep dreaming of the Prince of Peace, the great sage and lyrical prophet. "Am I defeating death?" he asked. I wanted to answer.

That would have been all. That should have been all. That might have been all if strange events had not led me, a few years later, to work in New York for a Mrs. Lena Goss, an art crook. Mrs. Goss employed me as a secretary, working mornings typing, answering her phone, cleaning her silver, dusting books, and paying bills. Mrs. Goss was in the art smuggling business, and she would dictate various nefarious letters to me that always, in Spanish, dear senor so-and-so, went on in a fashion not too puzzling if you knew the code. Please put the sleeve inside the banana and turn the apricot into the polka dot in Sweden, which, probably, decoded, meant please take the Goya and slip it inside the couch which is going to Sweden. At that job, I began dreaming of the Prince of Peace, daydreaming, because he was a friend of Mrs. Goss and he often telephoned and I answered in my Our Miss Brooks voice and it was his voice on the phone. One day I remember—fate of fate—I asked him if I might interview him for a magazine. He agreed. I reminded him that I had met him in the gathering at the college reading, in the winter in the Carriage Barn. He did not remember. He agreed, however, to meet me for lunch the next day.

Cupid's bow has poison arrows. I do not recommend love if you *want* to survive. I sat, Miss Little Lulu, in my red tight-under-the-armpits dress. I was sweating like mad, and he came into the Russian Tea Room and seemed to be walking in a fog. He looked romantic with his beard and his feet shuffling and his weirdo smile that didn't belong with his eyes. It was as if his eyes and mouth didn't belong together, didn't fit, as if the pieces of two faces got put together. And his smile was constant, like the smile of a headwaiter, I thought. I sat there in my Little Lulu dress and wondered what I might ask him. I was very young, frightened of the Prince of Peace. And when he sat down, he immediately held my hand, and I felt his palm sweat, and he said in a way supposed, I am sure, to be gallant and amorous, "My, Lulu, but I don't remember you as being so attractive."

What he meant was, "My, but I don't remember you at all," and I began asking my interview questions and the seconds seemed infinite because I knew the answers. I knew where he was born, I knew about his World War II period, his ashram period. I knew everything about him. I had studied him in the library and could recite backwards his farewell poems, the long love poems that told about fluids, ferns, rib cages. The interview continued until the lunch was over. Then we walked out of the restaurant and walked hand in hand in Central Park.

"You must see me as someone who has been looking for you all my life. I have been lonely waiting for you. And I think we should live together. We will have a maid, of course. And we will pay her two dollars an hour. We will make visits to all my friends. And when you die, you will be buried in my family graveyard in Bombay. How does it sound?"

I looked at the pond. I looked at the water. I looked at the pigeons. It sounded mad. It was mad. Mahindra was the Prince of Peace, but he was mad. A middle-class tragedy: The man I love is mad. I hailed a taxi and beat it away from the park and the Prince of Peace.

Meanwhile, back at my adopted house, everything was ridiculous.

I was living a comic-strip life with my father. I was Little Lulu, the dependent one. Father had given me the maid's room to unravel in, and I made that my base of operations. I had come back to New York from abroad to study the domestic communications satellites. "Communications is power," J. William Fulbright told the Senate Subcommittee on Communications in 1970. "And exclusive access to it is a dangerous, unchecked power."

On my own, I was investigating the matter of domestic communications satellites facilities by nongovernment entities. I was haunted by the private ownership of domestic satellites which allowed certain firms virtual command of the communications process. I sat in my father's maid's room charting my attack on the Federal Communications Commission. In the midst of my operation the phone rang. It was Mahindra. He wanted to see me. When I met him at the St. Regis Bar, he seemed so crazy. I had lost so much time with Abraham I didn't need another crazy artist. He was carrying a suitcase and a statue of Napoleon. He looked nuts.

"We are moving," he said, "into an apartment together."

"You are mad," I said. "I can't live with you. I'm living with my father. And I'm busy."

It was then that he launched into his dialogue and epilogue and all other kinds of logues. He loved me. He was a great poet. He had to *have* me.

"There is no place for love in my life," I said, lying.

But he was not to be put off. He revolved in his own poetic universe. He quoted Allen Tate. T. S. Eliot.

A few days later he called me again. This time he had something to tell me. He was Jesus Christ, the Prince of Peace. I went to see my analyst. At that time my analyst was a woman from Vienna, Dr. Lazer. In the middle of my being analyzed,

I always had to get up and answer the doorbell because Dr. Lazer was too old to do it. I was combination valet/analyzand. I talked about the Prince of Peace.

"Dr. Lazer, he thinks he's Jesus Christ."

She looked at me. "Vat is so crazy about that?" she asked. "Don't exaggerate, Lulu. You always exaggerate."

Oh, it was no exaggeration. Besides thinking he was the Prince of Peace, the poet gave a surprise party to which he invited all of New York's literary set. I didn't know any of the people, but I had read their works while at college. The Prince of Peace got into an argument with one of America's leading novelists. The argument? Who was worse, Hitler or Stalin? The novelist said Stalin. The Prince of Peace said Hitler. Most sided with the novelist. Of course, Hitler was worse, I found myself saying. I hated this kind of repartee and wished I was home with my satellite investigation. All the guests left instantly.

With the people gone from the party, Mahindra goose-stepped toward me. His eyes were popping out of their sockets. He looked like a disinterred Adolf Hitler.

Suddenly, he had his heavy hands around my throat.

"I'll kill you for not taking my side," he said.

I was being choked to death by India's greatest poet. A distinction of sorts. Oh, well. It's better than dying at a sale at Ohrbach's, I thought. What a way to go. And I might have gone but the poet stopped choking me. He was sweating and began gurgling. I was petrified that he was having an attack of the sort I had no name for. Was *this* a Hindu fit? I had heard of them. Did they take the form of choking people to death, then stopping to sweat? We were in the uptight town house of Mahindra's best friend, another Brahmin. I ran up to his room, but he had locked his door. I banged on the door. Mahindra was covered with schizophrenic sweat. He was a borderline person, but I realized all this too late.

"Come out, come out and help me. Your friend and mine, India's greatest poet, is flipping."

But the friend kept his door closed. In true Brahmin fashion, he was hoping to ignore the situation. He didn't want to get choked. He was no fool.

I ran down the antique steps, noticing how the parquet floors kept their varnish even after being shuffled on by so many guests. Mahindra had passed out. I lifted him and dragged him to the steps. I felt as if I were the killer, not the *victim*. I lugged him up the stairs. He was wearing tan loafers with pennies in them. (My father used to say, "Never trust a man in loafers.") I finally got him to a bedroom and unloaded him on the bed. He was either fast asleep or passed out permanently. His skin was green. I didn't know what to do, so I tucked him into bed. In the morning another Indian came. I had sat up all night watching the Prince breathe. I didn't know what else to do. The friend who arrived in the morning was wearing a tan turban. He behaved like a maharaja. He was very official. His voice was high Hindi.

"I'm afraid Mahindra has had another one of his manic attacks. He has had them in Detroit, Guadeloupe, and South Africa, but this is the first one he has had in New York City."

Was I lucky? To be present and almost strangled by his first New York attack?

"You know, when he got manic, he thought he was Adolf Hitler. He tried to strangle me. I didn't mind when he thought he was Adolf Hitler, that is. But when he tried to choke me, well, I mean, I came to a literary party, and I wasn't expecting psychosis."

The friend looked at me. "Quite right. I'm afraid we have to take him to the hospital. There will be an ambulance here shortly. What is your name?"

"My name is Lulu."

"Lulu, Mahindra is psychotic. You will have to visit him

regularly in the hospital. You understand it is very important to be supportive at a time like this."

"I understand. But if he thinks he's Attila the Hun again, I don't want to go through another choking scene. It's bad for my throat."

The friend looked at me and gave me a meaningless laugh.

"He is not just your *ordinary* psychotic, you know. He is India's greatest poet. We must do for him things we would not do for others."

"Why?" I asked.

"Because people will be reading his works as long as there is an English and Hindi language. Does that mean anything to you?"

"My neck means more. My peace of mind is everything. I don't want a maid at two dollars an hour. I don't want to be buried in his family graveyard in Bombay. I want to live. And go home and work on the satellite program."

The friend said in a low voice, "You must be supportive."

I found myself spending seven hours a day at Payne Whitney Hospital. Mahindra giggled and suffered very little. We all suffered more. At his side was the number two Indian poet. A handsome tall man with a hearing aid whom I admired for his patience. He said to me privately, while we were having a pizza after hospital hours, "He will always be a sick Hindu. But you are healthy, talented, strong, young. Get away from him. You will bloom. He will *never* be well."

I *tried* to get away. I wanted my freedom. But Mahindra called me every half hour from the hospital. I dreaded his phone calls.

"We are going to be together as soon as I get out of the hospital," he said into the receiver. Then he whispered something erotic in Hindi. I did not, at that time, know a word of *Hindi*, and I would have rather received a dirty phone call with the heavy breaths and obscenity than this phone call from the Prince of Peace. Even as an outstanding psychotic celebrity from India. Didn't he see that I had my own life?

When Mahindra came out of the hospital, he looked fine. I looked awful. The hospital setting hadn't agreed with me. Visiting the wrong Whitney takes a lot out of an individual. I was nervous. Underweight. My skin looked green. I had hospital pallor. My father thought I was studying at Columbia University. But I had been supporting the Prince of Peace. And did I receive any benefit from this? Did my prince repay me with gratitude or kindness?

As soon as the prince got out of the hospital, he took his statue of Napoleon, his clothes, and went back to his wife in a huff. I hoped I would never hear of him again. But I did. I visited him in Bombay two years ago. He was still writing poetry, although the poems didn't interest me anymore. He looked dead when I saw him. I thought, *Poor Mahindra*, and that's all I thought, although I wished I had loved him as I loved him when I first heard his poems. He was a genius. Woe to the women reaching into his universe.

memory on the plane

PART II
the prefabricated husband

The prefabricated husband comes in several sizes. Several person-
alities—cold, hostile (like Mommy) or warm and violent (like
Daddy). Take your pick. Your prefabricated husband may be portable.
He may be put together in any state, until the license plates expire. You
may extend your driving privileges with the valid home state driver's
license in Stamford by getting a nonresident minor's certificate.

My life has been filled with one humiliation after another
with men. Once I became ill. There was turning and tossing. I
needed to be kissed. No kiss. I needed to be held. To be stroked.
To be liked. To feel home. To belong. Only strangeness. Until
death do you part. I thought men would cure the ache. That's
why I married for the second time.

I was a wife. I'd been around. Seen it all. Power and failure.
Ecstasy, horror, revolution, despair. Oh, where was the quiet
life, the good life, the life with a center? I wanted to prove to
myself you didn't always have to be miserable with sex instead

of love—sex feathers—always wanting love and getting instead sex. Now I lay me down to sleep, now you lay me down to sleep—lay—pray for a lay. I wanted peace and quiet and to go away and find my own person. I found Larry.

I found Larry when I had lost confidence in myself. Lost a sense of myself as a human being. As an independent person. I wasn't a woman. I was always a child. Crying when I was unhappy. Looking for arms to hold me. Frightened I couldn't write anything. Anxious in my stomach. Nervous sweats and diarrhea. Always in trouble for money. Always gaining weight. Never able to control all my impulses to eat and drink—the need to write. To be somebody else. To be funny. To write comedy. To write sad so it came pouring poetry and wisecracks and humor or grotesque comedy out of my gut. But never able to get a job. Never able to be hired. A failure in offices. Working for different offices—advertising (fired), public relations (fired), the council of learned societies (fired)—the whole gamut of trying to control my glands and horny moments in girdles and offices. Love me, love me, all the songs were saying when I was a girl and so lonely, so unwanted, would I ever grow up to be a woman or would I remain little in the same red dress all my life, the baby girl? I wasn't a woman; I was a retard. I didn't want to destroy anyone. I didn't like making apple pies or doing all the good housekeeping things. I wasn't a woman. I wouldn't play the role assigned to me, the roles created by Hollywood and the radio. I wouldn't take off my shoulder pads. I wouldn't lie down and play dead for Abraham. And then I became a wife seriously. My marriage to Larry was meant to be forever feminine.

Larry was a businessman and yachtsman, and we moved to Stamford to be near the world's largest boat basin. I studied the book on etiquette. I went on a diet. I stayed home droning away at my book about boats. I arranged flowers and took long walks and tried so hard to be seaworthy. At night Larry would come home, and I would conceal from myself that we had nothing to talk about. He talked all the time about boating on Long Island Sound. We talked boat talk. He talked, and I listened. He took off his coat and seersucker shirt and put on a sweat shirt and told me to fix him a drink, and then he began to get excited about the weekend and the fact that he was going to his sailboat, *The More Expense*, and he talked yacht talk to me. He talked yachting results. He talked racing. He talked about moorings and afterguards and yawls.

I remember living with my husband in Stamford. First, I met the commodore and his wife, a perfectly charming couple. He is an expert on yawls. I asked him about yawls. I had dreams of sailing a yawl, but unfortunately, very unfortunately, I was married to a yachtsman. It was inevitable. I had to stay home. I had to spend five years of my life as a nigger. Wife. Downtrodden, whining, empty-gut nigger. Not a yachtswoman. Not even Little Lulu. I became Mrs. Larry. And why? Why? Because for some reason that I cannot explain, without a shadow of a doubt, I was living out *Mission Impossible*. Or Mrs. Impossible. My life went on and on in the suburbs of Stamford and Greenwich.

Larry, the successful sportive businessman, was the prefabricated husband. It was as if the Hadassah gave an award to a single Jewish girl—a trip to meet the perfect bachelor—and I won the award. I met Larry on an airplane. We were married two months later. He was perfect from anyone's point of view. First of all, he had good teeth. Secondly, he was very blond. He had a topnotch education. He didn't drink or smoke. He lifted weights. He jogged. He had good manners. He wasn't pushy. And he looked good in sports clothes. Who could ask for anything more? The fact that he was forty and had never lived with a woman was overlooked. He ran his business honestly.

I thought, *Gee whiz,* if he's that honest with his business' money (he wouldn't take a stamp without putting the pennies back in the till), he will be honest in everything.

I was wrong. He was the perfect husband. You take him out of his box and you put the parts together. You first take out the head. The mouth should be able to speak. Even if it says such things as, "Chin up," or, "Calm down," or "Don't be so extravagant," the head at least says something. Then the chest. It has blond hair. The arms are strong. They fit into the chest. One arm should have a watch. That watch is constantly ticking. That watch is the main part of the prefabricated husband. Then the lower parts should fit together. Thick hips. Flat stomach. An ass. One, not two, but one prick. Two, not one, but two balls. Legs. Blond hair. And feet. Put together, the prefabricated husband can go to work. He can insult. He can flatten. He can destroy. He can sulk. He can be hostile. He can refuse to fuck. He can scowl. He can reproduce. He can smile. He can speak nicely. He can use charm tactics. He can participate in conversations on the condition that they have nothing to do with anything with your feelings. Most of all, he can sail. The prefabricated husband puts all his talent as a P.H. independently into sailing. He sails for hours. He works up a sweat. What is he sailing from? Why is he just sailing around and around? Why isn't he sailing in some direction? These questions about the prefabricated husband are never answered. The kit does not supply an answer book. It only supplies the husband. Another kit supplies his sailboat.

Larry. I remember conversations with Larry.

"Why don't you talk to me, Larry?"

(Larry undressing and getting into jogging shorts.)

"What is there to talk about?"

(Larry lifting barbells.)

"Larry, I have a secret to tell you."

"What is it?"

"Larry, I am miserable in this marriage. Do you think we should see a doctor who can help us?"

"What can a doctor do?"

"We can tell him our problems."

"I don't have any problems."

(Huffing and puffing now from barbells).

"Well, I do."

"What are they?"

"My problem is I am an unfulfilled person. I know that I can do something with my life. I know that I can accomplish something."

"You are accomplishing something."

"What? I can't write. You don't want me to practice law. You think it's absurd that I should think of creating films. You treat me always as if I were an atrophied bonsai tree. And that's what I have become in this fucking Stamford. A bonsai tree."

"Even a bonsai tree can grow."

"Like a dwarf."

"Don't complain. Don't explain."

"What does that mean?"

"It means put up or shut up."

"Put up what?"

At this point the barbells are released. Larry sits down on the bed.

"You need a vacation. Why don't we plan to go somewhere?"

"Where?"

"Guadeloupe."

"Mosquitoes."

"No. You can speak French."

Suddenly, we are in Guadeloupe. In an old French country inn. We are the only customers in Guadeloupe. It is out of season. We are in Gosier. I take a walk into town. I go to the general store. I buy crayons. I bring crayons back to the country inn. I begin drawing pictures. All my pictures say,

"Help me. I am not surviving." I talk to the other guest. A man from Montreal. Jacques. I want to throw myself at him. I want to say,

"Jacques, do you know what? My husband has not made love with me for seven months. For seven months I have been trying to kiss or hug him or try to get him to hug me. But he doesn't respond. He just doesn't respond. I know he loves me. But he is closed off. His body and soul have been buttressed in a cave. I can't reach him. Do you know what it's like, Jacques, to have someone reject you like that? Jacques, how would you like to have a drink with me? I would love to become an alcoholic. I have a child and a failed career. I was once a brilliant girl, Jacques. Honest I was. I was the smartest girl in boarding school. Then I got married to a cellist. We lived in France. I studied existentialism and anthropology at the École de France with Maurice Merleau-Ponty, and Claude Lévi-Strauss. I toured with my husband. He was bisexual. He showed me all Europe. I had a valet's eyeview. I washed and ironed my way through all the watering places on the Continent. But, Jacques, here I am, married for the second time—I chose security—and you know what? My husband doesn't have one bit of feeling for me. If I'm sick, I'm not supposed to complain. If something is wrong, I'm not supposed to explain.

"I'm going mad, Jacques. Hold me. Touch me. Please touch me."

I thought of saying all those things to Jacques in Guadeloupe. Instead, I just took a walk by the tennis court. They played night tennis. I asked Larry if he would play night tennis with me. He said no. He didn't want to play tennis with me because I didn't know how to play. I asked Larry if he wanted to go dancing. No. He didn't dance. It was true. He had no rhythm. That was the trouble. There was no rhythm between us.

I said, "Then let's take a walk."

Finally, he agreed. We took a walk. I noticed the full rich flowers, the red canna and tropical hydrangea. The plants were like huge leaves out of Rousseau's jungle. Bougainvillaea. Huge plants. Fronds that were ominous. In the dark, I felt that I was a misplaced person. Misplaced in Gosier with a box of crayons and a husband who hated me. I wanted to hide. I wanted to put my head down in the flowers and weep. Weep my life out in Guadeloupe.

"Larry, please don't be angry at me."

"I'm not angry at you, Lulu."

"I'm going to go back to work when we get home."

"That's a good idea. What will you do? You can't practice law."

"Why not?"

"You hate it. That's why."

"I can write comedy shows. I can work for an agency. They need writers. And packagers."

"Would you be happy doing that?"

"It is better than Stamford and going nuts. How long can I make wienerschnitzel and take pottery classes and go to the yacht club and not feel like a retard?"

"That's right, Lulu. You were so talented when I met you. You're really a very pushy broad. You have to work. I think the agency's a good idea. Watch out. Don't step in the mud."

"Thank you, Larry."

The walk ended.

Reborn back in Stamford, I took the train. I commuted to the agency. I worked. I met new people. I dressed up. I ate my pride at night. Now I, too, was tired at night. Two professional people. The Stamford executive. That was me.

My son looked at me with love. He was a baby, and we played together. I taught him his first words. I read him *Babar*. He said, as he stood up in his crib, "DERBY, DERBY." The elephant bought a derby. Babar. I am also lonely. I wrote a note to myself about that. I found that I was writing odd children's books, weird notes of loneliness.

"Larry," I said, "look what I've written."

"What?"

"A note about what I felt like yesterday."

"Show it to me later."

"Can't I show it to you now?"

"Don't you have to make dinner?"

"All I have to do is put soy sauce on the chicken and put it in the broiler."

(A thousand and one nights of soy sauce.)

"All right," he said. "SHOW IT TO ME."

All right, show it to him. Show him your soul and your blood and your nipples, Lulu. Go on. Try to make a friend out of this person who hates you with every hair in his nose, with every hair on his chest. This person who has totally withdrawn any warmth or human feeling from you. Show this person who never touches you what you are feeling. Show it.

I took out a piece of paper. *Here.* I read:

Babar is sitting at home in his easy chair.
Babar decides it is less tiring to watch himself
    on television
And so he sits in front of TV. He sees himself.
In a play. In a comedy. I say, "Babar, speak to me."

"So?" Larry said.

"*You* are Babar. You are the Babar I want to speak to me. Please, Larry. I'll go nuts if you just ignore me."

"Then go nuts. You are nuts anyway. You're from a broken home. You never had a decent life. You're not normal, Lulu."

"And you're normal? It's normal to lift barbells and go to be with another person without touching them? It's normal to be a withdrawn, hostile man?"

"So I'm hostile. So what? A lot of people are hostile. You better get used to it."

126

Larry. Stamford. David. Stamford. Summer. Loneliness. Stamford. "I've died," I said. "And I have gone not to hell, but to Stamford." I am afraid to cry.

I didn't cry for help. I slept in bed with the prefabricated husband. Not once in the Stamford house, which we rented, did he touch me. I was celibate. But not by choice. He didn't stroke. Touch. Or even talk. I was a prisoner in a marriage factory. And then what? Wasted years. Wasted energy. Wasted time. What a merger. What a conglomerate of lonely moments. What bankruptcy. What a bad gamble. What a drag.

Memory:

I begged the doctor to let me watch his birth. My stomach grew large as a pumpkin. Me, happy and tired in my new skin, stretched over a life. Larry and me in the pumpkin and squash fields of Connecticut, the feeling of joy in the lips and nipples and legs. The slow thermometer feeling of being large and slow, the newness of life. Green flowers in my stomach. The contentment.

I wrapped my son in soft blankets. I saw his face looking at me with great longing to be held, to be suckled. This opened me and joined me to the newness of things. The new child face. What happened, Lulu, in that good time or bad time? What made the London Bridge fall down on the tired head, the bridge falling in the mind, in the mind's eye? What happened?

What broke up my marriage with Larry wasn't his head, wasn't his prick. It wasn't the guy or another chick. It wasn't a clack, and it wasn't a click. And it wasn't a stone, and it wasn't a stick. Then what was it? Motherhood.

The yachtsman, Larry, quit his job. No alimony. Fifty-dollars-a-week child support. And he sailed off for the Galapagos Islands, leaving me without a career and not enough money to bring up a child. Did he care? He cared for his son. But not for his son's mother. While I worked at the agency, Larry, now at work in the Galapagos Islands, sent cheerful words to the baby:

127

Happy Monday, my sunshine
Hello, sweet little sailor
Dada has gone to the bank
Where there is a Donald Duck
That goes quack, quack cause
Dada is so thrifty. Soon, soon
Baby boy will come Galapagos to see
Toto, the talking turtle? Kisses
From the sun. Dada

It was surrealist. It was Dada! My life had *become* a nightmare. I had gone from sweet, innocent, chubby Little Lulu, the joker, the single woman, to a divorcée with domestic responsibilities and bills beyond belief. And still exotic postcards arrived. Along with the bills.

Marriage over. Larry gone.

After it was over, I just sat in a chair wondering what went wrong. While the glass buildings filled with clocks went tick-tock, tick-tock, I looked at the dark walls and wondered how I got to be that new person. Lulu, tired, wrinkled. In fact, a mass of black-eyed circles, sweaty arms, almost middle-aged, celibate. I was once filled with juices and life-forces. The life juice. Little Lulu. Little Pussycat. An oddball. I sat and looked at the wall. Sat in a chair. That was long before the new address books. The Billys, the Hannahs, the Nicoles, the Aarons, the Dannys, the new friends. Thank you, dear God, for making me friendly. And now the memory of those lost days in Stamford, the long days of sun and sea and studying French in my own bathrobe made out of green, drinking tea and eating fruit, and reading the Stamford news.

That was a long time ago. Ten years ago. Until recently, I wrote letters to Larry in my head.

"Dear Larry, I wanted my freedom, but freedom from what?"

Why was it impossible for me to realize that I controlled my own destiny? I was still the frightened person who couldn't cope with the idea of being alone. The goods had been sold, and I had bought them. The myth of marriage, the myth of motherhood. Sometimes I wanted to string a towel around my neck and jump through the air. It's a bird, it's a plane, it's supermom—the provider, the agitator, the lover of life. Get up. Make money. Take child to school. Keep going. Make love. Make trouble. Make—what was I making anyway? What was I making of my life?

I had failed with all of them. With Abraham, there had been fury and outrage. He had brought me to Paris, and I had virtually been his captive. My life was totally dependent, economically and emotionally, on his concerts. I had gotten so sick in the setup of his double-talk, his leaving me alone for days. I had looked for "another life," through other men, never dreaming that I wasn't a cripple and could just leave. And with Larry—finally the security I wanted. Why had he decided to marry me? He was perfectly happy, and I was perfectly happy, too, for a time. Nice house, some friends, dog, baby, summer vacations, the whole mania of middle-class life which I wasn't suited for at all. My temperament wasn't suited to the middle-class baby-Mafia bullshit of private schools and magic years and dull busybodies giving advice on understanding parenthood (when they obviously understood nothing themselves) and then the divorce. Larry safely back to his own life. And I back in New York with the kid and the house day after day and the need to make a living and all the insanity and harassments in the new divorced void with child, bills, more bills, and then one creep after another. Heartbreak Henry, the depressing, sordid primitive who preached to me about the wonders of family life and marriage (of course, he avoided it), whose dream in life was a color TV set and an instant family. And then Dumbo. It was the days with Dumbo that broke the camel's back. And I was the camel.

Was it any wonder that I became fat, that I was so desperate for a savior that I chose foot-rubbing Dumbo, who promised me that no one understood me better than he did, that all those people who promised me the moon couldn't mean it as much as he did? Dumbo—who didn't promise me anything. Was it any wonder I wanted to shoot them all, to just pick up and run away and start again my new Lulu life? But I didn't.

In love. The bullshit part of love. From the moment I was born, I heard love pushed on the radio. In the movies. Well, I was over that now, the myth of love. Love *yourself*, I wanted to say. But it was hard for me to love myself when I was sleeping with someone else, breaking into his memories, his life. I wanted my own life. That was all. No myth of marry me. Maybe there really wasn't anything that two people had in common really. How about taking all that energy and aggression and making art out of it—love art—not wasting time on genitalia? And it was all genitalia. All a comedy. A ball game. A ballroom. A group of narcissistic playboys in their Cardin suits, set out to war with narcissistic playgirls in their jeans and polo shirts or Puccis or Guccis or acute sensations which all landed up in fleshy matters.

And Lulu, the comedy conscience, the grown-up girl who wept for the jailed, the mad, the intimidated, in the mad modern world of genital ruins, where nothing took place the way it was supposed to be, where memory kept coming out of the skin, memory of Daddy and memory of Mommy. I wanted my own life, too, without the bullshit, without the gentlemen to advise me, without the surly haters with jowls filled with spit who came into my life like lovers, selfish nonlovers. I had once been an adolescent made for love—layers ago, lawyers ago—and I had life exploding inside me. Little Lulu had one dress—wonder-world of little girl who can't do anything except open up her dress—and sex was at the heart of her dreams. How monstrous. Six million women killed in the suburbs, victims of marriage. If I could only make some sense out of it. But I couldn't make any sense out of it, only nonsense, nonlove nonsense, which was why, after Larry left me, even though I had no bank account and my life was a mess, I kept laughing.

I knew all along that I would sing in the vast eternity of comedy and love loss and injustice and ectoplasm and try to get myself out of the sick Little Lulu world where no one was anyone. But that was the trouble. Everyone said he or she was against violence, but did the most violent things to each other. They hated their parents, their kids, their friends. They created "love" instead of acting love out, and that was the plot, the life plot, where everyone was performing indecent acts against everyone else. After I divorced Larry, after I broke up my second marriage, before I met Dumbo, I saw it all and wept. It wasn't until later that I stopped crying and tried to function on my own. David and I needed each other. I had to take care of him.

Dear Abby:

My life has not been devoid of failure. I have had two husbands and many other men interested in me. But, Abby, here is my problem. I am taking a rest from the heterosexual world, and I find that for the first time I am really having a good time. I am really enlarging my vistas. I am really having fun going to movies with my friends. I am really looking forward to getting up in the morning. I am really finished with all the creeps and I don't care if I ever have another "relationship" again. Abby, here is my problem. Am I a celibate? Is something wrong with me?

Yours,
Worried

Dear Worried:

It seems to me that you should consult a doctor. It is not normal for a woman still in the prime of life to no longer look forward to intimate relationships unless, of course, she is too involved in her career to have time to care about another. If money is not your serious consideration and if you are not a businesswoman, I suggest that you have your blood pressure taken and ask your general doctor to recommend a good workup for you. If your tests show that there is nothing wrong with you physically, I suggest you consult a therapist.

Yours,
Abby

Dear Abby

I have consulted a therapist since my divorce. There is nothing wrong with me physically, except that I am a little overweight and have a rash on my backside which gets very red around the Christmas holidays. I do have a career. I am now a successful comedy writer. I have also written TV plays, films and have worked in the satellite control program as a researcher. So I guess you could say I have a career. But the real reason I am so sexually signed off is that all my experiences have taught me that although I might find happiness with a man, happiness is too much trouble. Am I wrong?

Yours,
Worried

Dear Worried:

I am happy to meet a comedy writer through my column. I have serious admiration for the kind of work you do. I love laughing. As for your problem, is something wrong with you because you do not wish to have another relationship with man—or woman, I take it? I suggest you do the following things to relieve your anxiety. Firstly, join a health spa, such as Jack LaLanne's. There you will relieve yourself of much of the anxiety that you suffer over not suffering. Secondly, do something for others. Enroll in a nursing program in your neighborhood. Carrying a bedpan makes most women feel good. Thirdly, keep a notebook of everything you are feeling. You never know when those notes will come in handy. Fourthly, consider looking up one of your

old beaus. Things change quickly in this society. A married man today
may be tomorrow's superbachelor, or parabachelor. Good luck and keep
making us laugh.

Yours,
Abby

Well, maybe Abby knew about looking up an old beau—
like looking up cancer or psoriasis . . . or Raymond or Heartbreak Henry or Dumbo. My past is a shadow-play box of all
the times I said yes instead of no.

I feel like Little Lulu falling down Alice in Wonderland's
hole. Dumbo had told me it was his "destiny" to meet me. That
we had been "together" in other lifetimes. He had insisted that
I go with him to the Ansonia Hotel to meet Madame Acuri. To
be in her church.

At the Ansonia we entered the corridor, where we wrote
down questions on a little piece of folded paper. I wrote "Will
Dumbo marry me? And can I make him happy?" We gave the
papers, folded up, to a man, who later delivered them to Madame
Acuri. That was during the time I believed that "thoughts are
things." If you think well about something, it will happen. I
thought well of Dumbo. He was very polite and well mannered.
At that time as Lulu, the schmuck, I didn't know that he was a
homosexual who was using me to "better" his career. Later we
went into the church. Madame Acuri read the answers to several
people's questions. When she got to mine, she held the paper in
her hand and said, "I can see you marrying this man. You can be
happy with him. You should give him piano lessons."

I left the church at the Ansonia feeling elated. My life was
to be with Dumbo. All he needed was some piano lessons. And
we would have happiness.

Isn't it terrible, but certain events with Dumbo keep
coming back to me? I remember the day he took me to meet
Jerry. Took me "home" to meet Jerry. Dumbo had lived with

Jerry. I was upset by the fact that he had lived with a man. Not that it made any difference. I was afraid to meet Jerry. It was like meeting Dumbo's ex-wife.

I had given a party, and a friend of Jerry's—Jacob—had come to my house. I like Jacob very much. I thought, If Jacob's nice, can Jerry be so bad? Dumbo had wanted me to meet Jerry ever since he knew me. Finally, one Saturday morning, we drove by Jerry's house. Jerry lived on the ground floor of a brownstone on West End Avenue. We were sitting in the car.

"Come on," said Dumbo, "I want you to meet Jerry."

I had never had the experience of meeting any guy's ex-boyfriend. It was weird.

"Look, I can't do it," I said.

"Why not?"

"Because I can't. I'm afraid."

"There's nothing to be afraid of. You'll love Jerry, and Jerry will love you."

"All right," I said. "I'll come and meet Jerry."

I was greeted at the door by Jacob, Jerry's friend. Jacob was visiting Jerry. I walked into the house. Jerry was in the kitchen wearing what looked like a housedress but was actually a terry-cloth bathrobe. He was washing dishes. He dried his hands. I noticed that Jerry had hands like a girl. He wore several rings, had large veins and long fingernails. I couldn't understand *why* he had long fingernails. Maybe he just didn't have time for a manicure. He had fuzzy gray hair, a friendly face with large green eyes; he was short.

"Hello, Lulu," he said as if he knew all about me.

It was Dumbo, Jacob, Jerry, and me, all cozy in the Colonial kitchen.

"Sit down," Jerry said. "Would you like a cup of coffee?"

"All right," I said. I was petrified. My heart was pounding as loud as it ever had.

"What do you do?" Jerry asked me.

"I am doing research on the *Female Comedy*," I said in a voice that was hardly my own.

"Dumbo told me you're very intelligent," Jerry said, smiling. "But he didn't tell me you look like Sophia Loren. Doesn't she look like Sophia Loren, Jacob? The same lips. The same eyes. Lulu, you are a ringer for Sophia Loren," Jerry said. "Same type."

Dumbo was standing near the stove. I hoped he wouldn't put on an apron because if he did, I would faint.

"Jerry's a casting director," Dumbo said. "When he's not a producer. He's about to produce a very big show on Broadway."

Jerry looked at me from the sink where he was sudsing up the dishes. He looked like an advertisement for *House Beautiful*.

"Yeah, Thorpe O'Schwartz is doing it."

I could tell that I was supposed to faint when I heard those three words, Thorpe O'Schwartz. He had won all the pennants this year, all the little plastic and cast-iron awards—Emmys, Oscars, Pulitzers, Obies, Faggies, Poopies, Pippies—all the goodies.

"That's *big time*, Thorpe O'Schwartz," I said. Immediately, I knew I had said the wrong thing.

"I really like you," said Jerry. "You know, I was wondering what you were like. Dumbo told me all about you."

Just then a man who looked like one of the two killers in Truman Capote's *In Cold Blood*, or maybe both of them combined, walked through the hallway.

"Hello, Jim," Jerry said in a disgusted monotone. He looked at me. "Jim's my roommate."

There was a pause. Jim came through the hallway again.

"Where are you going, Jim?" Jerry asked.

"To the Carole King concert in the park," Jim also said in a monotone. He walked out, closing the door.

Jerry looked at me. "He's very difficult. He doesn't do anything. Can't find himself. He's now into calligraphy lessons." He raised his eyes to the sky as if he were saddled with a terrible burden.

Dumbo said, "Jerry's been really good to him. He even had his tattoos removed. Isn't that so, Jerry?"

Jerry said, "I'm just a masochist. I go and see my shrink twice a week. As far as Jim goes, I'm very masochistic. I just can't help myself."

"Was it masochistic to live with Dumbo?"

Jerry laughed. "Dumbo's impossible. First, he hooks you in by being nice. And then he becomes very cold. I told him a thousand times that it affects his voice. And his acting. He can't loosen up."

Dumbo laughed for the first time. I realized I had never seen Dumbo laugh. Jacob, who looked like Job, sitting with his hands on his knees, laughed, too. We all laughed in Jerry's kitchen.

Jacob said, "I knew you two would like each other," referring to Jerry and me.

Jerry stopped washing the dishes. He dried his hands and came over to look at me more closely. I couldn't tell if he was looking at me as Dumbo's ex-lover, as a casting director, or just as one looks, in curiosity, at another's wrinkles, skin color, eyes, taking it all in. I could tell that this sweetness of Jerry's was full of shit. I was being stared at by a machine that wanted to know all about another machine. It was as if we were two satellites bumping against each other. I tried not to think about Dumbo having sex with Jerry.

"Would you like to see the apartment?" Jerry asked.

"Yes, I would."

Jerry led the way into the dining room/living room. It was the worst taste I had ever seen and I tried to be polite. The dining room/living room was decorated in the style of Mamma Leone's Italian restaurant. There were rocks (fake) appliquéd to the wall. It was supposed to suggest an Italian grotto. The dining-room table was formal, glass top. There was a patio feeling to one side of the room. The other side of the room—it was more or less split down the middle—was an attempt to imitate an imitation of Versailles. The chairs were overstuffed as if the entire apartment had had to live on stuffing alone. We were following Jerry now. He led us into his boudoir. Not bedroom, darling—boudoir. Here there was an attempt to imitate a Spanish castle. There were two large beds covered with green velvet. The bedspread was not unlike the bedspread in Dumbo's apartment. I realized that Dumbo had adopted Jerry's taste. I imagined Jerry and Dumbo together for three years. Jim was Dumbo's replacement. Jim was a karate expert, Dumbo told me. Just as Dumbo was a baseball player. Jerry liked tough guys. Suddenly, as I looked at the bed with the green bedspread, I remembered the first time I had made love with Dumbo.

It had been in his apartment on the velvet bedspread. No, he had not taken the bedspread off. I remember that he had switched on a lamp with a red bulb—a *boudoir* lamp, he said. He had gotten up and gone into the bathroom and come back with jelly. He lifted himself up from the bed as if he were doing a reverse push-up. Obviously, there was a technique to all this that I didn't know.

"I want you to feel my prostate gland," he had said. He guided my hands, now covered with this sticky jelly, to his gland, which I couldn't find. I wondered how I got myself into this bed? Was this Romeo and Juliet? Was this Tristan and Isolde? No. And I was a lonely woman who didn't like spending evenings alone in New York, who hated dating, who liked romance and being with one guy, who needed "help" because my life was falling apart and the comedy program was too much for me to handle. Lulu, who had wanted love, to be a free person, who had written a paper on the Grand Inquisitor when she was in boarding school and had said, "Everyone is offered the alternatives of the Grand Inquisitor or Christ, the alternatives of Authority or Freedom, and must choose, because there is no other way." Lulu, the girl in the boarding school who wanted to be an artist, here, involved in this atrocious, humiliating act, being asked to titillate this man's prostate, so coldly, without feeling, so that he could be making love to a Lulu and still feel as if he were with a Jerry. I felt full of shame at what I was being asked to do. I didn't enjoy it and felt in some way that the entire sexual exchange of you do for me, I do for you, the entire pari passu of sex, one for you, one for me, was absurd. And without love. Very sad. And it was with the remembrance of this event that I looked at Jerry. What had happened between him and Dumbo?

Dumbo had said, "It wasn't where my head was at. I wanted to go out with girls and Jerry knew it."

I wondered why Dumbo wanted to be with girls. His life with me had been an attempt to masculinize me.

Jerry looked at me and said, "Are you a Virgo?"
I said, "Yes."
"You see," he said to Jacob as we walked back to the table in the kitchen, "I could tell she was a Virgo. She's just like me."
Dumbo smiled. "She's the image of you, Jerry. She's so much like you, Jerry, I can't believe it."
At that time I began to wonder if I was like Jerry.
After a few hours in Jerry's apartment we went to a movie. Jerry sat next to me, and we got very chummy.
"Dumbo has to open up. I keep telling him that. I can see that you're very good for him."
"What went wrong between you and Dumbo?" I asked.
The movie began. We were whispering in the dark.
"He was into *girls*. I always knew that."
I sat in the dark. "But for three years, you were together. Three years is a long time, Jerry, if he was into *girls*."

Even in the dark I saw that Jerry was wearing Braggi to give him a suntan. I began to wonder, "Do I look like Jerry? Am I like Jerry? Am I the Jerry replacement in Dumbo's life?" I also was wearing *Braggi*. A gift from Dumbo. We sat in the dark with our fake suntans. The movie wasn't all that interesting. I was holding Jerry's hand and Dumbo's hand. I felt close to Jerry. I began to wonder if maybe I *was* Jerry.

After the movie Jerry went off in one direction, Jacob in another, and Dumbo and I went to have some Chinese food. Dumbo was looking happier than I had ever seen him look before. He had introduced me to Jerry. When Jerry asked me if I was a Virgo, a very important question, I hadn't gone through my schtick of that's all a lot of nonsense. I had said, "Yes, I am a Virgo." I have Virgo characteristics and I had even let slip that my son's horoscope had been cast by Carroll Richter. But I had to be very careful not to drop names with Dumbo's friends because they were dropping names like mad, and it would have been competing if my names were bigger than their names. So I just dropped names of people no one had ever heard of, like Fasil Bunk or Elle Metuck or Anna Lowe, innocent nice names that wouldn't put Jerry or Jacob down while they dropped all their names like Tony Bennett, Frank Sinatra, Gwen Verdon. I could have dropped a couple of names of women in the movement like Ti-Grace Atkinson or Flo Kennedy or I could have dropped Fidel Castro or Pablo Neruda. But why drop anything? I was eating egg-drop soup with Dumbo and listening to him compare me to Jerry.

"You are exactly like Jerry. Did you like him?"

"I loved him."

"Maybe you and Jerry could go out together."

"What do you mean?"

"Why don't you go out with him?"

"Why? Because he's your ex-roommate. Is that a good enough reason? And he lives with Jim, the butcher karate expert. Is that another reason? Is that good enough?"

Dumbo ordered two more drinks. (I began figuring the bill in my head. At that time I was paying for everything, which I didn't mind, but I always wondered if I had enough cash with me.) Dumbo began to lay out his plan for me.

"Look. You are perfect for Jerry. Jim upsets him, and he and Jim aren't getting along. Jerry likes girls, too. Honest. He used to go out with a girl called Lisa Lee. Ever hear of Fred Lee? This was his ex-wife. And they even went together. Jerry really would prefer girls."

"Oh, yeah? So why is he living with a guy?"

"That's just because he hasn't found the right girl for him. Lulu, you are the right girl."

"But I'm with you."

"You'd be much better off with Jerry. You and Jerry would really get along. Why don't you marry Jerry? I'd be best man at your wedding. You and he are a great combination. Maybe we could even go to bed, all three of us." Pause. "How would you like that?"

"I wouldn't." I continued eating my Chinese dinner.

I didn't know this at the time, but while he was with me, Dumbo was looking for another patron, and he found one in Rudy, the art peddler. Rudy was an old white-haired queen who devoted his life to being piss elegant. He was always talking about his marvelous apartment, which he paid eight hundred dollars a month for, his house in Spain, his decorator, his business.

"Money doesn't mean anything to me," he said with a sweep of his hands.

I first met Rudy when Dumbo took me to this art shop called The Genuine. I was picking out paintings, original lithographs, signed by the artists, and Dumbo kept saying, "Try this one," or, "Take that one." Soon we had the old man himself, Rudy, prancing around. Rudy threw his hands up in the air.

"This painting looks just mar-vel-ous, just fan-tas-tic. Really, Lulu, I don't want to pressure you, but you should take all of them, for God's sake. I mean, what does money mean when art is so fantastic? So alive. So vibrant. And that lithograph's a bargain, too, for God's sake. A bargain. These are all my original masterpieces. They are all genuine works of art. They cost hundreds and hundreds of dollars to buy, and I'm letting you have them for no-thing. Nothing at all, because you are a friend of Dumbo's."

Dumbo insisted that we invite Rudy to my house when I gave a small cocktail party. Rudy came wearing dark sunglasses and raved about everything. Dumbo had some other friends at the party, and Rudy insisted on taking everyone out.

"This whole party is on me," he said. "I insist on paying for everything and everyone. What does money mean?"

After the dinner, which we had at the Grotto Azzurro, we all went to the Continental Baths. I had never been there before. It was sort of like fag heaven. Steam baths were available, and all the men walked around with little towels around them. There was entertainment in the middle of the ground floor. And meanwhile, like goldfish, naked men swam in huge pools. The pool looked so cool and blue, the water so inviting.

"Lulu, why don't you take a swim?" Dumbo said sarcastically.

I remembered when I was a little girl at the zoo, I tried to jump in the pool with the seals. And suddenly I jumped in the Continental pool, wearing my clothes, jewelry and all. I just swam and swam underwater. The manager of the Continental Baths, a woman, had a fit of hysteria. She was a thin woman who had taken our tickets at the door. She screamed, "Get her out of there," as if I were contaminating her pool, ruining the chlorine or something for the guys.

"We don't allow women in the baths. Only men. Get her out of there. She's a girl. Get her out of there."

I looked up from the pool and saw all the men climbing out on the ladders, bare-assed, as quickly as they could.

"I'm integrating the pool," I called to her.

"Get her out, get her out."

So I got out, dripping wet. Someone gave me a towel, which I wrapped around my head. Meanwhile, Rudy was shocked.

We all went back to Rudy's home. Rudy gave Dumbo long desirous looks.

He turned to me, "You are such a marvelous girl. Such an original marvelous girl. Dumbo is so lucky."

And I thought that might be the last of Rudy.

Nope. On Father's Day, Rudy invited us to the ballet. His children had forgotten him, and he was moaning and groaning on Dumbo's shoulder.

"Never mind," said Rudy, waving his hand. "We will have the most marvelous time. We are going to see Elizabeth Towel. I gave her her first genuine painting when she came to New York. She didn't have a penny. Mind you, not a penny. But I gave her her art for nothing, and her house looked like a million dollars."

(Rudy has a thousand and one stories about how he loved to help out the unfortunate. He was always bringing a painting to someone dying of cancer or dressing a waif who later turned out to be a star. According to Rudy, he was the world's kindest and most generous benefactor of the talented.)

In Rudy, Dumbo saw a chance to make it on Broadway. I had been springing for his singing lessons, his dancing lessons, his Frenching lessons, his rent, his food, and his clothes. But the real reason, as it turned out, that Dumbo was with me was that he thought he was going to have the leading male role in my movie *Spy*. When it turned out that the movie might not be financed, Rudy seemed the next best bet. Dumbo went to him and told him his old story about how he was a great actor-singer struggling to make it in New York, how he had to have money to live on, he had no credit cards, and how he might starve. Rudy, of course, couldn't say no to him. This was while Dumbo was still my wife.

Enter into the scene Brigitte. Who is Brigitte? Brigitte is a lovable voyeur who is always touching her own breasts. A fiftyish French teacher with a love for one thing and one thing only—her Pierre.

"My Pierre is the greatest lover in the world. And the greatest husband. No one can be happier than I am."

It was to Brigitte, my beloved friend—Brigitte, short, hellish eyes, wrinkled face, drab hair, gypsy temperament, troublemaking, spirited, impossible, busybody cozy to whom I confided my life. My confidence in the matter of the *Homo sapiens* heart. Of the sap heart! For those were the days when I still believed in happiness.

Brigitte loved Dumbo.

"What a wonderful voice. So sweet. And kind. Look how affectionate he is to you. How he loves you. How he loves you."

"Do you really think so, Brigitte?"

"Think so? I *know* so. Dumbo is the finest man who ever lived after my Pierre. He is not of your *milieu*, that is true. He has no education whatsoever. In fact, I hope you don't mind me telling you this, but he is stupid. So uncultured. But nevertheless, it is so difficult to find a man. Look at my other pupil, Mabel. Her lover left her. How do you think she feels? Now she has no one but her husband. It's terrible when a lover leaves. But it is a thousand times better when you throw the lover out, not the other way around. My dear, you may never see me again, but I must tell you what I think. You will never find anyone on earth as honest as Brigitte. You will never find a better friend to you than Brigitte. Believe me, you have no friends, all those people who come to your house for dinner. Forgive me, but they don't care about you. I am your friend."

Perhaps Brigitte was right. Perhaps I had no friends. Perhaps Dumbo was a good person.

Brigitte called me every day. It was her life mission to see that I stayed with Dumbo.

I said to her, "You know, Brigitte, I really think he's hustling me."

Brigitte said, "What means this word 'hustling'?"

"It means, Brigitte, that I pay for everything. For all our food. He borrows money from me to pay for his telephone, his rent. Sometimes he stops in front of stores and says, 'How would you like to buy me that suede jacket? It's a hundred and fifty dollars. And I like it.' In other words, Brigitte, he's a gigolo. He's always asking for money. And whenever I 'lend' him some money to walk around New York, it's never enough. I've introduced him to all sorts of people who are making films, and I've gotten him readings, but he can't speak. Let's face it, he makes a fool out of me. I called up Frank Perkins, who was casting for his film in New York City and needed some young men to play the parts of priests. Dumbo went to read for him. I called him on the phone and I asked him directly why Dumbo hadn't gotten the part. 'So since you were so straight with me, I'll be straight with you,' Perkins said. 'He didn't read well. He just didn't read well. I'm sorry. I like you, and I wanted to cast him, but I just couldn't. It doesn't mean he wouldn't be right for something else.' "

Brigitte says, "*So what? He's so right for you.*"

"So what is he right for, Brigitte? He won't take a job. He'd rather borrow money from me than work. I've had my friends doing all sorts of favors for him. My friend Dee-Dee took photographs of him to use for modeling jobs. My friend Rick Orens called someone at the Stewart Agency. The man is passive; he has no drive or flare. I have to pay Dee for the photographs. And you know what he had the nerve to say? That the photographs didn't 'tell a story.' He wants his face to tell a story. I'll tell you a story. Once upon a time there was a man called Dumbo. He hustled another man called Jerry. Then he hustled a woman called Lulu. He saw in my life a way to survive in New York for a few more months. And that's not the end of the story. Dumbo went through a great deal of my money. He 'helped' me go from a calm and collected person to a collection case. When I first met him, he said it was destiny. Now it's destiny that he have his freedom. And so it's over, Brigitte. I'll tell you something else. Dear Dumbo has been screwing everything in pants during the daytime before he meets me in the evening. He says that he has appointments all day long. His appointments are with other fags. He talks constantly about respect and eternal values and calls himself the Renaissance man. Meanwhile, he's out hustling."

Brigitte started to cry. "Not my Dumbo. He's such a sweet boy."

Another conversation: Brigitte came to visit me. "That Dumbo is adorable. He is trying to help you in every way that he can. He is good for you. You know you can't be without a man. Why not? Because you are a passionate woman. That's why. We passionate women must have a man with us. We cannot do without one and be happy. And where do you find a man in this city? With all the homosexuals running about. Now Dumbo is a real manly man. He was a baseball player. He is trying to be an actor. Believe me, you are lucky."

"But, Brigitte, he also has a homosexual problem. He used to live with a man."

"Really. Are you sure? You are not making this up?"

"No, Brigitte. And he's always looking at other men."

"So he looks. Don't be so fussy. He has a lovely voice. He dresses so nicely. So clean. Always a fresh shirt. Listen to me. Even if you never see me again, I must tell you what's on my mind. That other monster? That hairy Henry? I wouldn't give you two cents for him. Henry was a man. But not for you. He's too primitive. You don't need a primitive man. A beast, an animal, someone who has no respect for your education and your quality. Now this lovely Dumbo has such nice manners. He doesn't humiliate you with your friends. Remember what that ugly Henry used to do? I remember. Brigitte never forgets.

Whenever you were speaking about your *Female Comedy* project, such an important project, my Pierre says that your work is highly important to society, what did that stupid Henry say? He put you down. So negative. Now Dumbo adores you. He appreciates you."

Why hadn't I thought about Dumbo being better than Henry in the first place? It's a difficult question to answer. To answer that, I would have to tell the story of Henry, how I desperately wanted to get out of that relationship. How I clung to Dumbo as a means of getting free. Unfortunately, the man I clung to to get out of the Henry situation was worse than Henry himself. But that is the Female Comedy.

After Brigitte went home, she woke Pierre up. It was twelve o'clock at night, and Pierre was sleeping in his study. The apartment that they had shared for twenty years was the closest thing to Europe in New York. The building was old, and elevators creaked and groaned as they went up and down on pulleys. The apartment itself was filled with pictures, sculptures, collections of all sorts. Pierre was a collector. He brought presents home to Brigitte on any occasion—an anniversary, a birthday, the Fourth of July, Mother's Day. Pierre always had a painting for Brigitte, and the paintings were stacked one on top of the other.

"Wake up, Pierre. I have something very interesting to tell you."

Pierre woke up. "What is it, Brigitte?" he asked in his French accent.

"Pierre." Brigitte's eyes were bulging. "Pierre, I have just come from Lulu's apartment."

"So?"

"Pierre, Lulu has gone mad. Completely crazy. Dumbo has left her for—oh, Pierre, you won't believe this—another man."

Pierre woke up. He rubbed his eyes. "What do you mean, Brigitte?"

"I'm telling you the truth. As God is my witness. Dumbo told Lulu that he wanted his freedom. That she no longer

146

turned him on. He tried to choke her when she wanted to keep him with her. He said he was going to live with a Rudy. An art seller. It seems that Dumbo had Lulu buy lithographs from this Rudy. And Rudy started taking them to dinner. And now—my God, that this should happen to Lulu. She's so sensitive. He's left her for Rudy. She's home now taking sedation pills."

"Is he at least nice, this Rudy?"

"Oh, Pierre, this is no time to joke. How can you ask such a thing?"

Brigitte threw her arms up in the air.

"She loved him so much. And he was so wonderful to her. So affectionate. He used to call her Salty Dog—so sweet—and pinch her cheek. And now he's left her. I'm only afraid she will poison herself. She's so emotional."

Pierre was calm. "Don't worry, she won't poison herself. Poison is fattening, Brigitte."

"How can you be so matter-of-fact? She's like my sister. I love her. I always say Lulu is the most intelligent woman in New York. Even if she is a surrealist. So are you. So am I. So we must understand this poor girl."

"What is there to understand? She fell in love with the wrong man, Brigitte. She bought him a boat. She should not have gone overboard for him."

"Brigitte loves Pierre. But who will love Lulu? Everyone knows that a woman cannot live without love. It is impossible to think that this man who she poured everything into, her whole soul, has left her for an art peddler."

"Would it be better if he left her for a Congressman?" Pierre asked.

Pierre lit his pipe. He threw off his covers and was now wide awake.

"Now she will have to face her life alone. Which is the best thing for her, Brigitte. She loves her son, and her son loves her. But as far as men are concerned, she is alone and will always be alone. She is so high-strung. So emotional. No man can bear that."

And Dumbo ended up taking his K-Y Jelly and leaving my apartment, making sure to try to strangle me before he left. He wanted, he said, to go fishing with Rudy. He wanted his freedom.

"You were my enemy in another lifetime," he told me as he left. "You tried to poison me in Egypt."

What other lifetime?

"Dumbo, don't leave me."

"Go fuck yourself, you cunt," he says. "I'm no longer interested in your kid and your car, your movies which never come off. I have my own life."

Alone. Alone. I want to put a hex on you, bigshot of the singing world. A hex on your hair which has to be curled with a curler machine. A hex on your tiny eyes with wrinkles rubbed out by vitamin E. A hex on your capped teeth and your larynx and your tonsils, a hex on your throat and your voice. A hex on your hairy chest which you show off in see-through blouses, a hex on your tiny ass that you're so proud of, a hex on your cock which you can keep rubbing with vitamin E until the day it falls off, a hex on your legs and your arms, a hex on your prostate and pancreas, and may you come to nothing, may your fucking career come to nothing, may you have to stand out on Central Park West hustling and may no one pick you up. A hex on your career as an extra, a hex on your singing. May you go back to Alaska where you started out and be sucked into the Hoover Vacuum Company and may you turn into a Hoover. A hex on you and your phony mysticism. A hex on you for the way you treated me in this lifetime. A hex on you forever and into time eternal. May you clean vacuums the rest of your life. You have no heart. No soul. No sense of humor. You'll never make it in the comic-strip world.

I thought of all this on the airplane. Attacked by memory. I was starting a new life. As an executive. As the head of a studio.

But the old life came back like blood that refused to clot. I was bleeding out every pore. I remembered everything. I missed David. I took his picture out of my pocketbook and looked at it. It was a picture of David next to a huge orange pumpkin. I was the bad witch now. Flying on my broomstick to the Coast. I missed my pumpkin-boy, my sweet son, my darling. I remembered rocking him in the cradle of my knees. I mustn't fail. I mustn't fail him. I had to make something strong out of my life. For both of us. For my little boy. And for the child in me that had never died.

memory on the plane

PART III
humiliations i try to forget

Hollywood *and the golden era. The man who made* Gone with the Wind. *On the plane I was reading Selznick and another paperback,* The Arabs. *What exactly were the forces behind the Arab expansion?*

I put both books away. I imagine a movie called *The Arabs.* With David Selznick playing the Arab chief. Hollywood is Mecca. The Crusades are coming. . . .

While I am sitting on the airplane, I try to forget all about Larry and Dumbo. I look out the windows at the clouds. I think how I have spent a lot of my time doing extraordinary things. The years in Paris with Abraham. The world of music. Little Stravinsky world. The escape with Mahindra into the literary world. Agencies. Movies. Larry. Suburbia. Dumbo. Working. Producing. The life of a person begins spinning around in my mind. Odd life. Comic life.

I wonder what everyone is doing at this moment. I imagine Missy going through the mail. Answering the bills. Returning the phone calls. All the messages on little pieces of paper. I imagine Emma taking care of David. Playing softball with him in the living room. I imagine David reading. Dancing to pennywhistle music in his room. Calling his friends. Reading the *Sports Encyclopedia* to his secret delight deep under pillows. Martin. It's three in the afternoon. He's sitting at his desk in the office. Beloved Martin. A house. Beautiful kids. Gorgeous wife. Lots of money. Martin. Tall, sexy, and sweet Martin from the Lower East Side now telephones clients. I imagine all my friends, Sasha and Helen and Martin, the friends, and lawyers and city—New York City—little city of lights—a tiny universe in a tiny universe—maybe—they say—there are other worlds out there—mathematical calculations prove that other worlds do exist in the galaxy—worlds—other New Yorks— other agents—other people—of course must exist—floating. Wouldn't it be odd if there were other worlds all filled with divorced women with kids looking for the right relationship? Don't be silly. Wouldn't it be odd if there were other worlds filled with movie theaters? Think of the distribution possibilities.

I stop thinking of worlds.

I begin thinking of Peter Wall.

Peter Wall. His own man. Movie star. Producer. Director. The one person that Suck City really hadn't stamped out. Politicians' friend. Took off two years to work in politics. Sister a movie star. Peter Wall. What a ball. Oddball, sweet, degenerate, intelligent. It was hard not to think of Peter. He would be waiting for me in California. He knew who were the creeps and the kind of deals they were going to offer me. Peter said he wanted to "work" with me. I remembered meeting him. Right after I broke up with Larry.

I had gone to Los Angeles for the first time. While I was still working for the agency. I wanted to write a film about space.

A film based on the life of Goddard. I knew that Peter had an interest in politics, had known the Kennedys, and even had some interest in a project about the true American hero who spent his life developing rockets. I knew he would be perfect for the part, and I wanted to interest him in the project. It would be a film made with the cooperation of Goddard's wife, Esther. It would be filmed at the Goddard Space Center and in New Mexico. I had gone to Peter's friends, and they had arranged for me to meet him. Laura, a magnificent "gal," as she was called in Suck City Hollywood, was one of the best lyricists in the world. I adored her, and she arranged for me to go to the Beverly Wilshire and meet Peter himself. Talk with him. At the hotel the desk clerk announced me. I took the elevator up to the penthouse. I got off the elevator. I thought I had the wrong apartment. The place was a mess. Dirty dishes in trays on the floor. Dishes that looked as if they had been there for weeks. Yellow eggs on the eggcup, falling-apart bed, dirty windows, towels on the floor, jock shorts on the floor, magazines strewn on the bed. So this is where the great lover Peter lives? I wondered who could be sensual in a room like that. It was the hangout of a spoiled brat. I wondered how he could have "conferences" in an atmosphere of sloth. Well, I thought, I guess he has slothful conferences. I walked out on the terrace.

The movie star walked toward me.

He had black hair and a good body and tan skin. He had the kind of smile that all the smart-ass boys who tried to make out in boarding school had. I began calculating how much money it must have cost to keep in the shape he was in. What tailor cut his denims.

"Come on out in the sun." He smiled.

I walked onto the terrace.

Orange trees. And two white telephones. The city below. He was talking now on both phones. Not one. Two. He held them up to his ears as he sat down. He was staring at me. Not bad. Talks on both phones and tries to fuck me with his eyes. A regular Charlie McCarthy. He was being a "big shot" into one phone and an even more obnoxious big shot into the other. His words were few. He seemed to be laughing at everyone. Making fun of me. Making fun of the people on the phones. Who was this guy anyway? I wanted to leave. He hung up on both people at once. He came toward me.

"Wanna fuck?" I thought he said. But what he really said was: "Wanna talk?"

He had a way of twisting every word into some sort of sexual overtone. Wasn't he bored with this cupcake act? Didn't his own conceit bore himself? Wasn't he tired of looking in the mirror at his own pretty face?

"I hear you want to do a movie about Goddard," he said.

He came very close to me. I backed away.

"That's right."

He looked down into my face.

"I thought you were a comedy writer." He licked the words.

It was all a game. It was fun to play. But I was more interested in my living than making it with a silicone star.

"That's not all I write. I'm interested in doing a documentary film about space."

"Are *you* writing this?" he asked.

"Yes. I'm putting it together. Obviously, if you want to be involved, I have a better chance of having one of the studios agree to distribute it."

He came closer. Cat and mouse. Some cat. He had Lavoris on his breath. Arrid under his arms. Old Spice on his chin. Dental floss on his teeth crevices. Jesus Christ. He was a walking drugstore. He cocked his head when he spoke. He spoke slowly. Almost as if he weren't too bright. But he was bright all right. He baked his face in the sun and rubbed a little Vaseline on his lips. I knew I was supposed to cream in my pants when he rubbed his lips. I was thinking of how much money this guy was worth. Now that he was into producing his own films, he was making a fortune. He could at least afford a maid to clean his room after hours. So this was Hollywood's intellectual. I laughed to myself. He was the Einstein of the Hollyzoo Vic Tanney world. I couldn't help thinking how this guy must really hate himself. That restlessness in his eyes, as if he were always looking for the perfect cunt and never finding it, and yet he seemed polite. What he really was was a cunt-tease. Teasing meant more to him than actually knowing someone. Let him tease. I was interested in his name, not his balls.

"Are you interested in being involved in this project?" I asked.

The closer I got to him, the odder I felt. It was embarrassing. I mean, how was I going to get away with not pretending to be attracted to this guy? And he was attractive. If only he had one little bit of modesty. Or humility. Or compassion. I wanted to say to him, "You know, Peter, I have a son called David. I'm supporting him and bringing him up myself because his father moved to the Galapagos Islands. I'm divorced. And not gorgeous. So I guess you think I'm desperate. But I'm really here to get you to sign a contract."

I looked at him.

"Do you want to come back later and discuss this? I'd like to talk about it, but I have another conference coming up." He was smiling.

"Okay," I said.

But the conference never took place.

We became friends from a distance.

Now I was going to see him again. He was one of the first people to call me when I was named head of the studio. I guess now that I had some real power, it was all right to fuck me. I laughed when I thought of all the fun we might have if we were just friends. Maybe we could be. I doubted it. He was still into the notch-in-the-belt variety of relating to a woman. It was too bad. I'd probably have to avoid him.

Peter Wall.

The life of Peter Wall.

Up against the Wall.

Wall-to-Wall carpeting. Peter and his sister star in musical comedy. Peter Wall makes millions. Peter Wall becomes guru. Peter Wall runs for Congress. Peter Wall runs. The headlines twinkled on and off in my head. Well, compared to the rest of the guys out there, Peter Wall was one of the good guys. Under the "For Sale" sign was at least a strong will to survive. To step on everyone else's carcass. At least he had Hollywood by the tail. He could call his own shots. That was more than most people could do. He was not only fucking every piece of ass in sight, but he was fucking Hollywood. "Good for you, Peter," I said to myself. And imagined him in his limousine reading the poetry of Yevtushenko.

I looked at my watch. It was probably time to start making notes on some of the projects that I wanted to work on. But I couldn't get myself to do that. Instead . . . relax. Relax into memory. Wouldn't it be nice to make my own film? To make a film about the absurdity of my own life. Everyone's life a film. To be called "insane" all one's life. But to turn out to be sane. Bobby Shafto went to sea. Silver buttons on his knee. He'll come back and marry me. Pretty Bobby Shafto. I didn't want Bobby Shafto. At sea. In the air. I wasn't going to marry anybody. I was giving myself a week to look into the whole project. A power play a day keeps the fear doctor away. We were all together now. Den mother to millions. Hello. I am not Lulu. I am YOUR IMPORTANT FEMALE EXECUTIVE.

During the Second World War, I prayed for Lana Turner not to collapse, for Hitler to die. My mother had married again. Her husband was a millionaire from Palm Beach, and I did not live with her. Her husband didn't want me in his house. I was an outcast, an untouchable to my own mother. They didn't want me. And Papa didn't want me either. Both of them wanted me to get married as quickly as possible. In that way, they wouldn't have to worry about my future. This made me very nervous.

Doctor: *Did this affect your body?*

Lulu: *And how! I had rashes, hives; I stuttered; my bladder didn't work, I peed instead of crying all the time. I was nervous, high-strung, and always on the edge of a crisis. My body finally gave out. I collapsed and was born, collapsed and was born. You know, like now.*

Doctor: *Yes, Lulu, you are still collapsing and being born. Each day you give birth to yourself. But who are you giving birth to? Lulu, I have something to tell you. You must leave the world of fantasy and live in reality. It is reality that you will not ever have good parents. Never. No man will be a good parent to you. As for your lovers, they have played you for a sucker. You are no more to them than a filler-up of the moments. You mop up their time because their lives are very limited. The only thing for you to do is to say, "In reality is my salvation." People must live in reality. They must seek it the way lovers seek release.*

Rabbi: (low voice): Lulu, he won't ever come back. you must get used to change. Chance is *grief.*

"Fuck you! *You* get used to change. I want my daddy, daddy, daddy." Funeral sobs. Tears.

Enter—on a wing and a prayer—Pancho, Boy Aztec, Boy Pilot. Pancho, *mi corazón*, my soul. I met him on the trip I took with my father's girlfriend, Maria, after the shivah. Ten days after my father died.

My beautiful father, the typewriter ribbon king, had died of ptomaine poisoning. He, like Buddha, had been eating the wrong flesh at the wrong time, and zippo, zappo, zilch, that human blob of tranquillity and bright sayings and manipulations and fat fingers humor was reduced to a corpse with lipstick on his lips at the Riverside Funeral Chapel with a couple of sad, serious Chinese-looking rabbis saying their you-know-whats and the audience for the death show, the vaudeville, complete with casket and girlfriend, the girlfriend wrapped in fur. And me, the daughter, dressed in a black dress with black stockings on my legs. Weeping for my unbearable loss. *Give me back my daddy.*

Pancho, his name like his face, a huge, brown, flat areola, dark Aztec complexion. How did we meet exactly? Before getting on the plane, this brown pancake was looking at me. I noticed, as he stood behind the Aeronaves de Mexico counter, that he had eyes as huge as Drake's cupcakes. A strange-looking pilot with a crew cut that made him look like Tonto out of my favorite radio fantasy, *The Lone Ranger.* Once Maria and I were airborne, the stewardess came and asked us if we would like to come up to the cockpit.

"No thanks," I said.

The stewardess was wearing a bright blue uniform and smelled of too much Tabu.

Maria looked up. "Let's go."

So up the aisle we walked to the cockpit. In the machine room, the room of Coleman meters and tiny clocks that tick-tock, tick-tock, Captain Arreolla made his first move. He invited me to see the pyramids.

"Oh, yes," I said.

In Mexico City, Pancho the Aztec drove us around town. He had baby shoes hanging from his mirror in the battered car. That should have been the first clue. Later, over warm tacos, he told us his story. He had married a German girl, who gave him two children, but she had left him, taking the kids. Tears rolled down his face, huge whipped-cream tears out of the

Drake's cakes, and left him in despair. She had gone back, he said, to her father who had a sardine factory in Munich. Does that sound like bullshit? You bet your ass it didn't. The little twist of the sardine factory made it all too realistic, too stinky to be full of baloney. So what happened? For a year of my life I would sit in my apartment in New York, and every time a plane flew over my apartment I would say to myself, "It's a bird, it's a plane, it's superfuck."

Pancho, who couldn't speak a word of English, came to visit me once or twice a week. Soon, I was more Aztec than any girl in Guadalajara. I wore Mexican clothes. Spoke Spanish. Hung out in Mexican places. And Pancho, the Aztec captain, lived at my house when he was in New York.

Some strange things: He was always going to buy Supphose at the stocking stores. Supphose. For his grandmother. Grandmother, my ass. For his wife. And what did his wife do with the Supphose? She wore them to support her feet while she was taking care of her fourteen children in Mexico City. Fourteen! But this I did not find out until later.

As it happened, Señor Arreolla loved crystal vases, a crystal bird, all left to me by my father, the typewriter ribbon king. I gave them to him, one by one, for his bachelor apartment in Mexico City. Meanwhile, he was flying home, giving thematic piñata parties, with crystal gifts for all the kids.

I left a will, drawn up at Larry Gottlieb's office, with everything I owned in the world left to Pancho Arreolla. And why not? We were going to be married. Every time he saw me, he said, in Spanish, I want a son in your stomach, and sooner or later I bought out all the white dresses at Fred Leighton's and prepared for our wedding. Here comes the Pocahontas, all dressed in *tu escondido fuego, todas las transformas.*

One day, *mi corazón,* old Pancho, did not show up for dinner. All the pilots stayed at the Chatham Hotel, and I went down to the hotel to see where Pancho was. (*Mi corazón.*) The clerk at the desk told me my prospective bridegroom had gone out. I was wearing a turban à la Carmen Miranda and hung out in the coffee shop until I had coffee poisoning. I ate three dozen prune danishes, and finally, I felt ill. Blood rushed through my head, blood under the old Carmen Miranda turban. I ran up to a certain Captain Martel, also with Aeronaves, and said, "Captain Martel"—tico-tico-tock—"I would like you to come to my house and have dinner with me. I must speak to you *en tu vacilación indestructible estrella* oscura eres about a certain captain."

Martel obliged.

Martel picked his teeth after dinner, all of them gold and shiny, and spilled the beans.

"Arreolla is tired of living a double life. He didn't come on this trip. He changed his flight to Madrid."

"What double life?"

"His wife, Dolores, mother of fourteen and a salesgirl for the Verdes-Verdes department store, is no dope. She found out. All those crystal vases begin tinkling in her mind. She found out that Arreolla wasn't spending his time at the Chatham reading the flying manuals, and she put one and one together. Threatened to take all fourteen children and move to Guadalajara."

"Our wedding day? Our house?"

"*Sí,* senora, all a bag of shit."

So much for Pancho Arreolla. *Siempre amigos. Mi corazón—* my soul.

And don't forget Raymond.

Into my house walked Raymond, the talking model. Talk? He couldn't stop talking. His father was dying of cancer at a hospital near my home. He sat on my falling-apart sofa and talked and talked.

He had been dropping off to have breakfast with his cousin Lisa on his way to visit his father at the hospital. Actually, I love

Lisa, and she had been crying about how badly her mother and father treated her, and I got impatient with the entire weepery and told her to pull herself together and stop getting drunk so much. I invited her and her cousin, whose father was dying of cancer, to my house the next evening for a dinner party. She came. Her cousin didn't come. Instead, he called. He called from a phone booth to say his father was dying of cancer and he couldn't come to dinner.

Later, after all the guests left and I was lying in bed trying to sleep, he called again. More talk about cancer. His father. What a good man he was. How he had worked all his life. His mother.

"Do you want to come over?" I asked.

He did. He arrived. Then followed details about his father. His father's bowels. I listened to all this wondering if he would ever climb into my noncancerous bed. The conversations continued. Catheters. Death. I began to feel sick. I said I thought it was time for him to leave. He continued talking about his career. How difficult it is to be a male model. He wanted to show me his book. Not his novel. His book of pictures and clippings. Another male model had come into my life. What was I? The Ford Agency? (Why did all these models want to show me their book? Their photographs?)

The next day he called me from the hospital. My dog was dying. Flops, whom I loved more than any human being in the world outside my son, was dying. I told him my dog was dying.

"You compare your dog to my father?" he asked, incredulous. "My dad to your Flops?"

"Yes, I do. Because I love my dog as much as you love your father. Maybe more."

Woof, woof, how's that for a surprise? The next day he called again and told me about cancer. Later he came to my house.

"Do you really want to make love?" I asked him. "Is this the time?"

"Yes," he said. "My father's death has made me aware of my own mortality."

With that, he took off his clothes.

Some body. Nice. It made me feel overweight. I crawled underneath the blankets. I couldn't take off my pajamas which my mother had given me for my thirty-sixth birthday. I was virginal. Faced with a male model body. Into bed he got. Talking about cancer all the way. How can you have an orgasm when a guy is talking about cancer? In the face of death, who can come? He felt nice. (Human hands had not been on my back for a year.) We managed to make love. Nothing exciting. Right after making love, he jumped into his bikini. He had a booking the next day and couldn't afford to have bags under his eyes. Boy, the way the guy took care of himself. It was inspiring. No drinking. No smoking. Quick fucking. Just looking after himself so he would look rugged.

"Ray, that was nice, but you were too worried about your father to enjoy it. Also, don't take offense, but I think I'm too old for you."

"Why too old?"

"Well, I just feel I am."

"Don't be silly. You are a warm, lovely, sensual woman. That means something to me."

"Does it? What does it mean?"

"It means that we have lots to talk about."

I wanted to say, "Please stop talking about cancer all the time. It's depressing me." But he was out the door so quickly, leaving behind some male model photographs. Pictures of him in swimming trunks with his arm around a tight-nippled bikini-clad Venus. I felt like the Rock of Gibraltar carved into a female divorced writer living in New York.

"I like you because you are so together," he said.

I hate the word "together." I'm falling apart at the bone, you idiot, I wanted to say. I'm lonely, and I hate living with a kid and housekeeper in fucking lonely sick city. New York filled with sickies. Did you know my last boyfriend was a famous black actor who screamed at me, and the guy before that was a married maniac who painted boxes, and the fella before that was a plumber pilot who went to Yugoslavia, and the guy before that was a fag model actor who is now rubbing feet for a living? Do you know my bank account goes down and my blood pressure goes up? That my dog died? My dog died, my only friend on this planet, has died. Did you know that I have hopes of not being on this planet very long? That I want to jump out of the universe of married divorced women with bills and children? And you think I'm together? When I'm practically screaming from nonattachment?

Ho hum. He called the next day from the hospital. A blow-by-blow description of comas. Later he called. His father had died. I felt bad. What could I do? Would I listen to a eulogy he was writing? He was in his apartment sleeping in the same bed as his mummy. And he had, he told me, a queen bed. As a writer would I listen to his eulogy? He called at four in the morning. All to get laid. I am listening to all this to get laid, I thought. And I'll go to any lengths just to get laid. Isn't that stupid? Isn't that ill? Isn't that insane? But the heart has its reasons, reasons I do not know. I listened to the eulogy. The next day he called. More funeral preparations were taking place. The funeral was going to be in the Bronx. On Jerome Avenue. Would I like to come? He was inviting several of his girlfriends to the funeral. If I didn't mind that, I was welcome to come to the funeral. No, I didn't mind anything. I was beyond minding anything. I was beyond everything.

And yet I found myself going by subway to a funeral in the Bronx. I had never been in the Bronx. I took the subway downtown by mistake. It was the worst day of winter. It was snowing. Slushing. Huge snowballs fell out of the sky. Finally, I was on an elevated platform leading to the Bronx. I got off. I was in strange streets. A world of empty sad houses. Where was I? I couldn't find the Knisher Funeral Home. My boots had holes in them. My feet were wet. I found a cab. As I arrived at the funeral home, a casket was being pushed into a truck. Or hearse. Whatever it's called. Was that Ray's father? Was I too late? I rushed into the funeral parlor. No, nothing had started yet. Standing in a yarmulke, looking happy, was Ray. This was his moment. All his girlfriends had arrived for the funeral. I walked into a huge room. Six women sat with straight hair. It was like Billy Rose's revue. Six showgirls in the Bronx on a bench in a funeral home. The man in the box was the father of the guy I was trying to lay. I was only at the funeral home on Jerome Avenue to get laid. All the people there were weeping. I was there because a male model-*cum*-actor had walked into my living room and I had to be a nice person to get to see him.

How many days of sitting shivah would I have to go through in order to actually get to go to bed with him?

The eulogy was read. I sneaked out of the funeral home.

Two days later I called Raymond. He was sitting shivah in the Bronx. He was weeping. His family was with him. Another long conversation ensued about cancer. Funerals. Papers. Medicare. Insurance. The Bronx. He read me some information over the phone. Maximum payable. A covered person will have a fifty-thousand-dollar maximum for each separate and unrelated illness or injury. His father was a covered person. But how covered? Why was I listening to this? Why into this phone were all these details floating into my eardrum like snowflakes? Do you have color TV? Yes. Do I have to wear a tie? No. Because I can dress if you want me to. No, don't dress.

That night I prepared the house for our physical uniting. Incense everywhere. A cook came in to cook a candlelight supper. My son was tucked into bed. The house was quiet.

Mementos of Flops were taken away so as not to remind me of my dead dog. Every book on cancer was hidden away with the phone book under a couch. He arrived, finally. We ate. He got up from the table.

"I hate myself," he said. "Dad loved me the way I was. Before he died, he said to me, 'Son, I am proud of you, you handsome brute.' He didn't care if I was a model. After sending me to Fieldston and Harvard on a scholarship, he loved me for what I am. Even if I am not successful."

I led Raymond to the bedroom.

"Of course you are successful. You are a successful person, Raymond."

Raymond took off his clothes. That body flashed its warm skin. He turned on the TV.

"Mind if I get under the covers?"

"No, go ahead."

At this moment the phone rang. My girlfriend wanted to come and spend the night.

"Tell her not to come," said Raymond, watching the film.

"Why not?"

Eyes glued to the TV set: "Don't you feel like making love?"

Sperm, sperm, you are always in the flesh and mind. I took off my clothes. We started making love. He stopped. Watched TV. We started again during the commercial. He interspersed his lovemaking with talk about weight, smoking.

"Dad died of cancer."

Maybe the only accomplishment of my thirties will be that I gave up smoking and started fucking.

I was getting more and more depressed. My hands went over his body. I reached down for his prick. Lo and behold, I found only a *knee*. A *knee*? Not erectile tissue. Please say it isn't your knee, say it's something else. But it's only a knee, only a huge knee. His lack of puff didn't seem to bother him. He kept on talking and talking—his gym, Dad died of cancer, and I was determined to keep myself in good shape, I was determined to take care of my body.

Later that night he confessed that since his father died, he hadn't felt up to making love. He put on his Bimini bikini and left me a photograph and a résumé, which I promised to give to a producer who "handles" actors—handle me, I'll handle you, handle music, hand dull in sheets finds human male—in hospital. My home is not a hospital. I wanted to scream. A hospital is an institution which is primarily engaged in providing medical care and treatment to the sick and injured on an inpatient basis at the patient's request. I began to feel that my bed was an insane asylum, a psychiatric clinic into which I took inpatients and outpatients. And Raymond was definitely an outpatient.

After the TV fiasco I saw him one more time. It was at a dinner party that I gave for a friend who had arrived from Poland several years ago to teach Brecht in America and never went back to Poland. To this dinner of Brechtian wit, fireplace, and candles came Sir Raymond with a black eye. His needs were immediately to have an ice pack. He had been hit at the Y by a basketball while keeping his body fit. All evening he absorbed sympathy at the dinner party, and then it was time to take his duffle and go home. I found myself sitting in my white silk dress (white for Medicare) and softly saying, "I don't like you, Raymond, I don't like you." I picked up my beloved Flops, who was whimpering near the bed, and covered him.

Then I went into my kitchen and took out a piece of bread and a lot of strawberry jam, and I began eating. I ate my heart out. When I came back to my bedroom, Raymond had left. He called the next day. I didn't take the call. I hated him. I didn't dislike him. I hated him. He had told me that he hated himself. Now there were two of us. I prayed to never see Raymond again. But Raymond had led to another experience. He had led to celibacy.

Christmas memory: Flops, my beloved dog, died. Oh, Flops. Your death was the final catastrophe. I mothered you. I held you. I took you to Dr. Higgins when you started bleeding around Christmas time. You were really my best friend, and then some. At Christmas your blood was all over the Galaxie, and I took you to the private dog hospital. Dr. Higgins admitted you and promised to make you well. This was followed by a telephone call on New Year's Eve from a Dr. Bigelman. Dr. Bigelman said that you had been drinking water excessively and, after he had run a report on your kidneys, that your kidneys were almost gone. He was trying, he said, to reverse this. I got furious at Dr. Bigelman. Who asked him to run a report on your kidneys? Couldn't he have just healed your wounds and left it at that? No. He had to give you intravenous shots, fiddle around with catheters. I could not believe that he was doing this.

"He is a much sicker dog than you think."

He did not tell me you were dying. At the same time that you were in the clutches of Dr. Higgins, I was in the clutches of Dr. Bears, an analyst. I was going through my own pain. I was bringing out all the pain of my relationships—all flops, not hits—and I was digging into amazing capacity for self-destructive behavior. I was feeling a lot of pain.

"Pain is when you are more aware," Dr. Bears told me.

The awareness led me to despair. And you were dying.

Then, one day, I took you out of Dr. Higgins' hospital. You had been admitted as a fluffy white-haired Shih Tzu with a wagging tail, big brown eyes, bad bit (crooked teeth—I loved your crooked teeth), a keen sense of humor (your grin), a cold black nose, sweep paws, and you knew all my secrets. You had kept me company through the horrible years of divorce, the years of Henry the Heartless, and the many affairs which had all led to my nervous condition. Then they gave you back to me—all bones. Shivering. Flesh gone. Your eyes looked up at me. "Help me," they said. A helpless loving animal. I hugged you. I wept. I knew that I would have given my life for you.

"Please let Flops live," I prayed to the Great Universal Power that may (or may not) decide such things. You would not eat. You refused food. Finally, I began crying all the time. You might actually be dying. I fed you the medicine. I stayed near you.

One day, in the beauty parlor on Fifty-fifth Street, a certain Miss Myra found me crying.

"Take Flops to the Animal Medical Center," she said, and she arranged for me to meet a Miss Michel.

I carried you in my arms. My dog-baby. My sweet old man. My bones and fluff. My dearest buddy from the world of innocence and woof. I cuddled you and cradled you, and then I waited, one of the deep animal lovers, Flops lover. You were called by name. So was I. "Mrs. Lulu Cartwright and Flops," and we went into the cubicle. The white room. You did not, I remember, want to walk up the ramp. You had resisted the long ramp filled with dog turd. It was like leading you up to your death. You were so mad at me. Even then, in the animal hospital, you managed to smile at me. An awful smile of a helpless animal being led to slaughter. I waited there in the cubicle for an hour. I heard the cries of animals in pain, the cries of dogs, the yelping dogs. Then a doctor came in. He found me weeping and holding your paw.

"Please, dear Flops, get well. You can't die and leave me. How will I live without you?"

Flops looked up at me. The silent understanding of the thought. The doctor came in. He was a young man with a reddish, almost purple beard. He was nasty, sardonic, biting.

"I have to run tests on him. It will cost three hundred dollars. You have to leave him here. I've spoken with Dr. Higgins. The kidney is nothing to fool around with, you know. Chances are not good."

I am you, Flops. I am growing older. Will I live? Will I die? Don't leave me. I am Lulu in the mirror. Who am I? My life one flop after another. I flopped. I failed myself.

Another flop in the personal relations department.

I imagined him sitting in an office which resembled the tent of the Mahdi in *Lawrence of Arabia*. (Why is every Jewish boy from the Bronx's ambition to be an agent called Yosef with a white office decorated in arches and swords?) And now here he is, ladies and gentlemen of show business and the industry, the hottest hot, hot producer in New York, Mr. Yosef Fleishkeit himself, complete with his own airplane, his own hit, his own monogrammed shirts. And what is he doing? He is schlepping up to my apartment to tell me his problems. I feel I should be charging or giving lessons in the new form of disappearing act—new jitsu—where you can make yourself disappear or get larger or smaller. And he arrives just at eleven o'clock to have a drink and relax after a hard day of screwing and telephone passion.

Yosef Fleishkeit, all five feet three of him, walks into my apartment smelling of Old Spice. His brace only makes him more attractive. It brings out the maternal feeling in me. Have you ever had a maternal feeling for a cobra? He is the original cobra man. He curls up on my couch. One drink leads to another. I have had seven drinks.

"What do you think I'm like?" he asks, smiling at me.

He is the Mahdi. I am the Mahdi.

"I think you're warm, sensitive, very aggressive, compassionate, cool, extremely smart, attractive."

He looks at me. "I'm a winner. I never touch anything I don't get."

(How about touching me? I think.) I am turned on by his swarthy face, his deep eyes, the sense of vulnerability (the cast) that goes along with his power (at casting Sol Cantini). What the hell. He's a man. It's twelve o'clock. I'm exhausted and probably at the nadir of the nervous breakdown I've been having all month. I've just come from seeing a ballet and arguing with my best friend Jacquie, a feminist actress, potentially a star, from San Francisco. I'm exhausted, and I haven't gone to bed with anyone since my fiasco with Raymond. At least this guy wouldn't talk about cancer. He'd talk about the film industry. That's one step up from cancer. Besides, I've never made it with a guy with a brace. It must make him even more sensitive. I'd love to cuddle him.

But he is now telling me about his life. His wife, whom he identifies as looking like Elizabeth Taylor, is the smartest woman he has ever met. Jacqueline Onassis.

"You're smart," he says to me. "And aggressive. But not as smart as my wife."

I'm gonna let that one pass. I'm not out to get into smarts. I'm out to get into bed. And this agent/producer who just dropped in from heaven or wherever he came from is sitting there across from me. He is probably the pushiest man on earth. Probably if there were a Nobel Prize for power and aggression and ruthlessness, this guy would get it. I can see him in Sweden picking up the award. He is sitting there.

"Go on, now, what do you know about me?"

I search my mind for the facts.

"Okay, you were born in the Bronx."

"Go on."

"You married a woman named Mary Lou who is Gentile. She probably is interested in politics and horses."

"So far, you're right," he says. "Do you have a cigar?" he asks, interrupting me.

"No. I have a cigar holder but no cigar. Do you want me to see if I can get the elevator man to get one?"

"I have one in my car," he says. "But if I go to my car, I might be too tired to come back."

(Step number one—don't let old serpentine powerhouse out of apartment.)

"Forget the cigar," I say, trying not to sound aggressive.

"Would you like another drink? Now, don't you feel better?

"I know that you're probably having an affair with Geraldine, the girl in your film."

"That's right," he says. "Geraldine's a lovely gal. I met her three years ago. She's been going with me for a long time. Actually, giving her a career just gives me something to do. She's playing the game perfectly. She never makes one wrong step. She may even get me to marry her."

And what about your wife? I wonder, staring at him. He is attractive. A good face. Full lips. Nice eyes. He's handsome in an undignified way. Greasy. If you like greasy guys, Yosef Fleishkeit is as greased up as you can get. Suave greasy. Sort of pomade and deodorant mixed together. Nice skin. Chapped lips. That's no problem. The cast fascinates me—it's leather. Is there really something wrong with his leg? Or does he just wear it for sympathy? Doesn't every woman of my age and weight want to meet a guy who reminds her of Philip in *Of Human Bondage*? He could play Philip. I could play Mildred. There I am, casting. But I'm Philip. He's Mildred. It's all mixed up. I never guessed he'd ever come up to my apartment. Boy, this must be an off day. He can have any tootsie in the film world. Maybe he doesn't like tootsies. My one shot is that I'm a comedy writer. But I'm aggressive. How to get laid? That is the question.

"You know what?" he says after his sixth glass of white wine. "I think you're a very attractive, a very sexy woman. I thought so last year when I first set eyes on you."

(I love his expression "set"—all this jewelry imagery.) Here I am with Valley of the Dolls, only this is no doll. No, sir. This is the world's most greasy and powerful manager and producer. He touches shit, and it starts singing. Everything he touches turns to box-office receipts. I wonder if he will touch me. Even for an evening. Just for the hell of it, I think.

"I think you're a sexy woman."

I bolt from my chair, which my child has torn to pieces. Candles are burning so he doesn't see the holes.

He says, "How long have you lived here?"

"Since I've been divorced. Larry and I lived here."

And I'm frustrated. (Should I ask him to take off his pants? Or use a lighter touch? He's probably turned on by aggression. He should only know I'm desperate, not aggressive.) More apartment talk.

"I'm looking for an apartment. Tomorrow I'm leaving my wife."

(I see the memo pad. Meeting with Peckinpah, it says. Meeting with accountant. Barber. Leave wife. Afternoon meeting at Paramount. Opening at the Maisonette.)

"Tomorrow? You're leaving your wife tomorrow?"

(No wonder he's here. Loose-ends syndrome.)

"Yes. Do you want to know what I want more than anything else in the world?"

Yosef Fleishkeit is asking me something. Actually asking me a question. I want to say, "Of course I do," but I'm silent.

"I want to live alone."

(You and Greta Garbo.)

"I want to see Geraldine, who has a nice little apartment—she has money, you know. She was adopted by one of the Rothschilds."

(Adopted? Why didn't someone adopt me?)

"And my wife, who rides horses but lives alone. . . . You know we have a huge fourteen-room apartment. We have two in help. I'm sick of the whole thing. I need to be on my own and think for a while."

(I hate being alone. And so would you.)

I rush up to him and begin to kiss him. I can take just so much talk about maids and apartments. We are actually necking on my couch. He tackles like a captain of the basketball team. Some kisser. We neck. He pulls away.

"This is wonderful. Can I come back and see you for lunch tomorrow?"

Here I become ruthless. What the hell——when in Rome, do as the Romans do.

"No. We have to go to bed now."

"I can't."

"Why not?"

"My wife is expecting me at home. We were having dinner with the Rosenblooms. . . ."

(He forgets I have no idea who the Rosenblooms are.)

". . . and I sneaked back to my office to get your phone number. It's late, and I don't know what to tell her."

"You've been married to her for twenty years, and you're leaving her tomorrow, and you don't know what to tell her? Tell her you are stuck in an elevator accident."

(It's probably Geraldine he has to call. Geraldine, the adopted shiksa.)

"Listen, I'm going to be frank with you, Yosef. Shoot from the hip. I wanted to make it with you at the very getgo. . . ."

(I'm now using his lingo.) I continue (talking agent talk).

". . . You are the kind of guy, you've got the kind of looks that turn me on. Do you think I'm going to wait for you to shlep up from your office at IFA tomorrow? You'll have a thousand meetings. I'll never get through your army of secretaries . . ."

(All called Maria. Why are so many Jewish agents surrounded by so many shiksas?)

". . . and I want you now."

"All right," Yosef says.

"Take your clothes off."

He limps into the bedroom.

"I'm right behind you."

Oops, I forgot the candles in the bedroom. It's a mess. The kid's crayons all over the place. Never mind.

"I've got to call my wife."

He picks up the phone. Stricken with megalophonia, he puts it back.

"I can't call her now. It's too late. I can't just make love and leave like an animal."

"Yosef, don't be silly."

I'd love you to leave like an animal. (Better you leave like an animal than like an agent who changed his mind.) I locked the bedroom door. That's the only way to deal with these powerful guys in the industry. You have to be one jump ahead at all times.

"What are you doing, Lulu?"

"I'm locking the door."

"Oh, all right, take your clothes off."

(What endearment. What words of caress. What a romantic. What suave manners. He must have learned them in Suck City.)

I run into the bathroom. Douche quickly. Get myself all prepared. And come out of the bathroom in my old purple nightgown. But better my nightgown than my nude body. One thing is with models, I always felt like a fat slob. At least with a guy with a slight physical impediment, with a cripple, I feel more relaxed. After all, I'm an emotional cripple. I'm the desperate Mrs. Cartwright, aren't I? Two cripples together under the sheets. Get into bed. Good. Lights out. Now or never. He is amazed by my tactics. It's now three in the morning.

"Listen," he says, "I gotta call my wife. She's waiting for me."

(Isn't that the name of the game? How could he have an erection without a goyish wife who looks like Elizabeth Taylor and rides horses waiting for him?)

"Call her."

"Oh, never mind. Take your clothes off."

"They are off. This is my body."

(Did he think it was my clothes?)

We begin kissing. Suddenly, we start making love. He's a good lover. At least he's passionate. Now comes the real kicker. I start telling him what to do. What the hell, I'll never bump into him again. I might as well give a couple of orders. Do this and this and this, I say. I feel like Sidney Lumet directing *Felony*. He listens.

For the first time in his whole life, he's following orders. I'm having a wonderful time. He is, too, I guess. He says so. In those very words.

"I'm having a wonderful time. I hate to leave you."

He gets up immediately and starts strapping on his brace. I have to hand it to him. No embarrassment. Jesus Christ, if I had a brace, I'd be nervous. I guess Jewish producers are at such a premium these days they lose their shyness. It takes him a long time to get himself together.

"Don't leave," I shout. I'm still directing.

"All right," he says.

(He's now completely passive.)

"I'll stay."

He starts kissing me again.

Finally, I get up.

"Now you can leave."

I unlock the door.

He says, "I'll call you tomorrow."

"No, don't call me. I'll call you."

Why am I pursuing happiness with this man? The next morning I go to my psychiatrist. I tell him the story.

"It's unreal," I say. "It's impossible."

Dr. Bears is always growling in my corner.

"Why is it so impossible? You say he's leaving his wife? You say he has the same interests you do? Why do you give up so easily?"

"Give up? He's leaving his wife for Connie, the adopted blond shiksa, and he's leaving his wife to do movies. What does he want with me? I'm overweight. Old. A hag. Aggressive. In other words, I don't fit in with the industry."

"That's your trouble," says the analyst. "You always under-sell yourself."

"Anyway, I've written a play about him."

I decided to take my play over to IFA and give it to Yosef Fleishkeit.

I write a note. It doesn't do justice to the way I feel. But it's honest. Dear Yosef, I loved being with you. I wrote a new play. And I wrote it about you. I bet you're the only producer in America who has plays written for you.

But I get shy. Suppose I just look like a delivery girl bringing a play to IFA. No, I have a better idea. My friend Jingles who is a cabdriver and wants to do something in films—a little weird but a kind person—will bring it. My friend Jingles who is a playwright-cabdriver is with me the next day.

"I'll deliver it."

"Don't give it to the secretary," I say to Jingles. "Deliver it in person."

I seal the play in an envelope marked "Private." I tape it and seal it with wax.

Jingles, wearing his old torn hat, carries the play. I go with him. It is six o'clock. I wait for him in front of the building. He goes up. Tick-tock. I'm a fugitive. Why should I feel like a fugitive because I'm delivering a love play to Yosef Fleishkeit? Am I doing something awful? What kind of person am I? Just because I'm divorced and lonely and overweight, I can't do lovely things anymore? I wait like a criminal in front of the building.

Jingles comes down (did I mention that he is sometimes violent?). He looks angry. He is carrying the play.

"Those motherfuckers asked me what I was there for. I said I had to see Mr. Fleishkeit about something personal. Then this tall guy comes out and looks me over. Maybe they thought I was trying to rob something. 'What have you got there, boy?'

178

he asks me. 'None of your fucking business,' I tell him. 'I have something that has to be hand delivered. And hand delivered means hand delivered. Now, where's this Fleishkeit?' Two secretaries ran out. 'He's not in,' one said. I knew fucking well he was there. So I said, 'You motherfuckers, let me into him.' They thought I was some kind of desperado actor trying to get Mr. Fleishkeit to see a résumé. The tall guy started pushing me. I would have knifed him, but I mighta dropped the play. 'No, sir. I won't give it to any of you. I have a sacred object here, an object none of youse would understand. To tell you the truth, it's from a goddess—right on your ass—from a goddess. And it's for your boss, not for you, you motherfuckers.' "

Jingles paused.

"They started to call the police. So I beat it. They started to call the cops."

I start to sweat. This may ruin my new relationship. Why are guys with casts on their legs so paranoid? Or maybe it's just the industry.

"Never mind, Jingles. I'll take it up myself."

I go into the lobby and hail IFA. I know Mr. Fleishkeit is *up there* because I checked with the elevator attendants.

"Hello? May I speak to Mr. Fleishkeit," I ask.

I get Maria. Or maybe it's Mary. Mary is on the phone.

"Yes? Look, it's Mrs. Lulu Cartwright, a friend of mine just came up to deliver a play to Mr. Fleishkeit."

"A what?"

"A play."

"I see."

"Well, you don't see. They wouldn't let him in. And it's private."

"Well, Mrs. Cartwright, he looked awfully weird. And he said he had a holy message."

"What's wrong with that? Hasn't a holy message ever come up the elevator shaft to IFA?"

"If we knew it was you, Mrs. Cartwright. . . ."

179

"It is me," I say, crying in the phone booth. Two minutes later up the elevator I go into the IFA crematorium, where thousands of so many talented actresses and actors have turned into ashes. I give the play to an old white-haired woman with a mop. I ask her to give it to anyone. I hear Yosef's voice in the voice-over style he uses on the phone.

Three days later, I call Yosef. "How did you like the play?" I want to ask him. But he's in a meeting.

Seven messages. One to his office. One to mine. Pari passu. Finally he is on the phone. The Mr. Fleishkeit—tara-tara.

"Hello, gorgeous. How's your life?"

"I feel wonderful," I say. "Did you read the play? How did you like it?"

A pause.

"I'll get back to you. I wanta read your script."

Then he gets back to me. Back to me. Or at me.

"I think the script is not commercial. It's a comedy. And no one wants a comedy. There's only one gal today who's commercial and that's Barbra; otherwise no one wants it. It's like a Woody Allen comedy without Woody Allen. Let me go down the list of movies today."

"Fuck the list, Yosef. Never mind the script. Did you find an apartment? Because I found one. You can have mine. I think I'm going away. Anywhere. I just want to go someplace."

"No, yours is too big. I just want a small one."

"How about the Hampshire House?"

"The Hampshire House?"

An incredulous pause.

"You mean on Central Park South, with the hookers?"

"What do you want? An apartment overlooking St. Patrick's Cathedral?"

"Naw, I've listed myself with Pat Palmer. She'll find one. Meanwhile, about your script. I loved it, it's funny. But it will never be commercial."

My fantasy takes over. I'll pal around with Fleishkeit until he gives me the shakes. Or he gets the shakes. My whole new comedy will be about guess who? Yosef, the producer. My son the producer.

Meanwhile, I am beginning to think that my real son is the only person in this Female Comedy that means anything to me. I'd like him to be able to feel things, not to be ashamed to be whoever the hell he wants to be.

It's time to go back to comedy writing. Let's see. I think I'll write a script about a gay housewife. *I Was a Gay Housewife.* I sat home all day until out of isolation and tonsillitis, I got lonely and rang up my best friend, another woman with child-rearing problems and no career to speak of. Another woman chained to the emptiness of the kitchen and kinder. She comes over. We talk about how people are starving all over the world and how difficult it is to be political when you don't have anything to eat. Priorities. However, over Maxwell coffee, we chat about how people use that as an excuse not to kick ass or do anything with their lives. We decide to demonstrate, boycott, do other things to make trouble. We talk about our houses and our husbands.

"Does your husband give a fuck about you?" I ask.

"No. He doesn't. And he doesn't fuck me either."

We chat about public versus private school. We chat about our childhoods and go deep into discovering who we were before we were people. We chat about loneliness, isolation. I talk about boarding school days when I wanted to be something, someone. That's what misery is, to have nothing at your heart, no one in your arms, to feel a person close to you, wanting to talk to you, but saying nothing. And suddenly, the other housewife looks at me and makes it clear to me she, too, is lonely. *I Was a Gay Housewife.* Starring Gertrude Stein, Jr. Or *I Was a Celibate* for the CIA. Ever since I could be grown-up enough to cry, I cried for a place to belong in the world. I was nowhere.

181

Memory on the plane: Listen to this: Richard Knowland, lawyer at Greer, Greer & Knowland. Introduced to Richard Knowland by Helen. Helen is always hearing about men about to divorce. Previous men she has introduced me to are a married bird-watcher and an accountant in show business. The married bird-watcher was bananas. The accountant was also crazy, not interesting crazy, dull crazy. But Richard Knowland was the weirdest. Weird occurrences took place. To begin with, he explained that he had left his wife and was living with a female stockbroker. But he was not happy with this female stockbroker. ("It's not working out," was the operative phrase.) Richard Knowland of Greer, Greer & Knowland was driving me to celibacy. But slowly. To see him was to court disaster. First of all, it was all a question of lies. He lied to me.

Richard Knowland's thirteen reasons for breaking dates:

1. Had to take son skiing.
2. Had to take daughter to Connecticut.
3. Visit a friend with hernia in Nassau County.
4. Testify in court (Queens).
5. Had to fly to Michigan.
6. Working late at the office.
7. Daughter having crisis.
8. Son in Christmas pageant.
9. Mother with tonsillitis.
10. Sudden root canal to save front tooth.
11. Dog cut two tendons in park.
12. Funeral.
13. Funeral.

memory on the plane

PART IV
anxieties of
suck city

I am writing notes to myself. I am riding on a plane to my new destiny. But I am also dreaming. Can't make it out. What will I do when I reach Hollywood?

I am imagining all sorts of people. And events.

Anxieties. Entering anxieties' slipstream:

Another memory: Aunt Vagina stands behind the stove waiting for Dumbo. She has beautiful white teeth. She smiles. She cooks dinner for so many people. And why are her talents put into crying her eyes out? Because she's not crying, she's cooking. She's cooking up a storm. Only the grits are made with tears. Tears, thank you very much. Aunt Vagina cooks. She also smiles. She entertains. And she fucks. Lawdy me, she fucks. She gets her ass away from the stove and puts it on the bed. And then she fucks up to her ass in grits. And why is Aunt Vagina so willing to make a pancake out of herself? Because Aunt Vagina secretly doesn't feel that anybody would love her unless she was on the box of pancakes. If she said what she really thought, such as, "You motherfucker, why don't you try understanding what the hell my head is all about? I'm not wearing a bandanna, I'm wearing a bandage. I'm not a joke. My head hurts because I'm tired of being pushed and shoved into your fantasy of me." But Aunt Vagina—"MMMMMMMmmmmmm." She smiles. She says, "I'm Lulu, fly me to Miami," and appears in the National Airlines ad. Crash with National. Crash with Dumbo. Crash.

I am dreaming. How quickly the real world evaporates.

Welcome to Suck City. Ding Dong Bell. Hollywood is Hell. The Hollyzoo. I go to Columbus Films. The man who was a Columbus film executive welcomes me into his office. He is a bulgy-eyed mechanical man who seems to be made out of green wax. The decor of his office (all out of *House and Garden*) was complete with a huge basket of fake apples. Strange Garden of Eden. Suck City. Plastic apples. The gray croaker standing there to greet you. *Errk, errkkk.* His white hair is perfectly groomed. His face lotioned and perfectly shaved. Warts. Teeth capped. Green spotted sports shirt by Nat Wise. Underarms shaved, no doubt. Bottled toilet water keeping him smelling clean. *Erkkk, erkk.* Small exercised ass. Slightly slimy pressed white pants. Gucci loafers. No toes. Smile at the secretive toady of a man. But at the moment of introduction, the man turns into a tree frog. I keep talking. My mind goes over everything I know about frogs. Mouth-breeding frog (*Rhinodermatidae*). Charles Darwin discovered the inch-long Darwin's dwarf frog in the beech forests of southern Argentina and Chile, but it has another claim to fame, a breeding method among amphibians. After a female lays thirty to forty eggs, several males guard them until they are ready to hatch, whereupon each male inserts some in his elongated pouch. The frog speaks to me. I wonder what would happen if he turned into a man.

I tell him I'm fed up with the tripe that's been handed out as films about women's experience. What is Columbus doing about changing the image of women in films? And would they be interested in a different kind of script about a woman's experience, one that doesn't end with a woman going crazy or killing herself because she can't take being on her own without being a nun. The toad croaks into his toady phone.

"Hello, Lena? Lee, get down here this minute. I have Lulu Cartwright here, and that's what you are here for."

The token woman executive arrives. She's from New York. Tough. Smart. Brilliant, by Hollywood standards. The toad is proud. He is bursting. His warts swell.

"We are the only industry in Hollywood that has a woman executive. Why don't you gals go upstairs to Lena's office?"

I say good luck to the toad, and he says good luck to us. (Everyone in Suck City is always wishing everyone else good luck.) Lots of luck.

I follow Princess Lee to her office. It is decorated by the same decorator who "did" all the offices at Columbus. They are all in the style of Stench Provincial. A combination of fresh paint, checkered tablecloths, and Lysol. Lena is nice. Lena is the head of the story department. She talks Suck City talk.

"There are no actresses today," she laments. "There's only Faye Dunaway. And Jane Fonda. Nobody else in that age bracket. Well, right now I am looking for a feminist-oriented film project for Goldie Hawn. Is there anything in *Kill, Kill* for Goldie Hawn?"

"I don't think so," I say. "But here. Why don't you read the script? If you Xerox it, you can keep it."

Lee: "Is there anything in the other one for Goldie? Goldie Hawn?"

Me: "There's something in it for Goldie Meir. Do you handle her?" I want to ask these people, "Why are you the way you are?"

From Columbus I take a cab to World to see Roscoe Bibb. Information about Roscoe: This guy's a prince. He's black. He has a number one executive position for black men in Hollywood. He understands what I am talking about. He digs rage. He will understand my anger at seeing women represented to each other as female niggers whose only theme seems to be the male promise her anything but give her an old cock to shut her up.

I want to say to Roscoe, how many films have gone into the minds and hearts of women's dreams?

Think of how a generation of black women must have felt about their femininity watching films in which femininity was always out of grasp for them. For the black woman, growing up meant that her problems only began because she now attracted the attention of the Big Man, who turned her beauty into the service of his own cock or kitchen. She could either be Lena Horne or Aunt Jemima (Aunt Vagina). The black woman's negative psychology, which was to protect herself by being ugly and repellent, was also shared by the white woman. Beautiful and dumb or smart and ugly were the two alternatives. It was impossible to be blond and brainy or black and brainy. I understood how black women, for example, watching the white movies, felt themselves to be mutilated. I felt mutilated, too. The Negro woman's black face, African features, kinky hair were attributes which placed her far from the ideal of the American beauty and made her, in reference to the American ideal, ugly. When this feeling of ugliness was reinforced by the rejection of society, the black girl, especially as she was growing up seeing womanhood portrayed on the screen, imagined herself to be a freak. Under normal circumstances, the white adolescent girl had a compensatory blossoming of narcissism allowing her to feel satisfaction with herself. But the black woman's feelings of mutilation were strengthened since films showed her to be nonexistent or ugly or poor or a sex object or a nurturer.

If you were white and beautiful (MM), you were allowed to offer your breasts to guys to suck—who did and then left you. But if you were black, you got raped or you got the job of being a mother. And that has been the two dimensions of Miss White America and Miss Black America in the movies. Black was not beautiful. Blond was beautiful. But black or blond, you wound up in every movie the same way: You had no influence except through your husband, your child, or your lover. If you were a tough babe, at the end you always gave in to some dumb man. Movies instructed us in how to live, how to love. They were shadows etched on our soul. And they taught us to hate ourselves. I thought of this riding in a cab to World.

In Roscoe Bibb's shiny black-and-white-chrome-decorated office, I start kicking ass right away. Bibb calls in a black casting director. The black minority now makes way for the women's minority.

"Can you understand what I am talking about, Mr. Bibb? I am going to see that World goes out of business. Do you dig that?"

"Wait a minute, sister," says Bibb. "I'm going to get you to the president. I was talking to him the other day and I told him I was tired of being the token Negro. He told me that if I could come up with a script that he liked, he might even let me produce it, so give it to me, and if I like it, I'll show it to him. World is a wonderful place, you know. They have all the money right there in the bank."

He pointed up to the heavens of the executive offices.

The corridors of World were huge labyrinths filled with overblown cardboard photographs of ex-glamour. Photographs of a thousand and one actors who all looked like a combination of Gary Cooper and Red Buttons. All the photographs are weird. Like ones the great Diane Arbus must have taken. I thought of Diane. What her camera would have done to World. The city within a city. The sick galaxy of stars.

That afternoon, I found myself at the high point of World, in the executive offices. Flo's motto—"Out of the streets, into the suites"—rang through my ears.

I said to Mark Simon's secretary, "When we liberate this joint, you'll be sitting in the executive offices instead of out here."

The secretary looked at me as if I'd gone stark raving bonkers.

"No. Don't look at me as if I am mad, dear madam. The time has come. Women really don't have to be niggers if you know what I mean. You've been making coffee and waiting on Mr. Simon for how many *thousands of hours?* When do you think you'll get a chance to have a little power? Soon he'll be out here waiting on you. By the way, where is he? *He's late.* If he doesn't arrive in ten minutes, I'm leaving."

I go into Simon's office and begin using the phone and eating some of the fresh fruit. Every executive in the Hollywood Labyrinth syndrome has fresh fruit. It's a status symbol. A leftover no doubt from poor Carmen Miranda's hat.

I use the phone to call my friends in Hong Kong. I love using Mark Simon's office. I am beginning to taste power. I call my friend Teddy.

"Hey, Teddy, guess where I am. In the Muck's office. Oops, here he comes."

Simon walks into the room. He cannot *believe* what he sees. A girl. Rather, a gal (all women are gals in Hollywood and don't you forget it) eating *his* fresh fruit and talking on *his* phone. Was he seeing things? His eyes popped out of their sockets. He is truly more like a frog than the guy at Columbus. No. He was a baboon. A gray-haired baboon. Mr. Apeshit himself. Famous for having been shot in the behind in a parking lot (such were the credentials of the head of the production department at World).

I said to Teddy in Hong Kong, "I think this guy is the president of something," and I turned to Simon, putting my hand over the receiver. The secretary stood behind with her mouth open. I thought she was going to call for help. Or break into an aria.

"Hey, are you the president?" I asked Simon.

"No," he said, "I am not."

I continued on the phone, ignoring Simon and talking long distance. Actually, it was overseas, but what's the difference to World? They owned everything, including all the property in Hollywood. What did they care if the new black flicks they were pushing didn't make millions? They owned the ghettos. They probably also owned the seas. Jesus Christ, they owned everything. But they didn't own me, so I kept on chatting while Mark Simon had a fit. Then I figured enough was enough. I hung up.

"Okay, Mark, I'm ready to talk to you about World doing the first feminist feature film. It's called *Kill, Kill*, and it's about women and violence and power. I'd like to use a lot of political figures in it just to give it some starface without paying for it, and the movie ends with a shoddy mess. I'm going to be the executive producer and we need World money. Maybe your company would be interested."

Simon looks at me now as if I might have a gun in my pocketbook. I guess he's afraid that I might shoot him in the behind.

"Keep calm, Mark. I'm not going to hurt you. I'm just talking to you about a deal."

I got up, eating a banana, and Mark goes behind his desk, where he feels more secure. He pulls out a fountain pen and begins signing a few checks. Down to the old paycheck. It was a sort of Librium for him. He asked for a moment of silence. Signing checks got his head together. Meanwhile, I cased his office. It is the office of a pimp all right. A few pictures of Carol Burnett on the piano to create dignity. But we all knew better. I waited for him to begin.

He looked at me and started talking about *Kill, Kill*, He had heard of the women's movement all right. I suggested that World would be a good place to picket. They had not one woman executive.

"Have you ever heard of a class action suit?" I ask, rolling my eyes. "Because if you ain't heard of one, you are gonna hear of one. Especially in your fucking TV department where you have to get an FCC license to appear on the air. And I'm gonna see you ain't gonna get one renewed."

(I hate speaking like that, by the way. But those morons from the Catskill Mountains don't exactly understand the Queen's English. They were all pseudo-Mafia types anyway—Mafia rejects—and you had to talk deese, dems, and dose.)

"Listen, Simon," I say, "your time has come. You are an idiot, and everyone knows it."

Just then the telephone rings. It is Sidney, the president. I listened carefully while Simon talks jock talk to him.

"Hey, Sid. We done it. We offered five million for the F.P., and they took it—er—ass—ugo—booba—bomba—ugo ugh ugh," which translated meant that Billy Wilder and Simon had bought the rights to some two-bit 1930s kind of *My Gal Friday* gig and are going to make a big movie out of it.

After the grunts are over, Simon begins grunting at me. In a businesslike way, of course. In the middle of the conversation, he stops and says, "You have great tits."

I let that one pass. If that's how he addresses a woman executive, I can imagine how he had talked to Marilyn Monroe. But I let it pass because I didn't think that saying, "And you have a nice cock," is appropriate. The days of tit for tat were over. It's all getting closer to the truth.

I looked at the motherfucker and thought, Gee, Simon, with an ape face like yours, you're going to look great behind bars. Because, baby, your time has come. You and the other ape-frog executives of the world are going to be thrown out of the industry with your mouths open. And your film fascist Mafia pseudo-financial power is about over. It really is, old boy. So keep your Guccis on, and keep talking like a smart ass.

Leaving Mark Simon's office, I descend into the real world

of huge cars. My elevator left me off in the garage. I got into the car of a friend. She drives around in a hearse, and we got on the highway. I see a woman with a wedding veil driving a Volvo alone. A lonely runaway bride driving ninety-five miles an hour down the highway. Is she an actress taking her lunch break? Speeding to her lover? Or a real runaway bride?

In my dream, I wanted to see the president of Pix. Mr. Pepperberg. Mr. Pepperberg had been told that I am going to see him to talk about how women had been misrepresented in films. Oddly enough, I got an appointment to see him the next day. What I, dear Superlu of the imagination, didn't realize was that NOBODY, nobody wants to see the president of Pix. He's lonely. He sisses and makes poopie in his executive toilet, which has, by the way, bars on the windows. He sitzbathes in his executive bathroom. He goes out to lunch at the commissary—no one recognizes him. After all, the *higher up* you are, the *more isolated* you are in corporate Suck City until you're so important you become anonymous. He gets yelled at for parking his car in the president's spot of the parking lot by blue-suited policemen until he explains, quietly, that he is the president. He is hamsteresque. But it ain't he who runs the corporation. No, ma'am. The corporation is run by the stockholders. He's just a figure of a man, a house mouse who says the right things. A lawyer who goggles at papers, a house mouse who is harmless and para-attractive. Rodentia exists at the very top.

It came as a shock. The president of Pix is really a hamster. His Royal Hamster was happy to get rid of me.

At Globe, Z.M. shows me into his office, which is early Irving Trust. Z.M., president of Globe, had a large brown office with Jasper Johns lithographs, stainless steel tables, imitation Ming vases, brown walls, a sitting-room couch made of suede. He had, in the Suck City sense, "taste," although you can take the plastic flowers out of the boy, but you can't take the boy out of the plastic flowers. Mr. Pepperberg's office is what Z.M.'s office must have looked like before Z.M. got taste. Z.M.'s blond secretary was cheerful as she showed me in. She is a Bronx producer's dream——English accent, *class*, a perfect depilatated automaton.

I got down to biz. I ask him what was Globe going to do about making different kinds of films about women's experiences? Sexist hatred flared up immediately. Z.M. isn't going to have any of this women crap. He got nasty and explained that since he had come to Globe, there had been *a lot* of changes made and no uppity executive from God knows where——*New York*——is going to tell *him* that anything was wrong with his corporation. I try to explain to Z.M. that the woman shown as a depreciated object only enforced the rage of the depreciated male.

Z.M. sat in his chair. *His* was the office of a powerful man. It was the office of a corporation executive. What is this madwoman doing here? Who let her in? Should he push a button and have her removed? Will there be any repercussions? All this goes through his head. I keep taking notes on everything he says. His teeth begin to show under his upper lip. His ferretlike fingers become nervous.

"If you are so dissatisfied with Globe, why don't you talk to our stockholders?" he asked.

"That's just what I'm going to do," I say. "But that ain't all I'm gonna do."

"Listen you . . ." he begins.

"Don't mind me," I said, rolling my Superlu eyes. "I'm just writing this all down for the *New York Times*. I'm writing an article about male power in Hollywood."

In Suck City a lot of people haven't heard of the *New York Times*, but Z.M. has.

"Why didn't you tell me you were interviewing me? I don't allow myself to be interviewed. I never would have agreed to see you. I saw you only because you are new here in Hollywood. I had no idea you were taking an interview."

I talk to him confidentially. "Globe is in a lot of trouble. There's something called the women's market, and we are tired of sending our mothers, sisters, daughters to movies to learn how to hate themselves. And we are tired of giving our dollars to bolster this sick industry, which is antidemocratic, antisexist, and antiracist. For women, retaliation is not out of the question. Oppression has produced fear and paranoia. Women under threat of power have gone mad. We consider that we have gone *sane*. If women are frightened, consider what frightens them and consider what happens when they feel cornered, when there is no further lie they can believe, when one sees that they are permanently cast as victims, and finally what happens when the sleeping woman wakes up and turns against her masters."

Z.M. was anxious to get me out of his office. He suggested we go to the commissary.

The commissary is a huge automat. Z.M. seems very jocular and friendly on the line, but nobody seems to care. In the commissary were a few bewigged chorus types, superbunnies, who were obviously being "shot" that day in some films on location. The lot itself, needless to say, is a stage set of papier-mâché buildings. Every type of street is there. It all seems empty. The commissary, too, has an empty feeling. As if dead people were, by rote, going through the motions of eating plastic food. Z.M. suggests that I try the "Texasburgers." I waited while a sweating chef came up with two plastic-looking heaps of rodent food put together under a spongelike bun. When I get to the register, in a gesture of largess, Z.M. refuses to let me pay for the lunch. He waved to the cashier. Obviously, one person knew who he was as he passed us by. Then he goes into his noble nigger act. He actually "buses" his own tray.

"I'm no different from anyone else," he said, smiling.

His effort to show me the efficiency of the corporation, the thrift of it all was wasted. I don't care how much money Globe is saving by having everyone bus his or her own cafeteria. I sit down and begin talking.

He said to me, "Look around you at this commissary. You see all these dark faces? All these Mexican faces?" He smiled. "This is all *my* doing. When I came to Globe three years ago, this was the only lily-white organization in the industry. Not a dark face. I showed that to practice what you preach is important. I saw to it that from the grass roots upward we had to have all sorts of men represented here."

I get up from lunch. I am late for my next appointment. Z.M. walks me back to my car.

"Hope to see you again." He smiles.

"Don't worry, you will."

I leave him standing in front of his limousine, looking like a con man, cemented in the doorway of his life. Anxieties' slipstream. I am with the self-sufficient ghosts of my own Hollywood anxieties. My dreams throw me a lifeline.

In my dream, Richard Marks is a desperado in Suck City and he keeps calling me and leaving messages at my hotel. The little white messages with his name and number begin to pile up. Finally, I call him back. I get his machine tape. What a performance. He would get the Oscar if Oscars were given for answering service tapes, which they should be given for, since they are the best performances in Suck City. King Lear alias Richard Marks speaks meaningfully into the tape. Deep, deep voice. French accent.

"Hello." (Sorrowful.) "This is Richard Marks." (Affirmative, full of hope.) "Thank you for calling me." (Pitiful, lonely.) "I have gone out for just a small moment." (Redundant but effective.) The real Richard Marks, in pain from his pinched shoulder, broke, desperado, has gone to the unemployment line in Santa Monica. "Please leave your name and number and I will call you . . . as soon as I come back."

(Direct personal attention will be given by Richard Marks to you no matter who you are. You can even be a crazy woman demanding women's rights on all the tapes of Suck City and Richard Marks will call you back.) A magnificent tape, I think to myself. The end is perfect. Just the right amount of suspense and hesitation between the "I will call you" and the "as soon as I come back."

How did Richard Marks know that he would be gone for just a short moment (as opposed to a long moment?) Richard Marks' life is one moment to another tied into his telephone answering machine. It gave him his only roots; the only thing he had to return to was his machine. Does someone want me? Is someone calling? At night he played all the tapes back. Being a "director," he always has young actresses and actors calling him and asking if he is directing a scene or a movie. He listens to those young voices, those requests for work. It was as if he and all the other "hopefuls" in Suck City spent their days and nights calling each other's services, speaking into each other's machines, and playing back each other's voices. Richard Marks listens to my voice on the machine which said, "Please call me. I received your message and am returning your call. Hope you are having a nice day. Lulu."

I am like a plaster Joan of Arc.

In my dream, Z.M. called me at my hotel to see if there was anything he could do for me. I ask him if he wants to have a drink later that evening. He is sorry but he is the dinner partner of Elizabeth Taylor. Elizabeth Taylor is now in Suck City being feted by Roddy McDowall, Edie Goetz, and others. Her dinner partner was none other than Mr. Head himself, Z.M.

197

In my dream, I realize Elizabeth Taylor is the quintessential exploited female. Despite her breasts, her love of squirrels, her outstanding beauty, she had gone from one jockfag to another. I wondered why she had never found one person able to give her the gift of understanding. Elizabeth Taylor. She sure could pick 'em. But was she any different from me? Was Dumbo or Abraham or Larry or Raymond worse than these guys? It was all part of the Female Comedy.

In my dream I compare notes with a friend who works for the *Hollywood Reporter* and is about to leave Suck City. Caroline listens to every story I tell her about my dates and counts them one of her own. But if Elizabeth Taylor didn't do so well, who was I to think I could do better? What makes people kill themselves? What makes people ill? What makes mental illness? You don't have to be a genius to answer that one. An Eddie Fisher or Dumbo Lavitch.

In my dream my first big date in Suck City is arranged by Sir Pimpo, Z.M. He was busy dating Elizabeth Taylor, but he kindly introduced me to a leading millionaire celebrity, the young writer-director Jonny Cragmore. Actually, I admired Cragmore's bestselling book *The Space Drain*. I had read it while I was getting divorced. Jonny's claim to fame is that he was four feet eight. His other claim to fame was that he had gone to Harvard. And that he was—hold on to your hats, everyone, because in Suck City this is really a big thing—he is a doctor. A *real* doctor with his own certificate. Of course he never practiced. And no one knows exactly what kind of doctor he is.

In my dream I go into the Cragmore cutting room. The crew of editors and sound men are sitting around the control booths. They were sitting in the dark helping put together Jonny Cragmore's first movie. They played it, synchronizing the sound with the picture. I walk in in the middle. The picture is violent. I watch a scene where, in a barroom, the guys start beating each other up. As we used to say in boarding school, *Blood and gore all over the floor and me without a spoon.* What good is gore unless someone is watching? I can't believe how guys could take off on this violence, this sickness. Z.M. gives a couple of produceresque comments to Jonny.

"Keep the music low in that last take" or mumbo jumbo like that.

Jeez, I think, it's real tough work in Hollywood, and these guys sure take their profession seriously. In my dream I want to stand up and scream.

I say to myself, "I want to get out of here."

As I am leaving, the lights went on. I say good-bye to Cragmore, the violent pygmy.

"Where can I reach you?" he asks me, his monotone voice suggesting that perhaps, only perhaps, I might be lucky enough to see him again the the flesh.

"I'll reach you," I say, and leave.

Now begins a short dream between Superlu and Jonny Cragmore. It is simple. A date in Suck City with an important man (a man of power) begins with Mr. Important VIP telling you how busy he is. That is to immediately show that although you may think you are important and famous and busy, he is much more beautiful and famous and busy than you are and don't you gorge yourself on memories of how easy it used to be, used to be, for people just to get together, used to be, when we thought of one another, used to be, we'd all walk down to the lake together, used to be, before we learned to humiliate each other, used to be, used to be. Jonny Cragmore tells me in my dream how *busy* he is. He is seeing another gal that night and another gal the next day and he was, very important, he was *cutting.* In Suck City you never go out to dinner with someone important like Mr. Director Writer Cragmore.

You progress. Like in Thomas Mann? You remember *The Magic Mountain*? You go from one sick floor to another? Well, in Suck City, an important man like Jonny Cragmore takes you for breakfast first. Then, only then, can you progress to lunch, if he likes you, and finally, the ultimate hour, the dinner hour, but only if he was going to *allow* you to sleep with him. Otherwise, it was just breakfast.

Jonny Cragmore comes and picks me up for breakfast in his convertible Mercedes Benz. He takes me to a Pancake House in Beverly Hills for breakfast. In a few seconds in the convertible, he tells me that he hates aggressive women and that he had been married, in his own words, to a female chauvinist pig. I ask him what that is. He tells me his ex-wife always wanted to be waited on. I take mental notes. He is obviously very disturbed about things, this facocktadocta. At the Pancake House we order our food. I see this important little man staring at me. He was enraged. We get down to the nitty gritty.

"What did you think of my film?" he asks.

"I hated it," I say to him.

No point in being diplomatic.

"I think it is a crock of shit. I also hope to get a few dozen women to picket it, and I'm sure I will be able to."

He puts down his fork. He chokes on his bacon. His eyes narrow.

"What's wrong with anger?" he asks.

"Nothing," I say. "It's not anger. Or rage. It's your false bullshit malefag violence that I find so full of shit."

Here he went into his Harvard song-and-dance number. It's called I'm a real doctor, I know better.

"Listen," he says, "I'm a doctor. Did you know that at studies made at Harvard University, when students were given tests, it showed that the adrenaline-producing students who had the most violence did the best on their tests?"

"Is that so?" I ask, pouring maple syrup on my pancake and watching his white Adam's apple get very excited. Gee, I sure knew how to hurt a guy.

"And my film only expresses what I, as a doctor, know is absolutely true and it is this: Male violence is a natural condition."

His voice gets louder. I stared at my astrological place mat, which is under my pancakes, and tried not to laugh.

"Listen," I say. "I'm nervous. Let's get out of here."

My mat said: *Virgo. Often you are in danger, but your sweet nature does not make you suspicious.* I look at Jonny. His fork was pointed at me like a bayonet. But I decided to end the battle right here. I was getting combat fatigue and claustrophobia in the Pancake House.

After pancakes with Jonny, I was scheduled to go to another shindig, a cerebral palsy benefit at Hugh Hefner's house. I drive to the hotel with Jonny. We exchange banalities about Suck City.

"This place is a joke. You can't take it seriously. I love the anonymity of writing where nobody knows me," Jonny says as he drives.

(He speaks of himself as if he were a genius hiding from his fans. Actually, he has no fans. I mean, he is hardly the kind of guy that people hound for an autograph. What was all this anonymity for?)

Looking at him, I realize that he is coming unglued. He looks at me as I get out of the car and growls at me, "Come here."

I go back to his car. Was he going to Mace me? It was only breakfast. I mean, we didn't fuck or anything, so what was his problem? All I had done was break bread with him. Break bacon, as it were.

"You female chauvinist pig," he says, looking at me, spitting his words out. His violence level is rising. I have the vague idea that he is going to shut the door of his Mercedes on my fingers.

"I hate confrontations," he says, "but I'm going to confront you. I'm going home from breakfast with you, and I'm going to start drinking. I will probably drink all day. How do you dare talk about male violence? And what kind of remark was that you made when we got to the Pancake House? That you asked Simone Lefkowitz to ask her girfriend who went out with me if I was good in bed. Is that true or is that a joke?"

"It's true," I say. "What's wrong with that?"

He began to stuff chewing gum in his mouth. I thought he might choke, but he started chewing very quickly. He was an enraged little VIP behind the wheel of Suck City's favorite Nazi car, a Mercedes Benz.

"And listen," I say to him, "I have something to tell you. Listen carefully. Go suck yourself."

(At last I was no longer Lulu, the schmuck. I am kicking ass.)

Hugh Hefner's party was the quintessential of Suck City. A lot of well-groomed people, sad under their skin, getting on a bus to be taken to his house. Tennis matches by celebrities were being egomaniacally played on his tennis courts to benefit the palsied. Arriving at the Hefner house for the palsy party, I felt pretty shaky myself. It was hot. My first breakfast confrontation with Jonny Cragmore didn't do much for my state of health. I got off the bus and wandered by the tennis courts. A brat of twenty years, with a face made out of flour, came up to me. He smiled his white dough smile.

"Hi," he said, "my name is Al. My mother runs this charity event. Have you seen all the celebrities?"

"No," I said. "I'm fainting in the heat. Do you think you could be kind enough to get me a glass of water, please?"

"Get you some water?"

Obviously, no one had ever asked this little boy to get anything in his life.

Hugh Hefner's pool and sauna is the ultimate in fagjock ecstasy. Mr. Hefner is too important to be enjoying it, he's missing from the party, but all the other guests were wandering around. Is that Buddy Hackett standing on a hill among the celebs?

"Hello, Mr. Hackett, I think you are a great comedian," I say to him.

He doesn't look at me. He's too busy checking out the young drumsticks walking around. Chicks fascinate him.

"I think so, too," he says. "I was in *Love Bug*, which was the biggest grosser in history."

"Oh yeah? How'd you like to play the comedian in my film, *Kill, Kill?*"

"I'd like to," says Hackett, still not looking at me, eyes looking beyond me. "But I'm probably too expensive. Only one place on earth can afford me."

"Oh, yeah? Whazzat?"

"That's the Sands. I operate only out of the Sands, but send me the script anyway."

He disappears into the bushes.

I approach the pool boy in the Sauna Jacuzzi Cave.

"Excuse me, but I'm from *Harper's Bazaar*. Do you think I could borrow some of the house bikinis?"

I borrowed a bunny bikini. The suit made me look fantastic. They are built up and built in and have gold clasps at the breasts.

I go to the warm pool. It's nice. At the pool Walter, a plastic surgeon, talks to me. His specialty is fixing breasts, noses, wrinkles. He opens breasts and puts them back together again in Suck City. His specialty is women who need desperately to be desirable. Walter is all heart. He offers to take me for lunch. Then he withdraws his offer. And there in the Jacuzzi, as we're undergoing water therapy, Walter opens his soul. He tells me he's outraged at the idea of the abortion laws and women not getting married. Kicking his fat white feet in Hefner's pool, he says to me, "Listen, don't you realize that women were given breasts for a reason? To have milk and babies? What else do women have breasts for?"

Walter, the surgeon, should know. His life comes from the knife. In Suck City the plastic surgeon is king. That's why Walter drives around in a huge white Bentley that looks as if it has had a nose job. He has fixed up more men and women and their children in Hollywood than most surgeons ever dream of. Suck City is a plastic surgeon's dream. And Walter, a demi-fag, is the dream doctor. Dear Walter, with his carving knife.

A strange creature, a loser, is staring at me. Richard Marks. Richard Marks comes over to talk to me.

"You look very sexy," he says in his Belgian accent, which he carefully grooms. "I love your red dress."

"That's cool," I say, looking at him.

He has green eyes, pockmarked skin. He takes out not one, but two cards. He presses them into my hand. One says "Richard Marks Productions." The other says "Santa Monica Playhouse, Richard Marks, Artistic Director." What the cards do not say is that Richard Marks is not producing and he no longer works at the playhouse. In fact, he's washed up. A has-been that never has been. Although all this is incidental.

Marks is also an actor, he admits. Am I an actress? No, I'm not. What am I? I'm a writer who's just made my own film. Acted in it? No, written, directed, and coproduced it. Then we have a lot in common. I wonder. He's not bad-looking. The clothes are tacky. And something is phony. Something? Everything.

"Look at me," says Marks.

I look at him.

"You are the perfect person to play Caroline in my next pornographic movie, *Ted and Caroline*."

"Oh, really? Well, I don't act," I say.

"Where do you live?"

"Right now, I'm staying at the Beverly Wilshire. But I'm going back to New York."

"Really? I come to New York often. Of course, as a producer one travels a lot."

I look at him. A thought goes through my mind. I have found the King of the Losers in Suck City. Richard Marks is a certified lunatic-fringe, unglued producer, director, actor. I decide to see him for fun and political reasons. I know he will call me. He would call anybody who's a half-baked anything to do with producing. The con game.

As soon as I get back to the Beverly Wilshire, Marks calls me and asks me to come to his house the next day for breakfast. I can't make it for breakfast but will try to come for a drink. After all that producer-director traveling around the world bullshit, I am not surprised to find that Marks lives in a Levittown ghetto in Santa Monica. It is as down and out as a white person gets in Suck City. The house is so ugly I decide to keep a cab waiting while I talk to Marks. Marks comes to the door and asks why the cab.

"I have to leave in an hour," I confess. "I'm going for dinner at Danny Kaye's."

"I'll take you," he says.

I pay the cabdriver and notice that Marks has a Cadillac in his garage. That's Suck City. Marks is obviously starving. But his Cadillac is like an iron lung without which he cannot breathe. The interior of the Marks house is beyond what I imagined. It is a small tomb with testimonials to Richard's life as an actor. There is a glossy photo of Richard Marks everywhere in the house. Everywhere.

Richard Marks drove me in his Cadillac to Sylvia and Danny Kaye's house. He is going to "direct a scene" at the Actors Studio and says he will pick me up after dinner.

Marks arrives after the Actors Studio and drives me to my hotel. He has a small suitcase with him. Like an overnight kit. Obviously he is planning to spend the night with me. When we enter my room, he immediately turns out the light. I was revolted but fascinated. Was his body so horrible it had to be covered by darkness? He opens up the kit and climbs into bed. I wonder if he is going to climb on top of me immediately. No. He did something else which fascinated me in a horrible sort of way. I lie and watch him. He turns on a side light next to the bed, and out of his kit he pulls a gadget that I had never seen before.

"Have you ever used a vibrator?" he asks.

"No," I say.

"Would you like to?"

"Listen," I say, "if I wanted to go to bed with two guys, you and Con Edison, I'd say so. Now you just got in my bed without finding out if it was mutual."

"I'm sorry," he says. "I didn't know I had to ask."

It was true. In Suck City men could find a suck so easily that it was like winning the Pulitzer Prize, the Nobel Prize, to get anyone called male to go to bed with you.

The vibrator begins whirring. Richard puts it on his head. I wonder if he really thought of passing off his dandruff as sperm. It was such an odd sight, this short man with dark hair naked in my bed with a vibrator.

"Please, Dick," I say, "you are a lovely guy, and I'm sure your film *Prison Babies* is very interesting, but I'm awfully tired and I'd like you to go home. I think I am just going to read a book and go to bed."

"What are you reading?" he asks, stalling for time.

"It's not important. But if you want to know, I'm reading Stendhal on love."

"I love Stendhal," he said pleadingly. "Can't I stay and read it with you?"

"That's sweet," I say, "but I like to read alone. It's the sort of activity that's better done by yourself. I'm awfully tired."

He went to the bathroom, leaving the vibrator behind in my bed. I get up and wait for him like a trained nurse. He comes out of the bathroom.

"All right," he says, "but if you can find a way through your guilt to change your mind, you have my cards, don't you? Actually, I'd love to go to bed with you and a young actress I know called Soulhaila. I like nothing better than to sleep with two women. Soulhaila is beautiful."

"Listen," I say. "You can't get me to go to bed with you. With your vibrator. Or with Soulhaila. If I wanted to go to bed with a woman, what would I need you for?"

"I'd like to enjoy watching you."

"Dick, dear," I say, "put your clothes on. We can talk in the morning. I'll call you. I promise."

"I hate to be alone," he says. "I have such bad memories in my little hours. Do you know what the name Dick Marks means to young actors and actresses? You have no idea what it's like to be a genius in this city and have only young people love you."

He sighs and dresses. As he is leaving, he takes something out of his overnight kit. It was a present. I felt touched. After all, how many guys ever gave me a present?

"What is it?" I ask shyly.

"A vibrator."

Well, a present was a present. The ultimate Hollywood gift. Your own vibrator. When he left, I waved to him as he went down the corridor. The leading loser of Suck City.

I wake up. Lights below from the plane.

And fall asleep again.

At Aida Gray's beauty parlor, I feel at home. Just as the poor man returns to his old barbershop for a shave and sympathy, for me, lost and lonely, although purposeful, the beauty parlor was the one place where I could relax, sit around, and chat in a woman's atmosphere. The man who set my hair was called Bo-Bo. He was a friend of Piper Laurie, he told me right away. He asks me about my film *Kill, Kill* and I tell him

I am raising money independently for it, and that is part of the reason I am in Suck City. I am hoping to see Al Bolinsky, Mr. Liberal Money Bags who has produced all the new radical films. Sitting under a dryer next to me was a woman whom Bo-Bo introduced me to. I couldn't tell if she was young or old. All I saw was a smiling face under a huge plastic bubble and long white fingernails being polished. Ava-Maria Whitney.

I was lonely in my dream. Now I was back at the Beverly Wilshire and sat in the sun at the swimming pool. Two young fags with perfect little figures were out looking around the pool. Lonely young guys waiting for parts in something. I sat next to a businessman making a call to his girl in New York. I listened aimlessly to his phone call.

"Hello, Rhonda? Hi, gorgeous. It's Steve here. Yeah, of course. Yeah. Do you miss me? I went out to dinner by myself last night. Chasen's cracked crab. Very overpriced. What bracelet? Well, I thought I'd wait about that until I got back. You really miss me? It's lonely without you, gorgeous. You know what? When you said you wanted to come with me, it took the wind right out of my sails. You know, sweetheart, I need my freedom. Yeah. Yeah. But now I appreciate you. I like you. Like is love. How's the kid? And the folks. . . ."

His voice droned on. Then he hung up. We were separated by a palm tree. He made another call.

"Hello, Sonny. How's the game going? Can I come over and play? Listen, you wanta hear something cute? I just spoke to Rhonda in New York. Remember her? Yeah. The broad I'm shacked up with. You know what? She actually thinks I'm going to marry her. She's an old bitch, and she thinks she can tie me down. Yeah. With the kid. Eight. Shit. She's old and ugly. I dunno why I even bother with her. Necessity is the mother of invention. Anyway, it's a mistake, and I'm not even gonna call her again. Yeah. I moved my stuff out before I left. So how's the game? Any broads? Really? Young? No varicose veins on their legs? I'll be over in a little while. I'm just stretching out for a snooze."

In my dream I sat in my plastic chair sunning and listening. My rage and pus came back again. I thought, *Your time will come*. Just then I was paged over the telephone.

"Lulu Cartwright, paging a Miss Lulu Cartwright," said the voice.

I went to the phone. It was Ava-Maria Whitney. She had entered my dreams before. She swaddled, in her mind and body, all the emotional conflicts of aging women, their rage, their boredom, their struggle to achieve womanhood each day, to achieve love, sex and fulfillment against the backdrop of a young world. Hollywood. Youth City. Young Golden Calf world. Zoo of possible and impossible beasts. Baby peacocks, apes, and camels. False tits, false lashes, sutured hair. No love anywhere. Suck City. Young fatcalf city of mirrors and no miracles. Desert of loss, cheerleaders out on the street with trim asses and blond hair praising jockfag youth. Suck City. Where getting old is the only sin. Where age is worse than death.

Ava-Maria Whitney is talking so fast on the phone I can hardly keep up with her.

"Bo-Bo at Aida Gray's, golden boy that he is, told me that you're looking for investors, and I thought that maybe I could work with you," she says.

I ask her to come over to the hotel pool and we can talk.

Ava-Maria is glamorous in a 1930s way. She still wears all the jewelry fashionable in Hollywood in the Rin Tin Tin, Cecil B. DeMille, King Kong, Dracula, Frankenstein days. The old beasts of yore. She is aging and desperate. Her husband, in the real estate business, leaves her alone.

Ava comes and meets me at the pool. She is in her late fifties. Bored. No longer rich. Still pretty.

"I'm no longer working for charities. I've done that all my life. I've decided"—giggle—"to work for myself. If I make any money now, it's going to be for me. If I raise money for your film, what do I get out of it—giggle?"

Ava. The original paper doll. She has had two husbands she has called her own. With the first guy she has had two children. Now grown up. With the second guy she had found security. Now he was always busy. And she was bored. She wants "some action."

But the point, dear Ava, is that I like you. I'd love to work with you. I can see that you know your way around Suck City, and I've been looking for someone to work with me and lead me from one maniac to another.

"I'll give you ten percent of anything we raise. A finder's fee," I say. "But don't get your hopes up. This is a city of con men and women. In Suck City the biggest sucker is king. Or queen."

With Ava-Maria Whitney, once the curly-haired daughter of a movie circuit owner, Ava, who had sat on the lap of Clark Gable in her father's circuit, I begin driving around Suck City. Up one street and down another. Here we meet judges and lawyers. Here we meet the head of Palatrix Independent Films. All the men are rude. Here we meet Faoud of Cinamobile. Abu Faoud, Egyptian extra, discovered in *Cleopatra,* brought to America, student of photography, hustling photographer on *I Spy*, who got the idea to put equipment on a bus, thus revolutionizing the film industry. Sued by unions, defended by legal staff of Globe, imitated. Mafia breaks up competition. He buys Rolls-Royce. He sells Cinamobile to Taft Corporation for five million, now screws anyone he wants. Handles business of large corporations such as Fox and Warner's. Efficiency, action films. Whore, still the Alexandrian poor beggar boy, now in Rolls-Royce, Suck City kind. Wife from Vienna who leaves him. Screws chorus girls, topless bottomless life. Rolls-Royce, TV business, Warner's, Fox everything on clockwork. Nine million to invest in action films, kung fu world. Small little King Faoud in Suck City. He refuses to invest.

Later I drive with Ava-Maria Whitney to Warner Brothers, through jungles of blond hair, the false eyelash garden, meet movie moguls, meet Mr. Rich in independent offices filled with posters of successes. Meet animators. Patty DeFreelings. Meet the Sufis, owners of Independrix Productions; meet Screen Gems moguls, meet Mirisch Corporation sons-in-law, meet impotent castrated white witches' sons, black men in King Tut suits and white witches in Wild West outfits, cowboys of the meridian behind desert desks, crawling out of Twentieth Century-Fox. Warner Sisters. Screen Phlegms. United Fartists. I drive all over Suck City with Ava in her Mercedes Benz.

While we are trying to raise money, we talk about dead heroines. About Marilyn Monroe.

"Some who had known her well said her eyes were green. Others said that they were brown."

We drive around in Dead Marilyn City. We meet Bonny, kept by top agent. Meet blind date Bill, the photographer, once hairdresser, now looking for bankroll to make indy film. Meet drunken Jim, the lawyer liar. Meet Dick, the vibration zombie. Meet facocktadocta writer Jonny Cragmore. Meet lonely champions from Hell's Eden. Meet health food nuts eating honey. Lonely, I laugh and laugh. I enjoy being with Ava. But we can't raise money because no one in Suck City has money, and if they do have money, they don't want to put it into a feminist film.

They don't want to invest in the last laugh of the future.

I try to leave Suck City. I am coming to the end of my dream-glue. I have to leave. The pus is getting to me more than I can bear. But I have to see Al Bolinsky. I call him.

Al Bolinsky. HALL A LUYA. BO LIN SKY AL BOLINSKY. HA HA LA LUYAH.

Hal lulu ya. Hal a lulu yah. Lulu. Hal a lue ya.

Calling Bolinsky is like calling De Lord. De Lord of Suck City city titty. King of the Tits. Wasn't it Al Bolinsky who sold his business to Exxon for a hundred million dollars? Cash? Who put his money into McCarthy? And Tom Bradley's campaign? Who understood Watts? And watts his name—McGovern? Who backed McGovern? Whose ex-wife backed Shirley Chisholm, my candidate? Whose money it was rumored was available for causes and who, according to the testament of Nelson Rising, would be the perfect person to invest in the first feature feminist film? Al Bo lin sky. I called De Lawd.

Suck City was getting on my nerves. It was a city of bullshit and cowshit, and I felt there was so much ass to kick I was just making a small dent. It was at this point (about to leave point) that I reach Al Bolinsky's secretary. (You have to understand that in Suck City to get "through" to a man, you have to go through his *Doppelgänger*, his "secretary.") I spoke to Bolinsky's "girl," and she said, "Just a minute, I'll connect you with Mr. Bolinsky. If you hang up, he will call you right back."

I hung up. He called me from his car. He was en route to his plane.

"What a groove to be constantly available."

Bolinsky laughed. I could hear his laugh coming through the ether waves that separated him from my room in the hotel and his leather seat.

"Listen, I want to see you about possibly investing in the first feminist feature film," I say. "It's called *Kill, Kill,* and it's about a woman who doesn't go mad, she goes sane. It's about a woman turning against society instead of turning against herself."

Suddenly, out of nowhere, I remembered what it was like to be a child, to talk through cups with strings on them, to laugh at talking at a distance, to be joyful in playing games. I remember long hair and old clothes and laughing. I used to go out with my girlfriend on my grandfather's farm in Goshen, New York, and we would ride horses and play the telephone game. Now it was his car to my room. This was no game. I was trying to get Bolinsky to finance me to kick ass.

My film was about the cruelty of the American society which leaves girl children to find themselves, with courage, in a system that has no place for their courage and, in fact, punishes them if they have it. Bolinsky tells me he will be back in town the following week and I could meet him at one o'clock at a screening. He was screening a documentary on South Africa and apartheid. I can meet him there and he will speak with me. I feel as if the Lord of Suck City has spoken. Anyway, anyone who runs Presidential campaigns and mayoralty campaigns is powerful. I thank him and hang up.

That means hanging out in Suck City for a few more days. I decide to call up a guy I had known in New York City, an actor called Sherwood Sydel. I heard he was directing the free Shakespeare project. That's wonderful, I think. Free Shakespeare in Suck City.

Sydel comes over to the hotel. In the fifteen years I hadn't seen him he had become even more arrogant and alcoholic than I remembered him to be. His eyes are red, and he has a huge potbelly. He is still a Napoleonic little man; only now he is obviously on the balls of his ass. He is late. When he arrives, he goes immediately to the telephone in my room and starts making "important" phone calls. He asks somewhat impatiently if I will order him a drink. Of course, what did he want? He wanted a double martini. I order it and a drink for myself. When the drinks arrive, he picks up the martini as if he badly needs it.

"What are you doing at the Beverly Wilshire?" he asks. "You are a writer."

"Where am I supposed to stay, at the YWCA?"

I loved these noble niggers who made being a nigger such a wonderful experience. These phony artists who made staying at a broken-down joint the necessity of being talented.

"Are you rich?" he asks me.

Obviously he thinks I am a poor schlep in New York.

"No. But I'm not broke either."

"What are you doing in Los Angeles?"

"I'm confronting the media. I'm here for political purposes."

I want to tell him that I have just directed a film, but I knew it would kill him. He had come to Hollywood fifteen years earlier to direct films, and like Dick Marks, his main claim to fame is directing starving actresses at scene classes. He is really talented, too.

"Do you remember the last time I saw you in New York?" he asks arrogantly.

Actually, I did remember that I had spent an evening with him.

Suddenly he becomes very belligerent.

"Why is it rich people like you are always raising money?" he asks.

"Listen, Mr. Sydel, I think you'd better leave."

"I will," he says, finishing his drink.

And so he leaves. The free Shakespeare director in Suck City. But he comes back. He has forgotten his nasal spray, which he had left in the bathroom. He sprays his nose.

"Do you remember that we fucked?" he asks.

It was fifteen years ago. I didn't remember. I only remember that he helped me park my car.

"No, I don't," I say.

He begins stamping his feet like Rumpelstiltskin. I wonder if he is psychotic and if I will be called upon to practice my karate to get him out of the room.

"I'm a black belt in karate," I say quietly. "I wouldn't try getting violent."

He sees that I mean it and takes his nasal spray and leaves. I had had enough of these guys and their props. One guy has a vibrator. Another guy has a nasal spray. Well, I suppose these were the weapons of Suck City.

I sit down and read the publicity material for Harrison and Tyler. They are the only two women stand-up comedians in the world. I want to talk with them about kicking ass. What a relief it is to see them. We exchange stories leading to the discovery of our inner selves. They tell me about how they had dressed up in little cheerleader dresses and gotten the U.S. to send them on a USIA tour in Vietnam. And how they had surprised the Army by appearing in fatigues and making deliberate slams on the U.S. Army. They had their car blown up and barely escaped with their lives. They told me how they had gone out on the football field during a huge Los Angeles Rams game and protested that they wanted to play too, protesting against the jockocracy. They were Supercomics. And troublemakers.

Meeting Bolinsky in a dark screening room was meeting De Lawd as he made his decisions. Who shall live, who shall die, who shall get money, what shall not. We were watching the documentary about apartheid in South Africa. Ava-Maria Whitney had come with me. The documentary was unbearably truthful. It showed how the "colored" in South Africa were treated in the apartheid system. I began weeping during a part of it. It was as cruel as anything in Nazi Germany. It showed how black men worked on chain gangs. Women were forcibly separated from their husbands. School conditions. And all the humiliations of being in a racist land. The lights went on.

Bolinsky, short, black hair, deeply suntanned, black glasses, white shorts, sat there. Two black people were in the audience, one a young man with an Oxford accent. In the back of the theater sat a cool-looking woman in a white African smock. She had long fingers, very white skin, long black hair. The black man begins speaking about the film. Then the woman speaks. They are extremely articulate. The film must be seen. I realize that this is a fund-raising pitch, but rarely have I seen a documentary so worthy of the money. The pitch ends with a request for ten thousand dollars. Bolinsky speaks quickly. He will have to think about it, and he will let them know.

There is a feeling of arrogance that Bolinsky projects even in the screening room. Remember the sign that Harry Truman was supposed to have kept on his desk: "The Buck Ends Here." Only, with Bolinsky, it is "The Buck Starts Here." Bolinsky is a kind of Daddy Warbucks living in Palm Springs and Hollywood. He is the only person, the only person, in Suck City who invests money in "cause movies" or "cause candidates" or cause anything. He is Santa Cause. I look carefully at Bolinsky. He looks like some kind of dried power monger; an ad from the *Los Angeles Times* comes to mind: "Dry your own flowers and have floral beauty in your home the year round."

One could say this about Bolinsky. He has been a powerful, dynamic man who has somehow managed to be wrapped in tape, dumped in formaldehyde. But he was still living. A dried power pasha walking around with dead black power shades, sneakers, white ducks. Dead power, the stench of his money still coming out of his pockets, his shoes, his nose.

He invites me and Ava (giggling) to a restaurant near the screening room. It is the Sandwich Box. On the walls are photographs of Marilyn Monroe, Burt Lancaster, Kirk Douglas. The one of MM is just above our table. I explain to Al briefly about my film. He is bored out of his mind. I am probably the two-thousandth person who has come to him with a project that week. But he listens. In his dry-flowered, dry-powered way. Power is arrogance. But he has the intelligence to surround himself with smart people. But Bolinsky is, like many men in power, a dangler. I had the strong feeling that through his conglomerate ownership of theaters, he is dangling a hundred people a day with "possible" backing. I knew, as I drank my tea at the Sandwich Box, that feminism was the last thing in the world Bolinsky is interested in. You didn't need to read tea leaves to get that one.

Lunch is over, and we say farewell. Bolinsky gets into his understated Toyota and drives away. I have the feeling I will never see him again. I didn't want to. If there is any financing from Bolinsky, it will be to finance some jockfag. Women are not part of his cause. Even in the movies he has produced, women were backseat niggers, and likewise in the political campaigns, where they always made coffee, not policy. Like many big shots in all the movements, they can't cope with feminism because it is one movement where they can't fuck their secretary because they'd be fucking revolution. But most of all, they can't take charge. So it is in their interest to turn this movement down and blot this sexism thing out. No one wanted to finance something he or she couldn't control. It was too radical.

I am reading for the tenth time Virginia Woolf's *Mrs. Dalloway*, the story of a woman tortured beyond endurance by the lack of compassion in the world.

The dream is coming to an end. I hear a knock on my door. It is definitely the knock of an arrogant, although unhappy, fist. I put on my bathrobe and open the door. Bolinsky is standing there. He is still wearing his dark glasses so that you couldn't see his eyes. I suppose that like Homer, he is blind, his eyes scratched out, in order to have them scratched in again, his eyesight traded for insight.

But that isn't true. He is just a creep wearing glasses.

"Come in," I say. "Would you like a drink?"

Bolinsky looks so fastidious in his white outfit that he seems almost inhuman, as if something like "a drink" were beyond him.

"Yes, thank you, I would. I'd like a double scotch."

We drink the same drink, I observe to myself, and pick up the house phone.

"Would you please be kind enough to send two double scotches to room 725," I say. "Thank you."

Almost immediately the drinks arrive. Bolinsky pays the waiter before I can sign the bill. At least this is a first. He is the first guy to pick up a check in my room in Suck City. Suddenly, I decide that Bolinsky looks like a skinny Farouk. I compare him in my mind to that old slob King Farouk, who had dominated the newspaper headlines when I was a girl. Bolinsky reminds me of the king with gold faucets. What a drip.

"What do you want?" I ask him.

"I'm willing to offer you five thousand dollars to get the hell out of Los Angeles," he says quietly. "You could have seed money for your film about incipient female violence and leave us all alone."

I wonder as he is speaking if he has heard about my starting to stir up trouble with the newly organized black women's movement. They are fed up with Bradley, and his use of black is beautiful in his campaign. But only male black is beautiful. He is accused by many black women of being Bolinsky's Charlie McCarthy. Bolinsky is the Edgar Bergen, who pulls the strings and Bradley speaks. But woman, where was she? Where are the black women in Bradley's administration? Obviously Bolinsky knows I am creating more trouble than people thought in Los Angeles. I wasn't there just to raise money for an independent film.

That was my cover, and he knew it. He looked at me coolly. Ten thousand? For a moment, I think of all the trouble I can make with ten thousand dollars. Wouldn't it be fun to have an office at the Pan Am Building along with my lawyers, Botein, Harp, Sklar and Seapines, and the Joseph Kennedy Estate? Wouldn't it be great? What does Bolinsky know? Women are no longer a joke. The Female Comedy is over. This is for real. How does he catch on that it isn't just a bunch of old dykes or neurotic gals or female hippies or crazy nigger ladies getting together? That the patriarchy, held up as it was by the Bolinskys, the Bradleys, the Nixons and McGoverns and Robert Lowells and Eugene McCarthys and Charlie McCarthys and Wilbur Millses, and primal scream guys and psychologists, psychiatrists, podiatrists, pediatricians, proctologists—especially by the political proctologists—was over. With his sixth sense Bolinsky senses that the power structure is about to change.

"I'd love to take your money," I say, sipping my scotch, "but I'll take it another way. If you're really making me an offer, I'll take my ten thousand to those courageous people making a film on apartheid. As you may have guessed by now, I'm not Little Lulu, looking to make an art film."

He looks at me. "I guessed that."

"Then you know who I am?"

"I do. I've often thought of killing you," he says.

Bolinsky, like many other men in power, was excited by the very idea that he could rub people out. But it was going to be the other way around this time. Bolinsky unbuttoned his shirt, took off his pants. I watch him. He thinks we should seal our promise with a kiss. He is fairly well built and wears white fishnet bikini underwear. I throw my hand out and give him a karate chop, just a light one, across his neck so that he passes out. I leave him lying in his fishnet bikini on the bed of the Beverly Wilshire.

I clean out his pants pockets, finding twenty cents in odd change that he happens to be carrying with him. I look at him. He is still wearing his black glasses. His skin is very tanned. So this is the richest liberal on earth. I try not to make noise as I take out my Polaroid and take a picture of him. I'll send it to him next Valentine's Day. Nothing excites a man like Bolinsky more than a picture of himself.

"See you later," I say.

But it is just a fantasy. A late-at-night fantasy. Bolinsky isn't there and couldn't care less about my film or about feminism or about me. Raising money for a nonsexist film in jockfag corporate, fascist Suck City is like raising a Hadassah scholarship at a Bundist meeting. I had kicked enough ass in Suck City. I decide to leave.

I wake up. Anxieties remain.

lulu in hollywood

all that glitters is not gold, joan
all that glints is not armor
all that whispers is not

Rough Joan all that glistens
is not all that shouts

—JOHN RODGERS

Hello there! Hi! How ya doing! With a wink and whistle. The new boss. New-style exec. Oops. Here I am. The human buffer. The human token.

Hi! The boss. The Amazon who used to be Little Lulu. The new-style. Ah. The delightful strategy of being first. Hello there! HIYADOIN? How lovely to descend from the airplane and go right straight bonkers into the world of former promiscuity and deals—into the wacky and wormy world of hooligans

223

and con men, the world of semiliterates and illiterates. Little Suck City world of propaganda and popaganda. Dear Lord, I am going to be a boss of the movie world. How is that possible? Never mind. By accident. By work. By fortune. By history. By need. By bankruptcy. By sheer nature pattycaking the planet I am here. Hello there! Hi there!

AND NOW HERE'S LOOOOOOOOOOOOOOOLU.

Just before I got off the plane, I went over in my mind several of the questions that I would be confronting at the studio. I was sitting with my briefcase evaluating the company. I had looked over the financial statements. I had discarded unacceptable performances based on relationships within the income statement and balance sheet. I had looked over the new films planning to be made. I made some memos on the accountants' report. The net income for the year, the dividends on preferred stock. All this took my attention. Most of all, I planned the new projects.

Then I decided on the strategy for my personality.

It was not going to be too strong. Not too weak. Not too cupcake. Not too businesslike. Not too demanding. Not too innocent. Not too funny. Not too serious. A little bit of all of them. I'd remembered the button I once wore: "By any means necessary." I planned to use all the means available. And so I descended into what promised to be either hell or purgatory. Or maybe heaven. The powerland where I would make decisions. And set trends. My new life.

I got off the plane. OOOOPPS. Don't trip, you klutz. Stride. Smile. Hi! I remember I was wearing my simple power costume. Gray pant suit. Sneakers. Vuitton bag. Hair long. I had lost weight, and I looked good. Dark-rimmed glasses. Natural makeup. No one noticed me at first. I felt like a cosmonaut. I was going to shake hands with all Beverly Hills. Memo to Lulu Cartwright: Don't be nervous. Keep cool. What they don't know that you don't know doesn't hurt them. Hi there! Hi-dee-hi. Hi-dee-ho. Hello!

Immediately reporters spotted me. I spoke with the press.

"Miss Cartwright, how does it feel to be the first woman to take over a large studio?"

I answered quickly. "I really don't see the difference between being the head of the studio or being the head of a household. Most women have varied jobs that require them to be a combination executive, whore, hostess, mechanic, production manager, director, accountant, public relations expert, and planner. I can't see that running a company is any different. Maybe the words are changed. But one of the reasons a woman's probably never run one of the studios is that no one wants the word to get out how easy it is."

"How old are you?"

"I'm thirty-eight."

"Do you think you will like your new job?"

"I enjoy being a social critic. I think a certain influence over people's fantasy will enable me to make a small contribution to our society. I feel that I have an individual responsibility to shake up the status quo and deliver a different kind of media product to the public. Do not forget that films are seen by young people. These people must have a need to see themselves reflected, not as morons, but as more responsible citizens. The women who patronize films do not want to identify only with whores or drunks or flops. They want to see themselves portrayed for a change as winners. I think I have something to say to other women, who, in my opinion, are an oppressed class. I want to see women integrated into the working force of the industry. I am interested in political films. I am interested in seeing poetry in films. We *hear* as well as see films. I think that a lot of the pain that we have felt as Americans has been swept under the carpet. I want to look at that pain. Even if I look at it through comedy. I intend to effect internal and external change in this industry."

They took notes. They looked at me as if I were a nut. A genius. A bombshell. A female comedian. A pioneer.

"How do you feel about the press saying Little Lulu takes over Hollywood?"

I was walking quickly now. Toward the airport.

"I don't care whether they compare me to Karl or Groucho Marx. I don't care what anyone says. As long as they spell my name right on the check at the studio."

"What new kind of films are you going to make?"

"They will be announced project by project. But you can be sure they are not going to be about Blondie."

"Are you really going to dump the star system?"

"No. Just change it."

"What do you plan to get rid of first?"

"Metaphysical cannibalism."

"Could you explain that to the press?"

"It means that films about the joy of loserism are out. It's about time we had different fantasies to offer people."

"Do you consider yourself an average woman?"

"I don't have time to consider myself. But I can tell you that there is no point in women trying to mimic men or blacks trying to mimic whites. Also I am not in favor of discretion or realism."

"What does that mean?"

"I'm interested in the poetry of politics. In the imagination. In the feel of people as well as the look of people. Everyone worries about cancer and botulism and Pentagonareah. But nobody realizes that our greatest force in America is IMAGINATION. FREEDOM TO CREATE. That is what makes our society greater than other societies. I intend to bring that imaginative force to the industry of films. Which means, of course, a shake-up."

They followed.

"Thank you," I said.

I disappeared into the ladies' room. I had to pee. Then I arranged my hair. Checked on my false eyelashes. And walked swiftly to the entrance where Mr. Jacobs, an official from the studio, whom I had met in New York, was waiting by the limousine. He was one of the good gypsies of the Hollywood world-without-end industry, having floated around from one job to another. Nobody quite knew what to do with him, so understandably he had been sent to greet and meet me. I'm glad they weren't playing plantation. With a bunch of bowing people at the airport. My instructions had said definitely I did not want anyone at the airport. I guess they didn't consider poor Jacobs anybody. I intended to put him on my staff.

In the car I mumbled to Jacobs, "I intend making a few changes. I think the biggest one of all will be to scratch all films about women and love. If women were free, would they need love? Hollywood love."

Jacobs didn't quite know how to answer.

"If we were free, would we need *love?*" he repeated. It struck him like a gong.

"Did you know I intend to put a lot of old people on my staff?" I asked Jacobs.

We were speeding down the endless Hollywood-Los Angeles-Nonfreeway. Bumper to bumper. The Harbor Freeway.

"Really?" he asked. He was lighting a cigar.

"Of course. The whole concept of people being senior citizens is a bunch of propaganda. The concept of youth and strength and age and weakness is going to be thrown out the plate-glass window. I want to put a lot of the golden oldies on my staff. Only I don't want them called senior citizens. I want them to be referred to as newcomers. I'm not interested in picking the brains of people without experience. Older people have more energy, more guts, more fun, more under-standing. They are closer to death, you understand, and so they have less to lose by being safe. I don't want anyone on my staff who can't afford to be fired. That way I won't be surrounded by a bunch of yes-people and gofers. If people have families to support, they can work elsewhere. I want to hire artists, political revolutionaries, kids, and older experienced people with some knowledge of life. I don't want anyone on my staff with responsibilities. Get me a list of retired geniuses. I'm taking them out of mothballs. And the older, the better."

Jacobs listened. He made notes.

"Also," I said, "I'm calling a meeting in the morning of some technological experts. I'm investigating a new process where satellites can be useful in the creation of product. The high cost of films is ridiculous. The whole world has changed. But Hollywood hasn't changed with it. From a hardware product point of view. The whole world is talking Fortran while Hollywood is talking cobalt."

"Mmm. Wazzat?" he said.

"Just the names. The names of computer languages. I see no reason why films of the future do not make use of the development in technology. I have some gentlemen from the Space Center in Houston arriving in Los Angeles tomorrow to give us some pointers in the technological developments."

"That will cost money, too," Jacobs said.

"Not in the long run. And the long run counts.

"*And*," I said. I paused. "I'm calling a meeting of the unions tomorrow at my office. The fact that black people and women are not in the unions will be changed. Or I won't make union films. It's as simple as that. It's called the testicular approach. Getting them in the testicles. That's the approach I intend to use at all times."

The car swerved. Jacobs repeated after me as if he were reciting from the only book of poetry he probably knew— *The Prophet*.

"The testicular approach. Mmmmmm." He undid his tie. "What a girl," he said to me.

"Not girl. We don't like to be referred to as girl. Or gal. It's absurd. Like being known as someone's wife. Woman if you don't mind."

"Woman," he corrected himself.

"It's like the Israelis. They don't like to be called little kikes. It's the same principle."

The car was now out of the traffic jam. It was damp and hot, and Jacobs was sweating. He was about to faint. From the heat. Or me. I wasn't sure.

"Mr. Jacobs."

"Yes?"

"You know that I am planning a lot of changes. And I'd like you to be a member of the staff."

"Thank you," he said.

"The main thing is that the studio hired me because they want things done in a new way. They want the new style. That's why they went into bankruptcy. Because they had the old style. They think the new style is going to get them more of an audience. Which, after all, is what filmmaking is all about. Audience. It's no good making Laura of Arabia if no one comes to see it. Now they think they've picked out a new-style head in having me named, and I'm giving them their money's worth. They want change. They want the studio turned around. And I want the money. It's going to be a new-style studio. The first."

Jacobs asked, with a wonderkid look, what I meant by NEW STYLE.

"Okay," I said. "Old style was making films by formulas. Following trends. New style is making trends. Old style was politics didn't sell. New style is that everything is political. Old style was art is for the very few, trash is for the masses. Make it easy. That's all wrong. Old style was closed unions. New style is everybody gets in on the action. Old style was entertainment. New style is exciting futurism. Old style was separating genres. Animation. Porno. Musicals. Action. New style is everything at once. And jazz like that."

The car pulled up to the Beverly Wilshire. I bounded out in my sneakers.

"So long," I said to Jacobs. "See you in the morning. I would appreciate having the limo here for me at six thirty. That way I can get an early start."

Jacobs looked at me from behind the window of the car. He looked like a happy man. Cemented in the car. All he knew, all he cared about, was that he was going to keep his job. Maybe even have a job that would be fun. He waved at me. Made a V for victory sign with his hand. The limo pulled away. It was probably going to take him to a turkish bath where he could sweat out our conversation.

The desk clerk didn't recognize me. This was good. I asked for my key. The studio had reserved the presidential suite for me.

"Look," I said nicely to the room clerk. "This may come as a surprise to the Beverly Wilshire, but it doesn't interest me to sleep on a bed where Nixon has sneezed or Gerald Ford has had a sleepless night. Do you have anything more appropriate?"

"The bridal suite?" he asked overpolitely.

"I'll take a small room by the pool, please," I said.

He gave me the first room by the pool. I took my key and went to my room. Since I didn't have any luggage, I didn't have to go through the checking-in ceremony.

I sat on the bed. Picked up the phone. Asked for a wake-up call at five thirty and prepared to go to sleep. I browsed through my reading. Then I made a list of skills I was going to need for the next day.

Humor.

A professional sense of security.

A smile.

A wink.

A handshake.

An even-timbred voice.

I knew that the studio needed the kind of personality that spelled profit. Words came into my mind: The word "profit." Then "prophet." Then "pro." Then "fit." I went to bed dreaming of nothing.

The next morning I woke and did my routine exercises. I had coffee and grapefruit juice sent to my room. I looked at the papers in my briefcase. Read the *Los Angeles Times*, *New York Times*, the *Washington Post*, and *Variety*. I had arranged for these papers to be sent to my room every morning. Then I got dressed. As I put on my sneakers, I looked out at the pool. I had time for a quick swim. I got my bikini out of my briefcase. All alone at the pool. I dived in. Hello, little world of film companies. Price. Cost. Current income. Annual income. Current yield. New project. Hi! Memo to Lulu Cartwright: This is fun.

The well-oiled machinery of my new job was in motion. Jacobs was waiting for me outside the hotel. We got in the limo and got to the studio just as it opened. Jacobs took me to the part of the floor that was my office. Outside my office there was a place for the executive secretary. And the assistant secretary. My office was more or less what I expected. It was a large white room with plate-glass windows. I had asked to have it painted white and to have all the furniture outside of a desk and couch removed. No pictures on the wall. They had followed my instructions. It was a nice white empty room. Unfortunately, the trademark of the studios was in my room. Fresh fruit. And nuts. But nothing else. The nutcracker was an obscene object—a pair of wooden woman's legs. It might have been funny. It was funny. I asked Jacobs if he wanted the routine fruit and nuts for his office. He did. He took them away. I sat down at the desk. Took some of the papers out of my desk. Looked at the telephones. Looked at the intercom. I then made some notes. Took a few scripts that I had with me out of my briefcase.

At nine o'clock my staff arrived. They were on time. I was the new boss, and they were determined not to be fired. I had some laying on of palms to do. My secretary was, as I expected, a woman. She came into my office and introduced herself to me. She told me her name was Mrs. Dubrow.

I asked her, "What is your first name?"

Mrs. Dubrow looked at me as if she had just been accused of robbery. Apparently she had no first name. Or it had never been used. She was always Mrs. Dubrow. I wondered who Mr. Dubrow was and what he was up to that morning.

Finally she got it out. "Kate."

"Thank you for seeing that everything was arranged exactly as I asked it to be, Kate. Please call me Lulu. Now, Kate, let's just have an informal chat."

"Shoot," she said.

Kate sat down in front of my desk and started taking notes.

"No more notes," I said to Kate. I seemed to have wounded her feelings.

"It's like this. I like to dictate letters and memos into a little recorder that I have here."

I showed it to her.

"Very well."

"And afterward you can have your assistant just type up whatever I need. That way we can talk with each other, and it will save a lot of time."

"Very good," she said.

She decided to enjoy the idea of not taking notes.

"I assume the entire staff is here?" I said.

"That's correct."

"Very well. I'll meet everyone slowly. I'm sure they are all

232

curious to see what I am going to do, so I'm going to get busy doing it right away."

"Very good."

"The first thing is my appointments for the day. Let's go over them. This morning I will be receiving some gentlemen from the unions. Please send them in to me. Then I will be receiving some gentlemen from the Space Center in Houston. They will be my consultants for new technology. Then I will be receiving two women from Wall Street who will be working in the next office."

"What will they be doing?" she asked more out of curiosity than routine.

"Well, Kate, I've decided to hire a new staff. I'm going to get rid of the former employees of the studio. They have already received their notices and checks, and I'm bringing in my own people. You will not be surprised to see that they are mostly experts in their fields, and they are all people I am sure you will enjoy working with, Kate."

"Do we have room for them on this floor?"

"Yes. My strategy is to keep a few of the old guard but hire some new people also and bring in my own staff. I'm sure that my own people have arrived. To begin with, as I mentioned, I will have two women next door who are from Wall Street and whom I have great confidence in. Anne Small and Dolores Wrightsman. Anne and Dolores are both stockbrokers from Payne Webber and Hackson. They have a different approach to film investment, and they will advise me on everything that is financial. You might say that they are both wizards who are very knowledgeable about stocks, bonds, investment companies, insurance, banking services, and many other subjects. Both of them will work closely with me."

"Very good."

"I have also asked out a friend of mine called Elizabeth Reese. Liz is not only an expert on money, but a genius on the question of distribution."

"I look forward to meeting her."

"Then I have two specialists on technology who will work along with the three gentlemen who will be arriving here shortly. These people are all experts on satellite communications and media, as well as knowledgeable in the area of home entertainment and video tapes. It is a known fact that many movies will be seen directly in the home, and this is a new area where the studio has been sadly lacking. This kind of distribution will bring our product right into everyone's living room. It requires a different kind of expertise. To begin with, it's not just American living rooms that we are after. We are after aiming our product at the living rooms of the world. The huts of the world without living rooms are also up for grabs. Through satellite communications and cooperation with Fairchild and Western Union, I plan to make the company a pioneer in the field of home entertainment films, besides films which will be beamed cheaply and effectively to every single corner of the earth via satellite communication. We will be using a domestic satellite communications system and a more sophisticated kind of equipment. My staff will inform you of how we shall be making these changes."

"Very well," she said.

"Also, Kate, I intend to make experiments. That is to say, I won't be needing the usual story conferences because many of the new films that I am planning for the next five years won't have what you normally call stories. I intend to do away with the ridiculous expense of buying properties from most agencies."

She seemed shocked.

"What do you mean?" she asked.

"I'm just not interested in making films out of best-sellers and musical comedies per se. We will only commission and make original films. I know that the old-style way of making films is to film anything that is a best-seller because it comes with a built-in audience. If a book is well known or people can whistle the tune of a Broadway show, that is a surefire test which gives us a presold product. But I intend to let the other studios spend their millions of dollars on buying properties. We will not buy a single property as long as I am head of the studio."

"What kind of films will you make—I mean, what will you make them from?"

"Kate, I've been hired as a creative director," I said. "And I'm going to create. I will have a team of some of the best novelists and investigative reporters that are going to work together. And I'll have a special women's division that will make up for the gap in women-oriented films. About ten new people will be out here working together on new projects."

Kate didn't say anything. For a moment I thought she had lost her dentures. Then very quietly, she said, "Is that for real? Do you mean it?"

I looked at Kate.

"Of course I mean it. We want the studio to make money, don't we? We know from *Variety* and from the Harris Poll and from all the researchers that women are the biggest ticket buyers to films all over the world. Films appeal to the leisure class. And since most women can't get or don't want decent jobs, they go to the movies. They sit there in the dark and dream. So we will give them something to really dream about."

Kate looked at me. "What are you doing for the kids? Are you going to change the concept of films for children?"

"But of course," I said.

The first day passed quickly. What with one conference and another. That night, as I lay on my bed at the Beverly Wilshire, utterly exhausted, I thought of lots of things. First I called New York to talk to my son.

David was in his room. Emma answered the phone.

"My goodness," she said. "Missus, you are everywhere."

"How is David?" I asked.

"He's playing in his room. He's typing letters. He wants to go to California, missus."

"That's what I'm calling about, Emma. I've decided not to fly back to New York. There's too much to do here. I'm going to arrange for you and David to fly out here. Itzi will do all the arranging of tickets. My mother's coming with you, and Missy, too. I'm going to try and bring Martin out here for a few weeks."

"The whole company."

Emma laughed.

"I'm afraid I'll get homesick."

"For what?"

"Well, they don't have an Easter Parade in California, do they, missus?"

"You can create one, Emma. How's New York?"

"Missus, you're on the cover of *Newsweek* and *Time* magazine. The things they say about you. My picture is in *Newsweek,* too. I'm sending it to Europe. I'll get David."

I heard her cover the phone. "David, Mommy on the phone."

"Hi, Mom."

"Hi, pal."

"Momma, when are we coming to California?"

"Can you leave in three days?"

"Pack all my things?"

"Itzi will help Emma put everything in a warehouse. Just keep everything you really want. Pick out the books you love and the toys you want to take with you. And keep out anything you really love."

"What about my goldfish?"

"Keep the goldfish. You can take it on the plane in a cup with holes."

"Mom."

"Yes, sweetheart?"

"Mom, will I meet anyone out there I can play with?"

"Of course. You're going to go to school in the fall. And I'm going to find out if there's a day camp here. Like the Chevaliers. Where you play hockey and basketball and stuff like that."

"Can we go swimming?"

"Special treat. I'll find us an apartment at the beach. And we can stay there for a couple of weeks."

"Yippee. And run on the beach? And snorkel? What will my room be like?"

"A surprise."

"Momma. I miss you. It's hot here. I've been going to movies with Jacquie, and Grandma is here."

"All right, sweetheart. I'll see you very soon. Kisses. Give me a butterfly kiss."

A long kiss came into the phone.

"Now hear this: it's a baboon kiss. Baboons have fast kisses like little snorts. Catch it?"

"I caught it, Mommy."

"See you in a little."

I hung up the phone.

I called Itzi. She was now living at the Barbizon.

"Itzi, I need you to get everything ready for California. Call Manhattan Storage and arrange for them to put everything in the apartment in storage." I paused. "My mother will help you with the packing. There's a Mr. Godwin there who specializes in boxing antiques and furniture. They will do everything. I want you to make several calls for me. Call Helen. Tell her I'm taking a house at Malibu for a month and ask her if she wants to come out for a week's vacation. Call Martin. I'll speak to him later. I need him out here for insurance purposes. Call the agent and book five seats on Pan Am. Check with Martin, and if the time is all right, arrive on an afternoon flight and call me back as soon as you have the reservations."

"Righto."

237

"Itzi, I'll have a suite here at the hotel for Emma and David and me. I'll get rooms for you and my mother and Martin on the same floor. Bring light summer clothes. Don't let my mother bring too much. It's hot here, too. All you need is bathing suits and T-shirts and jeans. I've got a lot of paperwork piling up here. About twenty-five people from my staff have arrived, and they're already working with me at the studio. Everyone's staying in this hotel. It's like a Lulu Cartwright takeover. Any important calls?"

"No, I've had all of them transferred to the Coast."

"All right, Itzi. Sopher and Company has rented the apartment on a year's lease. Arrange to have the Watts line taken out of the office. I guess that's about it for this evening. I have an assistant here who seems capable. There's a lot of work, just personal letters, and I'll look forward to seeing you in a couple of days."

"Lulu, did you see *Newsweek?* And *Time?*"

"I have them here at the hotel. I look absurd in the Time cover. They were trying for their new-woman look."

"Did you know that *People* is going to do a cover on you next week? I spoke to John Dominus, and they're going to fly out to the Coast to photograph you. *MS.* is doing a cover also."

"Terrific. I'll be a floating target."

"And I have articles from *Paris-Match, Der Stern and Le France-Soir Illustré.* Wow!"

"Anything else?"

"Sy Peck called from the *Times.* They want a story on the new Hollywood. A whole schmear, and I think they're getting Anita Loos."

"Who are doing the *People* and *MS.* stories?"

"Gail Rock at *MS.*"

"She's terrific. I love Gail."

"And," Itzi said, "I have requests for interviews from Fairchild, Condé-Nast, and about fifteen publications."

"Okay."

"Is that a bombshell? That's a bombshell."

"Anything else?"

"What's it like on the Coast?"

"It's a nice place to visit. A lot of trivia. Incipient power-play machismo. The seventies haven't hit here yet. Only a few people have ever heard of the women's revolution. I've been busy. Am going to see Ralph Bakshi and ask him to come on the staff. The man's a genius. Jane Fonda and Liv Ullmann are going to be in my first two projects. Phones ring. Masculine thinking and personal achievement are the name of the game. I think the company thought they were getting a cocktail waitress instead of a bartender. Itzi, you know what?"

"What, Lulu?"

"When I was little, I read a book called *Babar's Castle*. I used to read it to David. That's just what I feel like I'm in. I swear to God. The studio, believe me, is like a little castle. And it really is like Castle Bonnetrope. Portraits of movie stars like portraits of ancestors. There's a big dining hall where they serve watercress soup. There are underground passages which lead to the hall of armor. There are parks. And libraries. And big cars. And royal robes. Tell David it's like moving to Bonnetrope. Tell him we can play Babar in the studio."

"I'll tell him," Itzi said.

"That's all, Itzi. Love from Bonnetrope."

I threw Itzi a final word. "You wouldn't believe it, but everything they ever said about the Dream Factory is true."

I hung up the phone and went back to work.

I had finished about fourteen strategy charts. Now, at last, I had memos to go over. The hotel had sent a phonograph to my room. I liked to work listening to Callas singing *Carmen*. I put the records on. They were soothing. What did I have to do next? Maybe I should just go around the city and refresh myself with the topography of Los Angeles and Beverly Hills.

I suddenly wished I had my bicycle with me and made a note to make sure Itzi had it sent out. I picked up the phone and reached Jacobs.

"I'd like to just take a tour around the city by myself for an hour or so, Mr. Jacobs. Can you have the limousine drive me around?"

"Of course. Is there anything else you want, Lulu? The directors have asked me to agree to anything and everything. They are looking forward to the first meeting with you tomorrow. Anything you want. There are a million people who want to take you to dinner."

"No. I don't want to see anyone while I'm working these first few days. I'm going to eat and stay in my room. I'm planning strategies."

"Strategies?" Jacobs cleared his throat.

"Haven't I told you? I'm making strategy plans. I feel that there are prorebellion people at the studio. And antirebellion people. I've had a check done, and I knew who they were before I arrived. So I'm planning to put my own pro rebellion people next to neutral people. Then there are the buffer people. And the board of directors. They are on my strategy chart number three. They're not sure what is happening yet. I want them to see how much I will negotiate and how much I won't negotiate. I have also done alternate oppressor strategy charts. Right now, I'm planning tactical strategy chart number thirteen and am picking out issues worth going to battle for, how things have shifted in my favor are included in my infiltration chart. I need some time alone to work on all this."

Jacobs was impressed. Bewildered. Depressed. It was all the kind of thing he only saw in war movies. I could hear him thinking, What kind of madwoman have we hired? All this talk about revolution and strategy and sexism and oppression and unions. Where were the good old days of casting on the couch? Is this woman a general? Is this a war?

"When do you want the car?" Jacobs asked.

"Right now, please."

"Tell me, just one thing. Where do I fit in on the strategy charts?"

I thought for a moment. I didn't want to hurt Jacobs' feelings. He was an old trouper. He had been through witchhunts and blacklistings and studio changes of guard and he had always been on the side of the good guys.

"Mr. Jacobs . . ." I paused.

"Yes?" He listened through the phone.

"On my strategy chart you are definitely in the position of a person who is an instrument for change. That puts you in the buffer section. The new studio that I am trying to put together has to be based on the principles of imagination and struggle. As well as fiscal and technological changes. It's all a game. Even the strategies are a sort of game. A war plan. Similar games involving millions of people have been devised by the large corporations that have succeeded. We are future-oriented. Future-forming. That's where the profit is."

"I agree," said Jacobs. And then again. "I agree totally."

"There's only one favor, Mr. Jacobs, if it's not too much trouble. I'd like you to find me an apartment in Malibu. My family's coming out here, and I'd like my son to be able to play and go swimming. I'll commute to the studio from there."

"The studio has a house at the beach that they own already. Don't forget, you have a house at the beach, a house in Beverly Hills, a house in Palm Beach, an apartment in New York at the Regency, and a small apartment in London and Paris," Jacobs said proudly.

"Yeah. I know. But I don't need a house. You can get rid of them. Just find me a small apartment at the beach."

"A house with a tennis court?" Jacobs said hopefully.

"No. Just an apartment. I think there's one out there that Fitzgerald once worked in and is now owned by David Lean. See if we can get that for a month."

I drove around the city. I asked the driver to take me around Beverly Hills. I had taped *Carmen* and listened to Callas singing as I went around the city. So they wanted new management. Everything was going harmoniously. Too harmoniously. My planning-programming-budgeting system combined with new creative projects was going into effect. The lights were on all over the city. What a strange empty place Los Angeles was. I started thinking about goals. The goals for the studio had to be formulated at the top. I still needed a lot of data collected. It was thrilling to manipulate the studio imaginatively. How to hit the universal public? That was the question that other heads of studios before me had asked. Well, with increased turnover, they were going to get their answer. They were in for a shock. The car kept driving. I drove out to the beach. I drove back from the beach. I drove into the hills. I drove down the freeways. And finally back to the hotel. It was midnight. I was tired and told the driver I would see him in the morning. Good night, good world.

In my room the phone rang. I was trying to sleep but forgot to give the operator a do not disturb message. Callas was still singing on the tape.

I was lying in the dark thinking of technocratic patter. Planners and managers. A rushing stream of wild and unorthodox eccentric or colorful ideas had been going through my head even as I was half awake. That I was thinking of tangible components, data, frameworks, strategies, technology, internal studio problems, color importance, revolutionary shifts, and power relationships meant that I should be sleeping.

The phone rang again and again.

I picked it up.

A soft voice said, "Hi, Lulu."

It was Peter Wall.

"Did you get my messages?"

"Yes," I said.

Silence.

"I got them when I arrived. And my secretary gave them to me at the office. I'm sorry I haven't had any time to call anyone except the key people in the new organization."

"I understand."

I couldn't understand whether he was calling me to acknowledge the fact that now that I was a winner I was now *eligible* to spend time with.

Peter Wall was polar ice. He was cool.

Peter Wall was as *indifferent as a croupier.*

He was intelligent. And his dark hair and sensitive hands were perfectly groomed. He'd make a wonderful Chopin to Liv Ullmann's George Sand. My God, I'm always casting. I'd better get over that. Yeah. Peter Wall was a croupier. Like a croupier, he stayed out in Hollywood on top of the Beverly Wilshire, throwing the dice, accumulating winnings.

A croupier accumulates no friends has no time, combines the lyric with the loss, combines the soul with the hand, there are never irritations.

Peter Wall was cold. He was also witty, and he could laugh his cosmic head off. He also was interested in me. After all, now I was the head of the studio.

"Still thinking about Goddard?" he asked.

The advance of polar ice. On my bed. Sitting there. Iceberg.

"Okay, I'll be straight with you, Peter. I confess that I would enjoy fucking. I have nothing else to do at this time of night."

I could see the ice-stale formula smile. The large eyes.

"But I still don't have time. I'm getting up early these days. Look, Peter, I was seriously thinking of not returning the messages."

I could hear Peter breathing.

"Don't talk," he said. "I'm coming down to your room. I know you're right by the pool. We can go swimming nude."

He hung up the phone.

I thought about it while he took the elevator down from the penthouse. He did have a great body. That was true. Mine was still a little bit too heavy. For a moment I remembered what it was like to make love. It occurred to me that I hadn't made love for a long time. Bart was the only person I enjoyed touching. I loved him, and I loved his body. And frankly, I didn't have time. *I'm too busy.*

I thought I'd explain that to Peter. It was interesting that when I first met him, he was a cunt-tease and now he was a winner wanter. He probably saw my puss on the cover of *Time* and *Newsweek* and figured he'd knock on my door just to make known his territorial rights. After all, this was his town. He was on top. Not only of the hotel, but of the whole system. He wasn't a star. He was a producer. He created projects. He didn't just produce them. He conceived them. He knocked on the door. I hid the strategies. And then I answered.

Peter walked in and sat down. He looked at me, and I looked at him like two animals sizing each other up. I was still impressed with the way he talked, his low, sexy voice, and the way he looked. He had gotten older since I had seen him seven years ago.

"Did you see my last movie?"

"Which one?"

"*Houseboy.*"

"Yeah. It was cute. All about a houseboy who fucks a lot of women. I suppose that's your fantasy."

"Did you like it?"

"No, not really. It was a big put-down. Anyway, it had a few funny moments, but basically I thought it was stupid."

"Are you gonna live here?"

"I might. I guess I'll be living at the beach for a couple of months."

"You could come up and stay in my apartment."

"Thank you. But my son's coming here in a few days."

"Wouldn't you like a sort of temporary marriage? For about two days? We could keep it a secret. Nobody would know about it but you and me."

"And the telephone operator. And the State Department. And Suzy."

"Who's Suzy?" he asked, bewildered.

"You know, the columnist. That's not exactly what the studio is paying me a million bucks to do. Come and fuck a star."

"I'm not a star."

"Please, Peter. Let's not play who's the star. Let's not play who wants to fuck. Let's play human condition. You try to imagine what it's like to be a real person. With feelings. And intelligence. And a sense of humor. And I'll talk to you."

"A lot of people say you have a great sense of humor," he said. "Do you mind if I order a drink? I'm thrifty." He ordered a ginger ale for himself and a scotch for me.

The bar was closed, but he could have anything he wanted. The drinks came. Suddenly I felt how embarrassing all this was. Peter was really a different kind of man from the one I had thought he was. It wasn't his fault if he was once a nice kid from Shreveport, Louisiana, whose sister was a star, who came to California and had the brains and taste to put deals together as well as become a star on his own. He was the only person out in that jungle, one of the only people, who cared about politics. I wanted to shout out at him, "Peter, this is intolerable. We are people. We are not judges of each other," but I looked at Peter instead.

"What is all this about?" I asked.

"I don't know," he said.

"I like you. I think I do. It's agonizing to be out here as a winner. But I've wanted this success all my life. I'm finally doing what I want. I'm no longer a victim."

"I understand," he said. "Do you want to be like a man?" he asked.

"Is that what you think it's about?"

"Isn't it?"

"No. Women used to gather in great conventions for eloquent speeches. Now they gather there, but they also rap among themselves. They used to fight for legal rights and the vote. Now they boycott. And they get where the action is. That's why I'm here. I'm not really interested in the myth of the vaginal orgasm. I'm more interested in how the *imagination* of women can be turned around so they can participate in their own time. I'm really not interested in that noble feeling of love in which people can be bought, sold, caressed, and crucified."

"I'm with you," he said.

"By the way, can you drive?" I asked.

"Sure. Why?"

"I know it sounds snobbish. But I can't drive. I used to drive, but I've forgotten, and I'm afraid to drive. I don't like being a prisoner in a limousine. I thought you might be able to tell me where I can rent a bicycle."

It was odd. Revolution. Bicycle. Handsome star. Politics. Little Lulu. Executive. Studio. Was this all a pleasure? Or a punishment?

"Do you like fucking?" Peter asked.

"I don't want to talk about it."

"Why?"

"Women and men don't have to always talk about fucking."

"Can you tell me it doesn't matter to you?"

"Not anymore it doesn't. Not the way it used to. Like a drug. Like a drink or a drug. To knock you out or make you feel good. I'm not interested in fucking as a narcotic."

"Don't you think it's good to fuck?"

"You mean good for your health?"

"Yeah. I guess you could say that."

"I do. But it's used by people to enforce attitudes. Women need free health programs. Free breakfast for children programs. Free day care centers. They need that more than they need a good fuck. If you see what I mean."

"What do you want?"

"To do my job and collect my check."

"That's what you say. But you're still an animal."

"That sounds like high school talk. You're not able to change the subject."

"Is there anything wrong with lust?"

"Is there anything wrong with dust?"

"What do you mean, Lulu?"

"Nothing. I was just making a rhyme. Lust. Dust. Sometimes at night, before I go to sleep, I think about what I'm trying to do in my work. Then I think about what it was like when I was a little girl. And I wanted to do something with my life. Something. I don't know what. I had no image of myself. And no real confidence. My father loved me, but he thought I should cater to a man and be taken care of. My mother had a career in musical therapy, and she had a good second marriage. She didn't think I had to be with a man to be anybody. She believed in me. Still does. But I was with a lot of men. And a lot of women. Not sexually. The women."

"Why not?"

"Just didn't feel like it. It's just that I've been around a lot. Had two divorces. I've been looking for a partner but never found one. Still think loving a man is possible. But for me, it's different. I want to do something else with my life. I don't have to go to touching school."

"I sympathize."

"Do you want to go swimming?"

"Sure. The light's off at the pool. No one will see us."

We took off our clothes and wrapped ourselves in the hotel towels. Like two dolphins flapping around in the cold water of the Beverly Wilshire pool. The moon was out.

As I swam deep into the water, holding my breath, I felt like a free dolphin. And yet I couldn't stop thinking about the unfinished revolution. The invisible revolution that was going to change the world, and nobody knew it—kind of weird—someone like Peter Wall didn't even know about it or understand it. I swam for what seemed like hours. In the water I felt good. I got the studio off my body. Back and forth across the pool. Peter swam next to me. Under me. Two nude people in the binary salt. I was thinking of *Carmen*. The music was still in my head. Callas kept singing. I kept thinking of all sorts of things. Katmandu. How I was once there. Salt. How I liked garlic in my food. A story I had read about consumerism. How sexism pervades all nature. I thought about Saul Bellow. How I loved his novel *Mr. Sammler's Planet*. I thought about Helen. Her poems. Under the water I thought about David. I thought about his waving good-bye to me at a bus station once when he went to school and how I walked home crying. I wondered if his goldfish could survive the flight. I thought of how I was once the golden goldfish girl. Rich daddy. Handsome husbands. Money. Everything you wanted. Not what I wanted. I thought about old age. I wasn't scared of growing old. I thought about being alive and dead and running an office and evaluating a company. I thought about women heroines. Movies I could do: Samson and Delilah. Peter Wall could play Samson. Maybe Julie Christie as Delilah. Shot in Israel. A lot of women heroine films. Judith with the head of Holofernes. Jane Fonda as Judith. Cicely Tyson as Judith. My head surfaced above the water. Universal mind connects with cosmic breath and women's revolution in future shock of political pioneer of kiss Hollywood good-bye environment à la Babar Castle in Karma circuit while everything women should touch. Pinocchio and Wonder Woman come out of

Wonder Womb and Jonathan Livingstone, Yertle the Turtle while star-bright storybook snoopyfare. Claude Lévi-Strauss in the Rape of the Sabines, while Abigail Adams, Flo Kennedy and Robert Kennedy, Sarah Grimké, Susan B. Anthony, Shulamith Firestone, Robin Morgan, Kate Millett, Norman Mailer and playtime water colors frightened of myself what meditation should I do, I have to call Yale Younger Power Award, Yale Younger Poet's Award. Call Bart. I should call Bart, it's that impossible to call Bart while Robert Lowell's poems are just out and freedom of dream. Who is freer than when they dream? I came out of the water. Wet. Dreaming. Tired.

"Dry yourself," Peter said.

He threw a towel at me.

I sank down in one of the plastic chairs at the pool.

"You look tired," Peter said.

"I'm not. I was just having such a nice time in the pool. Letting myself just dive and free associate and think of nothing but words."

"I'm going to put you to bed," Peter said.

"Thanks, pal."

"It's okay."

"I'm sorry about what I said about your movie. At least it was about the stupid life-style of a lot of dipsy people."

"It's okay. . . . I'm going to lift you up and take you back to your room."

"Don't. You'll get a hernia. I'm heavy."

"Come on, Lulu. You look tired."

We were sitting nude at the Beverly Wilshire. In the plastic chairs.

"Do you still read a lot?" I asked.

"Yeah."

"What do you read?"

"Poetry. I like poetry. I like to read about the earth. Right now I'm reading about the earth. Billions of years ago, the universe as we know it today did not exist. There was nothing but endless space—no stars, no planets, no sun, no moon, no earth. But drifting about in space were clouds of dust and gas. Although no one knows how the clouds and dust actually came into being, we know that the force of gravity exists between things as tiny as tiny particles of dust. It is believed that these particles were drawn to each other. They gathered in masses until they became spinning balls. Being retroactive, these balls became hotter and hotter until they were great blazing objects. One big hot mass, much larger than the others, was the beginning of the sun. With its force of gravity, the sun pulled on the other small bodies so that it pulled some of them into its own body, making itself larger and hotter than ever. Some of the balls, it is said, were strong enough to resist the pull and could not be drawn entirely to the sun. Instead, they went into orbit around the sun. These balls were the beginning of the planets. One of the balls circling the sun became the earth. A smaller ball in orbit around the sun became the moon. And here we are looking at the moon."

I listened. We looked at the moon.

"Come on," Peter said. "We're going up to my apartment."

"In my towel?"

"Yeah. In your towel."

"In the elevator?"

"Yeah. Sweetheart. On your mark, get set, go. In the elevator."

I was tired. But I walked with him. We walked into the elevator. The sleepy elevator operator took us up to the top of the hotel. We walked into Peter's bedroom and out onto the terrace. The city was there. The whole world of the bright lights.

"Okay," I said.

I walked into Peter's bedroom. It was just as messy as it was seven years before when I had come to his hotel to beg him to be in the story I was writing about rockets. I picked up a cigarette and lit it.

"Do you want a drink?"

"No thanks."

I lay down on the bed. Some few moments, hours, I don't know how long later, he was on top of me. Then me on top of him. Me sucking him. He began sucking me. We swam in galactica. His ass on my cunt on his cock on my tit in his tongue near his balls down my hair on his leg. Two mouths. Saying nothing. Two bodies. Releasing each other. Eating each other. Sucking each other.

Lying on Peter Wall's bed, it suddenly occurred to me as we were making love that it was entirely inappropriate to be doing this. Was Peter a stud? Was I so hard up? Certainly not. There are plenty of other things we could be doing. I had the feeling while Peter was sucking my breast that he was interested in yoga.

"Oh, it strikes me that you are beyond just ejecting sexual feelings. Are you by any chance interested in yoga?" I asked.

I was naked and exhausted but always managed to find the energy to talk with Peter.

"Yes. I've been seeing a guru. My guru is gentle and affable, and he has suggested that we both go to a hermitage in the autumn. Also, I've been reading the *Autobiography of a Yogi*."

"That would make an interesting movie," I said. "With you playing the levitating saint."

Peter nodded.

"I saw a yogi remain in the air several feet above the ground last year when I was in India. I have seen yogis perform unbelievable feats. The aura of peace after a storm is the way I felt after finding my first yogi."

"Is it still in your mind? Your first experience?"

"*Yes*. It was just like recognizing a high state of consciousness. It was the recognition of the superconsciousness, which is the exact opposite of the conscious mind."

"It's often confused with hypnotism," I said.

Peter began kissing my ass. I had heard people called "ass kissers" in high school, but he was *literally* kissing my tushie. All of it. He was under me. Over me. "My god," I thought to myself, "Peter Wall, the world's greatest star and stud, is kissing my tushie," but I didn't say anything. I didn't want it to seem this was anything unusual for me. I kept my dignity.

"Let him kiss," I said, continuing my conversation. "A person after all is not just defined by his or her actions," I said, keeping to the subject of yogis, "but we must also define ourselves by our spiritual nature."

Peter turned me over. He began kissing my stomach.

"When I was in India, I made a pilgrimage to an ancient Srinagar temple dedicated to Swami Shakara. As I looked on the hermitage, I fell into an ecstatic trance. I am planning, by the way, to visit the Self-Realization headquarters while I am out here in Los Angeles."

Suddenly a bell rang.

"What's that?" Peter asked.

"It's my alarm clock on my wristwatch."

I bounded out of bed.

"The limousine is picking me up in an hour, and I have to wash my hair. I get out to the studio at six in the morning, so I can go over my strategy charts and memos before anyone is there. You understand."

I got into my towel, put my watch on and ran for the door.

"Aren't you going to kiss me good-bye?" Peter asked from the bed. He looked like a wounded teddy, the bear. Winnie-the-Pooh as part stud, part yogandanda guru.

"I'll call you after I finish work," I said.

I rushed from the elevator, running around the pool, into the shower, a little Fermadil and No Tears Shampoo and then off to work. The limo was waiting. I dried my hair in the car.

At the studio the six men that I had to account to faced me as I sat at the head of the conference table. Lulu the Magnificent. Lulu the Noble took over.

"I'm going to get into the gut issues immediately," I said.

They faced me. Some of them had memo pads. This was unusual for them. Perhaps in their whole lives they had never taken orders, as it were, from a broad. They had probably never even sat at a conference table with a woman or listened to suggestions from one. Two of them were slobbish and fat. The others were in good shape. They all had extra-white skin—executive green—these were men who didn't spend their hours around a pool. These were men who were insulated against everything but work. They were workoholics. That's how they got where they were. They were all working for their boss. Whoever it was he kept his people with their nose to the grindstone. These men probably only knew two things: *pussy* and *balance sheet*. They did not look imaginative. They looked like old men who were worried about bankruptcy. They did not want the studio in the hole that it was now in. *Courage*, I said to myself. I remembered my favorite saying that I had once found when I was living in Stamford with Larry. I had found it in the public library in an article about the watercolors of Henry Miller. He had said DON'T LOOK FOR MIRACLES. YOU ARE THE MIRACLE. Wondergirl talks to aging management. That was my cue.

I cleared my throat.

"Gentlemen, I have now been at the studio for three days. I have had time to talk to everyone who is working for me in an executive and nonexecutive position. I have spoken with everyone on the staff that I inherited. And I asked each person simply one question: 'What the hell are you doing?' Each person then explained to me his function. I wrote down a memo on each person's performance and his verbal explanation of his work load. And my opinion is that only half of them are doing a goddamn thing. Therefore, we must immediately consider what dead management means. Dead management means dead business. So I have taken the liberty of firing exactly half my inherited staff. And I have replaced every four or five people with key people of my own. Each person that I have brought in has a salary that is exactly one-fourth of the salary of the person I fired. This way I am cutting down immediately on expenses. This is necessary to do if we want to turn this company around."

No one said a word. I continued.

"Secondly, I have gone right into the nitty gritty of how films are being made here, so I can cut costs. I have decided that the optioning and purchasing of properties is unnecessary in the 1970s. We have so many talented creative people that we can commission, project by project—nobody, of course, who is creative should be held on contract—that it makes the expense of bought properties absurd. I have already spoken with a group of fifteen writers and journalists who are interested in creating new projects. From now on, the *writer* will be the true *star* of our films. Not the director. This way the writer will have more control of the product, his or her ego will be involved, and she will work harder for less money. The script is the important element, as far as I'm concerned, in the film. I say this not only as a writer, but as a producer. Of course, once you have a *good* idea, then the writer can work with the actors improvising the dialogue. Improvisation can always be incorporated. But we are going to make film into a written medium. It has been a director's medium for a long time. And a star's medium. Only stars and directors were bankable. That, gentlemen, is why the studio has lost so goddamn much money. Fuck the star and the director. There are millions of them around. Let me tell you something. What do you need to be a director? Imagination and confidence in your ear and eye. Very nice. That's not what makes a good film. From now on, we will concentrate on writers. Each of them will have final cut.

"As for the directors, the ones we've been hiring are all lousy. I'm bringing in some women directors who have worked underground and directed films that already are classics. And I'm hiring William Wyler and Woody Allen as consultants for every film. Lina Wertmuller is coming to work with the studio for a year, and so is Fellini. Everyone else will be unknowns. That will cut costs. And bring into the studio new talent.

"As for stars, what stars? Three or four women artists that I know personally will be working in the projects. As for the rest, give them an opportunity for humility. Let them watch amateurs—amateurs who are a thousand times more cooperative than they are—work for small salaries and produce great film performances. All those slice-of-life films made in Italy that we are all so fond of use reportage actors that are the best. Each director will have to discover his or her own cast.

"Now for the trimmings," I continued. "The growth of the INTELSAT satellite system is an example of operational communications that are going to work for our company. I've brought here some of the men who worked on Early Bird, and they are going to be here for a year on a consultancy basis at the studio. The future of films is the future of satellite communications. That's where the capacity for growth comes in. When I say GROWTH, gentlemen, I'm talking about the next five years. Not any of the other studios have made a similar and thorough investigation of the possibility of satellite communications as they will figure in the film industry. Satellite communications means simply a faster and cheaper communications system. Films will be beamed by satellite to every corner of the globe. They will be picked up by earth stations and carried, without cable, into receivers in every hamlet and living room and hut in the world. Satellites have already shrunk the globe. Instant time programs via satellites now come into your living room and mine. But we, gentlemen, shall be the company to pioneer satellite communications and the film industry. It is my goal to be the first studio to set television trends and foreign distribution trends. In 1970 television via satellite averaged one hundred transmissions a month, compared to five a month in 1965 when INTELSAT ONE was the only satellite. Global satellite television increased by thirty-three percent during 1970. In 1971 it increased by almost fifty percent over 1970. Can you imagine what the increase is going to be for the rest of the seventies? Satellite communications is the key to growth in the film industry and to all media. I am looking into the research possibilities in our record division and our television division. This technology means a whole new concept in viewer-defined entertainment. We are not going to sit back and allow another studio to beat us in the race. We are, gentlemen, not here to make zero profit? Are we?"

They looked at me—every single one of them—all twelve eyes were glued to my eyes by Elmer's Glue.

"Our objective is to concentrate on new shifts in management, a cutdown of cash flow for properties, and a *stepup* of technological development in the satellite field so that we not only will show growth but will be the leaders, once more, in the industry."

I paused for a glass of water. Lit a small cigar. And continued.

"Now let me tell you guys something," I said confidentially. "I am not just interested in the balance sheets for this country. No, sir. I don't like to say anything as banal as tomorrow the world, but the world is, after all, our great big market. People will start buying our product, what with satellite receivers and cable TV used for home entertainment, in every part of the globe. And we have to aim our product, gentlemen, at the world. Not just at the American consumer, but the world consumer. After all, America spells Hollywood, doesn't it?"

No one disagreed.

"Now, I tell you what I am going to do." I took another puff on my cigar. "I am going to outline to you now, very briefly, the kind of product I think the world market is interested in, gentlemen. Let's start first with the kids. After all, we must give the devil his due and admit that one hell of a guy who made one hell of a pile of loot out here in the sands of California was a guy called Walt Disney. And he was no dummy. I give you my word that our studio profit will be closely linked to children's entertainment. No woman anywhere in the world, except perhaps in a few countries in the Middle East, and even that's changing, wants to sit home with the kids. Kids will be sent to study or dream or keep quiet in movies in the seventies and eighties more than ever before. And these kids all over the world are not dopes and morons anymore. Kids stop liking that *Sesame Street* bullshit now very shortly. And they are not interested in mice and pigs and bears and elephants that talk and cry. They have seen people killed on television. They have seen wars and documentaries on the sea and hunger and old age and insane asylums. They are exposed to these things, not only in conversation, but in images. And they want to know more. Our films will tell them more. We will make films for children about real things. About how the earth was born. About the bottom and secret place of the sea. How a seashell is made. About everything and anything that has to do with this planet and the wonders as well as the evils of it. You may say, 'Heck, kids don't want to see that,' but they are the future. And we cannot only change their way of thinking about the world, but show them how wondrous and varied the world is. They can also be exposed to the classics. It won't harm them. And they don't have to see a little pig or mouse speaking Shakespeare. I want to make films for kids that are made by kids."

No one said a word. But they seemed not to have heard me correctly. Lulu the Lay. At the bottom of the world. In charge of reality.

"That is correct, gentlemen. I am starting a new kids' department at the studio with kids as consultants about the kind of films they want to see. The first film, by the way, that I am going to make is going to be about the life of Goddard, and it will be shot on location in Worcester, Massachusetts, and at the Goddard Space Center. Kids will do the photography. The acting. The directing. Everything but the editing, which will be supervised. Kids' films will be a first. Believe me, those kids will put a lot of pros to shame. If you think *Jaws* made a lot of money, wait until you see a kid's version of what it's like to live underwater."

I looked through my notes. And took off my glasses. I sighed.

"Women, it's almost too banal to say this, but I suppose I have to, want to see films about themselves as winners. Not losers. Political films. Funny films. Porno films. Musical films. Even films about violence and danger. But they are interested in films about the truth. And so I have made a list of fifty new films for women that I am prepared to create with qualified writers and journalists and poets. I have Xeroxed this list, and I will pass it out to you so you can take it home and study. Fifty new projects. All with low budgets.

"The first film will be a semi-documentary called *Tichi*. It's a *Fem-Jep* film about Allende's widow. Tichi Allende will be in it. It will take place in Mexico. The second will be *Coyote*. A comedy. It's about the organization of whores in San Francisco by Margo St. James. Margo St. James will play herself. The third will be a porno musical. With lyrics by Comden and Green. And a fabulous sound track. The fourth will be a wacky comedy called *Siggy*. The life of Freud as told from the point of view of his mistress and daughter. Stuff like that.

"Now for what has been called black exploitation films. They have been losing a lot of money mainly because they have lacked qualified scripts. I am putting Afini Shakus in charge of that department, along with a group of Masai women who have trained in Italy at Cinecittà. Simone de Beauvoir, James Baldwin and Florynce Kennedy will head up the consulting department in that area. (How's that for the death of the Soul?)

"As for conventional Broadway musicals, well, they are just too expensive. Even if they do have a tie-in with the record industry. Frankly, I have investigated the sales of those records, and they don't do all that well. So scratch musicals at least for the time being.

"Documentaries? Yes. But with low budgets. I am going to head up that department myself. But I am going to work almost exclusively with the great women editors Dee Dee Allan, Patricia Powell. That will be my staff. Along with a select list of composers from every corner of the world. I have also chosen twenty-five outstanding American poets, who seem to be always out of work, to work with me particularly in that area. Documentaries mean sound tracks. And nothing sounds more beautiful than the voice, the human musical voice speaking poetry. The poetry will often be a counterbalance to the image seen. It will give dimension. And I believe that the world market is ripe for real stories about real people. And so I plan to produce one hundred outstanding documentaries in the next two years.

"Now, to basics. And I mean *very* basics. Gentlemen, it is my sorry duty to tell you that one out of every fifteen people here at the studio steals. And when I say steals, I am talking about corruption with a capital C. You guys don't want crooks. Surely you are aware of the crime. But what shall be the punishment? We are all aware of the various scandals that involved some of our key executives in corruption and, I hate to say this but, perversion. Daniel Stern exposed some of this in his fascinating study of corruption *Final Cut*, but that was just a beginning. And so, gentlemen, you will be DELIGHTED, just delighted, to know that I have hired Sergeant David Durk, former associate of the famed Serpico, and head of the New

York Police Department Special Investigative Force—recently dismissed for not taking bribes or playing the game—to head up our special investigative division. True, we will be paying Sergeant Durk a salary of seventy-five thousand dollars a year. But with that come four former investigative policemen who will be doing undercover work right here at the studio to make sure that there is no more hanky-panky between our executive staff and the people we want to have working for us. That will take care of the millions of dollars lost in corruption here at the studio, gentlemen. I take it none of you has anything to worry about."

There was a slight laugh.

"Then I am bringing out four bright lawyers whom I have worked with personally in New York. And one person will be here consulting with us for a month on our insurance program. The studio, I have discovered, wastes a million dollars every month on unnecessary insurance premiums and coverage. We will change all that immediately.

"Then, of course, all of our phony real estate deals will be exposed and done away with. My lawyers are working on that one."

"There will be a union shake-up. I am not interested in playing footsie with closed shop unions. That means either they hire blacks and women or they do not work for us. I think the photography union and art directors union are choking on that one. Let them choke. The bastards.

"Oh, yes, I have always the bad habit of leaving out the most important item, which is the team I've brought into the studio from Wall Street. You've heard of the Boiler Room Girls? Well, these are the Wall Street Wizards. They are women from Wall Street who are involved with negotiations with Arab money; we certainly don't want to take any anti-Semitic dollars, do we?"

The group of men who were Jewish looked away.

"On the other hand, if we can get their dollars, and get them to pay for interesting projects, such as my secret film project, *Arabesque*—which I haven't told you about yet—I say WHY NOT? Also, these Wall Street Wizards are going through all the books at this very moment. I just want to make sure that none of us, and that includes all of us, makes any mistake. The accounting department is just delighted to have these new people going through everything at the moment. THIS STUDIO IS BEING RUN ON PAPER PROFIT. WE HAVE OVERBOUGHT, UNDERSOLD, AND OVEROP-TIONED. WE HAVE A MINUS SIGN WHERE WE WANT A PLUS SIGN. WE MUST HAVE EVERY DOLLAR THAT WE SPEND ANALYZED. EVERY CENT ANALYZED. I AM TALKING ABOUT DOWN TO THE LAST PENNY. And that, gentlemen, is what I am here for.

"In conclusion, I wish to say that I have not neglected another tiny little way that we can save millions of dollars. And I am talking about utilities. Our electric, gas, telephone, water. All this will be scrutinized while I am head of this organiza-tion. That means everyone of us, I include myself, will have a telephone chart. We will mark down not only every call that goes out and every call that comes in. This means NO MORE WATTS LINES. Those lines are so extravagant. I had one at home, and I found that it NEVER PAID. Who needs to call the Aleutian Islands anyway? And as for lights and water, well, let's say that everyone is entitled to flush the toilet, but no one can flush our profits down the drain by using excess water. So that private shower and steamrooms are out. In fact, the plumbing division is removing all that travertine paraphernalia right now."

I smiled.

"In conclusion, gentlemen, you will find me always avail-able. I intend to work from six to six, so that you can always just buzz by my office. I have instituted a policy of no lunch breaks, so you can always find me doing business where business should be done, behind my desk. That's the first role of productivity. No lunches. Also, they say that women are less corrupt than men, but that's only because women have had fewer executive jobs. But you will find me constantly available to account for every personal cent I spend. No more charge cards, and I know that you will all be glad to follow suit. I want an air of stability brought to this studio. I want us to enter the 1980s as leaders. Not as bleeders. Thank you."

The gentlemen looked at me, and suddenly I heard something I had never expected. Quiet. Polite. Very reserved applause.

Frankly, I wanted to kiss them. After all, I was a newcomer. Kicking ass. And I hadn't even bugged them.

That night I had a drink with Peter Wall at the inevitable styrofoam Polo Lounge. I explained that my son and some friends were arriving, as well as some more of the staff. I would be moving out to Malibu to a small apartment. He asked if he could come out and play tennis with me. I explained that would have to be in the early morning, at five o'clock. He said he could get up that early if he wanted to. He kissed me good-night because I had to get up early and work on a new project that I was presenting to the writing group. He gave me a signed copy of the *Autobiography of a Yogi* and kissed me longer than I had ever been kissed. It lasted—that kiss—for twelve minutes. I timed it. Maybe he was a yogi or something. I decided to find out later that week.

I met the group at the airport. David was excited to see the limousine. Itzi wheeled her bicycle off the plane. Emma was wearing a hat that resembled the advertisement for *Jaws*. It seemed to look like a huge fish with some flowers on it. Martin was delighted to be in Los Angeles. He carried his briefcase filled with insurance papers and a hot dog from Nathan's. My momma wept when she saw me. I wasn't aware of the fact that she had had the cover of *Time* and *Newsweek* with my face on it mounted in a Chemex solution and she carried these artifacts of her daughter's success with her as if they were the most necessary objects. She looked as if she were picketing. The gang got into three different limos, and we sped toward the beach. Everyone couldn't wait to go swimming.

And that was how it all started. My working my way into the power structure. All I can say is: Nothing Great Was Ever Achieved Without Enthusiasm.

I was walking with David on the beach. We were walking down the water edge sand, in the morning, jogging and running past all the little shacks and Malibu beach houses in what my husband, Larry, used to call MNO country—money no object country. Past the tennis courts and the private worlds of property and wealth.

David looked at me. "Hey, Momma—look—it's Dumbo."

I didn't see him at first.

The car stopped in front of me. It was Dumbo all right. In a Maserati. He jumped out of the car. He was wearing a tight purple bikini that was practically painted on him and began running toward me.

"I heard you were here," he said. And lifted David in the air, kissing him.

Dumbo had changed. His hair had a slight gray streak in it. He still had a beautiful body; only he had gained weight, and his shoulders were even thicker, and I noticed, I couldn't help it, that he wore around his neck a tiny golden foot. On a chain.

As we walked, he spoke breathlessly to me. "I've opened reflexology centers all across the country," he said. "Foot parlors where people come and see the stars. Really. They have their feet rubbed, and they are healed. Healed of everything. Touching the foot does that."

"Touching anything does that," I said.

"Lulu. I have made an unbelievable amount of money in this. You can't imagine how many sick women and men there are who come to the reflexology parlors to have their bodies stimulated by foot therapy. It's amazing, but I had no idea how many lonely, sick women there were who wanted their feet rubbed. And men, too. This thing has caught on like wildfire."

"Good," I said.

"And I've become a vegetarian. I meditate. I've cured my body and mind of all impure thoughts."

"I'm glad of that, Dumbo."

"And hey, you've really done quite well for yourself. I read about you, and they even had my picture in *Newsweek*. They had a group of pictures on the men in your life. How did they get them? Pretty sneaky. And they had Abraham, your first husband, and Larry, your second husband, and old David there, and even a picture of me. I felt flattered."

"Good. I'm glad."

I wanted him to leave. I had nothing to say to my ex-wife, dumpy, dingy, delightful, sexual Dumbo.

"I've become a much more aesthetic person, Lulu. I realize now that I love you and it will really be possible for us to be together now as equals. I'm able not only to pay my rent and buy my own suits, but I could take care of you as if you were my queen. I could build you the Taj Mahal. I think we were right to wait."

"Wait?"

"I waited for youuuuuuuu," he began singing as we walked along the beach.

"Wait? You must be loco," I said. "Dumbo, I loved you. When you left me once, I had a sort of breakdown. That's true. I went into shock. That's true. I was *lost*. Helpless. Unloved. Frightened. All those things. But I think I'm okay now, Dumbo. I'm doing fine."

I looked at my watch. I didn't mean to seem rude, but I had work to do, and I wanted to go swimming with David.

"I'll call you tonight," Dumbo said. "And we can talk in the moonlight."

Was he kidding?

No. Apparently not. He ran on the sand. So gracefully I must admit. Back to his Maserati. Then he jumped in. And drove away. I could hear him singing:

Dream the impossible dream
Fight the unquenchable foe

I looked at David.

"He was nice, Mama," David said.

We raced each other to the sea. We ran over the granite rocks, David and I, past the acorn worms. He took the air in his lungs. We went right to the sea water. Water washed over us. Fine sand and silt going over us. Our hair in the current of the waves. Foam. And I was Venus going into the waves. Me. No longer Little Lulu. But the Botticelli woman, half giddy, half smiling, into the shell world and stepping out again, for the first time. It was thrilling.

I no longer thought of my terrible life. I had forced myself to be no longer a round-faced bespectacled child or a wife of a person who didn't know I was there. I was dealing with a pack of scoundrels, and I was emerging from this not as a liar or a traitor to myself, but as someone who was not only a collector of inquiries, hello, I am not only an executive of the imagination but someone who believes she is going to last. Hello! Hello!

"The ruler of reality is more unreal than the queen of fact," I said to David.

CPSIA information can be obtained
at www.ICGtesting.com
Printed in the USA
BVOW03s2158050417
480467BV00001B/9/P